Steel Magic

Steel Magic © 2016
by J.L. Gribble
Published by Dog Star Books
Bowie, MD
First Edition
Cover Image: Bradley Sharp
Book Design: M. Garrow Bourke
Printed in the United States of America
ISBN: 978-1-935738-85-5
Library of Congress Control Number: 2016940690

www.DogStarBooks.org

For Erik.

Steel Magic

J.L. Gribble

DOG STAR
BOOKS

Funerals were more for the living than the dead, but Toria imagined her old teacher scoffing at all the fuss. She and Kane sat on a wooden bench in the back of the chapel as the officiant droned on about remembrance and honor. As Toria toyed with the hem of her skirt, wrapping a loose thread around and around her slender fingers, Kane captured her hand in his darker one to stop her fidgeting.

While the heads in front of her bowed in prayer, Toria gazed at the stained glass window that filled the front wall of the chapel. The chapel was nondenominational, and the glassworks' abstract shapes were designed to be as inoffensive as possible. Master Procella had been a lifelong bachelor and not particular about his religious leanings, but his sister had planned the funeral. In all likelihood, Marcos would rather have had them carouse around a bonfire while the drinks kept flowing.

He'd been the first mage in Limani to welcome her and Kane, the city's first bonded warrior-mage pair in over a century, with open arms. He had fully supported the way they split their attention between the mage school and the local Mercenary Guildhall rather than insist they dedicate their increased power to the art of magic alone.

Kane nudged Toria up as he stood. Her partner was much better at paying attention to social cues, but he was also less affected by this loss. Marcos Procella had been Toria's original magic instructor, first leading her through exercises in sensing the power around her and later in the more delicate skill of manipulating bioelectricity. Her lessons had commenced at five years old, when she first showed evidence of mage talent. That was almost twenty years ago. He had been the only other storm mage in the city of Limani, and she had learned much from him over the years. He'd have been irritated to die peacefully in his sleep. She tried not to remember Master Procella as she had last seen him, frail and wheelchair-bound. She would much rather recall the vibrant man who had taught her to throw lightning. How to mesh her energy with Kane's earth power. How to appreciate fine wine.

The officiant led a final moment of silence while they all stood, then he stepped down from the podium, robes flowing around him. Toria waited with Kane while the majority of the funeral's attendees filed out of the chapel before leaving. The double doors at the rear were already thrown open, and the summer's oppressive humidity cut through the chapel's pitiful excuse for air conditioning. Toria pushed a lock of brown hair behind her ear, feeling the short hair at her neck frizz.

Kane captured her hand again as he led her out of the chapel into the bright sun. With her free hand, she pulled her sunglasses from the neck of her blouse and slipped them on. The body had been cremated and only family members were invited to the following dinner, so she and Kane milled about with the other friends and acquaintances.

She resisted the urge to call up a breeze. A summer storm threatened to break, and they didn't need the sudden deluge that the colder air would bring forth.

"Ms. Connor? Mr. Nalamas?"

They both turned at the hesitant voice approaching behind them, and Toria resisted the urge to correct her use of their titles to "Master." This was neither the time nor the place for being that sort of a stickler. A woman led two elementary school-aged children toward them, a boy and a girl. Toria had noticed them on the other side of the chapel during the service, sitting farther to the front. The girl's blouse had come untucked, and the boy's tie was loosened. Both had red-rimmed eyes that matched how hers must look under her shades.

Toria could sense the power emanating from the children, both of the element air. The summer's heat pressed heavy upon them, but she didn't feel the breeze that stirred the kids' blond hair. That meant their control still needed work, but at least they kept the current within shields. Master Procella had reprimanded her many times over her years of training for messing with the weather patterns as she grew into her power. These kids were doing pretty well for their age and obvious emotional stress.

"Yes?" Kane said. "Can we help you?"

"I'm sorry," the woman said. "You don't know me. I'm Dana Sjolander. These are my kids, Reed and Maggie."

Kane folded his tall frame to kneel in front of them. "Hey, guys. I'm Kane."

Maggie ducked behind her mother, but Reed stood his ground. "Hi. Is it true you grew that oak tree behind the mage school in less than a day?"

That startled Toria into a laugh, a welcome relief from the melancholy she'd felt since learning of Master Procella's death. She hadn't thought about that tree in years.

Kane echoed her with his own chuckle. "Hardly. A certain storm mage, who shall not be named, accidently struck it with lightning. I only repaired a lot of the damage. That tree stood there long before we were born."

Maggie also giggled, and Dana beamed at her kids. "I knew that couldn't be true," she said, "but who was I to tell them otherwise? They got the magic from my late husband. I'm just a nurse."

"It's nice to meet all of you." Kane shook Reed and Maggie's hands before standing to also shake their mother's.

"How can we help you?" Toria asked.

Dana glanced at the mourners clustered in little groups around them, though most had drifted toward their electric town-cars in the neighboring parking lot. "This probably isn't the right time for it, and I'm sorry for that. But I wanted you to meet the twins. They need your help."

Toria heard Kane ask what was wrong, but she had already called forth her magesight, bringing the magic that filled the world into focus around her. She faded out her familiar shields, violet prismatic structures that surrounded her and Kane. Kane's own fluid emerald shields, like forest shadows at dusk, faded next. Then she tuned out the chapel, which emanated with the benevolent ambient rainbow of power fueled by generations of worship.

Dana had spoken true. The mother had no magical ability to speak of, but her gentle cerulean aura was echoed by the whirlwind of azure and indigo hues that surrounded both of her children. Their shields needed work, but Toria's had been equally disjointed at their age.

At first inspection, she found no major problems. Smooth shields came more from experience than from power, and she saw none of the fluctuations that signaled illness or injury. There was also no tarnish that indicated a curse placed upon the children, nor any other signs of darker power.

"No, no," Dana said. "They're fine. It's just that we're in a bit of a dilemma. Were the two of you planning on taking over the mage school?"

Kane turned to Toria, an unspoken question reverberating down their mental link, but she shrugged in response. She'd heard nothing about the mage school in recent memory. To be fair, she and Kane had been wrapped up with finishing their college degrees in the past few months. Graduation had been less than two weeks before, and since then, their focus had shifted to relaxing and catching up on all the movies and books they'd missed with their overloaded schedules over the last two semesters.

"What's going on with the school, ma'am?" Kane said. "We graduated almost five years ago, and we haven't kept in touch very well."

"I guess not," Dana said. "Master Procella was the last master there. Without him, my kids have no one left to teach them."

No one left? Toria had no words. Maybe they should have kept in better contact.

Kane spoke first, ever the diplomat. "Well, that's definitely something we can look into," he said. "And I will keep you informed of what we decide. But I'm afraid we can't really make any commitments now."

"I understand," Dana said. "But if no one takes over the school here in Limani, and I can't find any other mages in the city to train them, the twins will have to go to school up north. I'm not embarrassed to say that I'm worried about being so far from them. Not to mention the tuition costs."

"They certainly can't go untrained," Toria said. "And I promise we won't let that happen. Something will work out."

"Thank you," Dana said. "Here's my number. Please, call me anytime." She pressed a business card into Toria's palm, then took each of her kids by the hand and led them toward the parking lot.

"Well," Kane said. "I did not expect that."

"I had no idea," Toria said. "You?" This was the distraction she had needed from mourning Master Procella's death, but not the one she might have wanted.

"Of course not. We've been living and breathing schoolwork for almost a year. I haven't spoken to another mage except you in ages." Kane tucked Toria's hand in the crook of his elbow as they ambled to their town-car.

It was true. Maximillian Asher, the head of Limani's Mercenary Guild, had sat them both down after the unfortunate events with the Roman army two summers ago to discuss their futures as mercenaries. He'd been polite, but firm. Chemistry and literature where honorable courses of study, but neither would help in their chosen career field. So they had added political studies to their course loads, overloading their schedules every semester to accommodate the extra classes and still graduate on time.

"We can't take on two students," Toria said, feeling the need to state the obvious. "Neither of us is air, we have no experience teaching, and Max will never let us push off our journeyman rotation any longer. Hell, we should have done it after high school."

"I know," Kane said. "But we can't let those kids go untrained. And they probably aren't the only students at the school right now. We have a responsibility to them." He unlocked their town-car when they reached it but didn't open the driver's side door.

Toria stared at him over the roof. "Looks like our vacation is over."

#

Their apartment door was unlocked again. But since a delicious aroma, combined with much-needed air conditioning, hit right as Toria entered, she once again forgave Syri's criminal tendencies. Seeing her friend's familiar black leather jacket tossed over the back of the couch, ever-present despite the heat, warmed a spot in her chest that had been chilled despite the summer heat. Though always dismissing every offer of her own key, their elven friend had kept them fed with balanced meals for most of the past year while they crammed for classes.

"Good, you're back," Syri said, calling from across the open-plan apartment. The petite elven girl spooned tomato sauce over pasta onto plates at the kitchen island. "Food." Sometime between now and when they'd last seen her two days ago, Syri had added a streak of cornflower blue to her spiky blond hair. The color matched the crystal stud in her nose.

"We see," Toria said. "Thank you." She kicked off her heels inside the door and hopped onto one of the stools at the island. "Any beer left?"

Kane loosened his tie and tossed it and his suit coat next to Syri's jacket before crossing to the refrigerator. "We polished it off last night."

"Savages," Syri said. "There's wine on the counter." She pointed with her ladle.

Kane poured three glasses of the red wine while Syri distributed plates, and within minutes, all three were inhaling the meal.

"Exactly what I needed," Toria said. "Thanks, hon."

"My pleasure," Syri said. "I figured neither of you would be in the mood to cook after the service. How was it?"

"Service itself was nice," Kane said. "After the service was odd."

"How so?" Syri quirked an eyebrow at him.

"Some lady came up to us with her two kids. Twins, maybe nine or ten years old?" Toria said, and Kane nodded at her estimation. "Wanted to know if we were taking over the mage school."

Syri gave a slow blink. "What's wrong with the mage school?"

"Apparently Master Procella was the only teacher left," Kane said. "I guess Masters Vilece and Bennett aren't there anymore?"

Toria snapped her fingers. "Master Vilece passed away three years go. Cancer."

11

"And Master Bennett moved to Eire almost four years ago," Syri said. "I remember him asking my uncle for advice on where to retire."

The apartment descended into silence. "Well, crap," Syri said, swirling the wine in her glass. "Where the hell are all the middle-aged masters? I think we're missing a generation somewhere. If everyone is either dead or old, you two might have to train them after all."

"Absolutely not," Toria said. "We are already four years behind in our merc careers. We are not taking off another five plus to train up some kids with an element we don't even have experience working with. And there might be more students we don't know about. The mom didn't say. We can't exactly accept two and leave the rest hanging."

"I know, I know," Syri said. "But untrained mages are dangerous."

"They won't go untrained," Toria said. "But Dana sounded like sending them to the school in New Angouleme would be cost prohibitive."

"Of course it would be," Kane said. "The mage school here is subsidized for Limani residents, like the university. She is a single mom on a nurse's salary. It'd be different if the kids were bonded, but we'd have heard of another warrior-mage pair."

"True," Toria said. "Any school would snap them up in a heartbeat. Or we'd have already been training them."

Warrior-mage pairs such as Toria and Kane were rare. When they had joined hands at age twelve, their magic had clicked together, forever linking Toria's affinity of storm with Kane's potential with earth. Mage schools as far away as Europa had fought for the honor of teaching the rare bonded pair. But their parents were in Limani, so they had stayed. Master Procella and the other local mages had managed to muddle through teaching them just fine.

"I'm surprised they're not bonded," Syri said. "Twins and all."

"They have the same element," Toria said. "I've never heard of a pair bond with the same element. Just a quirk, I guess." Her plate was only half empty, but she nursed her glass of wine until Kane kicked her ankle.

"Time to eat, not stress," he said. "We'll go by the school tomorrow morning and see what we can find. There's got to be a list somewhere of all the other mages in Limani. Maybe one of them is interested in taking over."

"I slaved over a hot stove for you," Syri said. "Don't let it go to waste."

Toria laughed, but ate another bite of pasta. "Fine, fine. We need a cheerier topic. So. We're still going to Europa soon?"

"Nope," Kane said. "I told you, we're going south first. For once in my life, I would like to be in a place where it does not snow in the winter."

This debate was almost half a decade old, but still no closer to a resolution. Time was running out. While they had received field promotions two summers ago, Toria and Kane still needed to complete eighteen months of travel to officially move from mercenary journeymen to full status. Max had checked the regulations, and their short summer trips with Toria's grandfather Asaron didn't count. Eighteen months in a row, unaccompanied by a senior mercenary, accepting and completing their own jobs and contracts.

Kane was serious about the warm weather, but Toria had grander plans. Her adopted parents originally hailed from Europa, and she was determined to visit their old stomping grounds. The world was a big place, and she had no plans to spend her whole life in Limani, or even on one continent.

"I'm with Kane," Syri said, and she and Kane clinked wine glasses. "Hell, the only reason I've stuck around the last two years is you kids. If you head south, I'll come along until I find a nice beach to park myself."

"This isn't over," Toria said, brandishing a fork at each of them in turn. "We've got eighteen months. I'll get us to Europa somehow."

#

The next morning found Toria and Kane on the stoop of Limani's local mage school. It had started life as an old manor, but rather than remaining rural, the city had grown in its direction. The land was bracketed on either side by a bakery and boutique. The school owned the large field that spread behind it, and there was still space for many more extensions to be added to the already sprawling building. The patchwork structure looked like a contented cat, shading itself under the large oak that spread over one side of the building. The welcoming feeling it exuded could only be the after-effect of decades of excited students.

The local businesses were used to the sort of havoc that untrained mages could create. Toria had once summoned a train of floating pastries from the bakery. That had embarrassed her more frying the large oak. Before mages learned to tap into the power in the world around them, magic ran on their internal energy. A young, growing mage was often a hungry mage, and a hungry twelve-year-old within nose range of baking sweets was a mage who might accidentally perform a summoning charm.

"It's been awhile," Kane said. He knocked on the front door. The rain that had threatened the day before had fallen overnight, but today the heat had returned with a vengeance.

They didn't wait long. The door opened a crack, and a young face peered out. "Hello?"

"Maggie?" Toria said. "What are you doing here?"

"Don't let the cold air out." Maggie opened the door farther and gestured them in.

Toria and Kane entered the school's large foyer, and Maggie shut the door behind them. As Toria remembered, a small office sat to her right and a lounge with comfortable sofas spread to the left. She saw a new scorch mark in the hardwood floor of the hallway, but someone had finally repaired the water damage on the plaster walls that had occurred shortly before she and Kane graduated. The air inside indeed felt cooler than the summer heat, present even during the early morning hours.

"I'll get Miss Lukis," Maggie said. She dashed down the hall, leaving the bewildered pair in her wake.

"If there aren't any teachers left," Kane said, "what is she still doing here?"

"I guess we'll find out." Toria led him to one of the couches in the lounge, but before they could settle in, Maggie ran back.

A woman a bit older than Toria trailed Maggie. She stood even more petite than Syri, with curly red hair that contrasted with her dusky skin. Though the red hair was a bright color not found in nature, Toria noted in a flash of magesight that the woman both possessed mage talent and her primary element was fire. Cliché, but the color suited her.

"Good morning," she said. "I'm Misty. You must be Toria and Kane. Maggie and Reed have been raving about you all morning." Misty shook both of their hands. "Why don't we talk in the office? Maggie, go keep an eye on your brother and Ian for me."

The young girl beamed at the responsibility and darted away again. Toria and Kane entered the office, and Misty shut the door behind her. Rather than sit behind the desk, she perched on the edge of a filing cabinet to the side of the room. "To have her energy again," Misty said. "I'm so glad you're both here."

Tori and Kane exchanged worried glances. Sounded like Misty had the wrong idea. "We just came by to get some information," Toria said. "There's got to be some sort of list of other local mages, or those with ties to Limani. We're certainly willing to contact them on your behalf."

"If there was such a list, I'd have found it by now," Misty said. "I've looked, believe me."

"Maggie's mom said the school was closing?" Kane asked.

"It pretty much has closed," Misty said. "I've been the house mom since my son started attendance here last year, but he's the only resident student since Maggie and Reed live with their mother. My contract runs out at the end of the summer, and Master Procella's estate will take care of selling the house."

"Why can't you teach them?" Kane said. "You're a mage."

Misty snapped her fingers, and a flicker of flame appeared. "Because that is the extent of my power," she said. "And my son and the twins are air mages. I have nothing to teach them. I promised Dana that she could keep dropping her two off in the morning so she doesn't have to find childcare for the summer. But I've mainly kept them occupied with arts and crafts and nature walks. I can supervise a bit of their shield practice, but I'm hesitant to try to teach them more. And there's only so much magical theory you can have ten-year-olds read from the library. I can't explain much of the theory myself. I never attended a school like this when I was young—my training was from my grandmother outside New Carthage!" Misty slumped back against the wall as her tirade wound down. "Sorry. This is a bit stressful for me. Not only am I worried for my son, I'm also losing my job."

Toria felt metaphorical lightning strike. "Wait a sec," she said. "I don't remember exactly getting a summer break. That was when we did more work, when we didn't have to worry about regular school. Where are the rest of the students?"

Misty gave a short shrug. "There are no other students. It's just my son and the twins. Two graduated last summer, and another left with her parents for New Angouleme a few months ago. There are no new apprentices scheduled for this year. Hell, apparently there haven't been any incoming apprentices for the last three years."

When Toria had first shown signs of magical ability at five years old, she'd received her rudimentary training at home. At eight years old, she'd joined the school as a formal apprentice, the youngest in the school.

While she attended the mage school, there had always been around a dozen students at any one time. All of them split their time between the mage school and the public school system. Though the warrior-mage bond allowed her and Kane to breeze through most of the necessary training on power control, they had stuck around for further lessons until formally graduating with the rest of their "class." They'd crammed to bring up their grades senior year of high school, and then started college at Jarimis University. Five years ago, there had still been half a dozen students. Toria had figured it was a lull of some sort, a gap between the generations.

The population of Limani hadn't drastically changed in that time. Not growing at a huge rate, but it certainly not declining. Toria's mother, from her position as a member of the city council, had mentioned a few weeks ago that they would have to look at redistricting soon to take into account some expansion west.

Kane spoke before she could bring herself to think the same scary realization. "The mages are disappearing."

"That's ridiculous," Misty said. "They're just not coming here. Maybe word got out that the school was shrinking, and parents found other places to send their kids." But she couldn't hide all hints of the doubt in her voice. "I have to figure out where to bring Ian, and how I'm going to afford it."

"Yeah, that was the same thing Dana was concerned about," Toria said. "She asked Kane and me whether we would train her kids."

Kane held up his hands against the flash of hope that crossed Misty's face. "We are in no way prepared to take on students. We are not experienced teachers, and we have other commitments that need to be fulfilled that we have already put off for too long."

"But you're storm," Misty said, turning a pleading look to Toria. "That can't be too different from air."

"Oh, it's different. Very different," Toria said. A bit of overlap, especially concerning weather manipulation, but air mages focused more on kinetic energy. Toria could call a bolt of lightning, but one of the major air tricks that came naturally to the youngest of apprentices, mimicking telekinesis, had been outside her purview until she'd figured out how to manipulate static electricity closer to graduation. "I'm sorry, Misty. But even if we could teach them, we couldn't leave them on hold for eighteen months while we finish our mercenary training."

"Have you or Dana approached any of the other mages in Limani?" Kane asked.

"Believe me, I've tried that. You two and Master Procella were the only master-level mages left," Misty said. "The rest are more like me. Limited power, limited skill sets. And no air mages."

"What about the elves?" Toria said. "Untrained mages are bad for all magic users. They use different power, but it all essentially comes from the same place."

"Master Procella mentioned a few months ago that he had sent them some messages," Misty said. "But I never heard anything come of it."

Odd. Kane touched Toria's hand, and she felt his own surprise echo through their link. The elves had always been intimately involved with the training of the mages during their time as students. They'd been especially interested in the prodigal amount of power Toria had shown as a child, then in the education of

Limani's warrior-mage pair, with elves traveling from both the British and Roman colonies to meet them. The idea that the elves had cut themselves off from the school troubled her.

Maggie burst into the office before anyone could continue. "Reed and Ian are fighting again!"

"I'm sorry," Misty said. "I have to go see what the boys are up to this time. But please reconsider. You might be these kids' only hope." At that, she let Maggie tug her out of the office.

Toria met Kane's brown eyes and saw the worry that must be reflected in hers. "I wonder whether the first mercenary contract we sign can be hiring ourselves," she said. "We've got to find a teacher for these kids."

"I've got a crazier idea," Kane said. "We'll have to run it by Max, first. But maybe we can get Limani to hire us to find out what's happening to the mages. We still on for dinner at the manor tonight?"

"Yep," Toria said. "Let's pick Mama's brain and see what we can pull off." Maybe more time with their more experienced family members would help.

#

Toria's childhood home resembled the mage school in size only. While the school was structured with classrooms, library, and a dormitory, the manor owned by Limani's Master of the City and her daywalker was a more formal affair, with spacious rooms filled with antiques and mementos from thousands of years of history. The former plantation dated back to before the Last War, and forest had long overrun the surrounding fields.

It was hard to feel formal, however, as Toria helped said daywalker chop ingredients for a salad, and the esteemed Master of the City of Limani sat hunched over a cup of coffee at the kitchen table.

"I hate summer," Victory said. "Waking up during daylight is awful and should not be allowed." She had pulled dark auburn hair that contrasted with pale skin back in a hasty braid and wore a wrinkled T-shirt over jeans. At the moment, she could not look less like a prestigious government official and one of the most feared and respected former mercenaries on two continents.

Toria's adopted mother even still scoffed at the title "Master of the City." She had that honor by virtue of being the only vampire with a permanent residence in Limani. The job came with a seat on the city council, the responsibility of keeping any passing vampires from preying on the city's inhabitants, and absolutely no perks. She had been with her daywalker Mikelos Connor close to a hundred years,

17

and the two had raised Toria from infancy. They had claimed Kane as a foster son when his parents died a year after he bonded with Toria.

"It's only once a week," Mikelos said, his voice filled with more humor than pity. He pushed up his sleeves to wash his hands after dumping the rest of the chopped green peppers in the salad. He wore khakis rather than jeans, which Toria knew meant he'd taught music lessons that day. "You're the one who wanted to increase the number of times the council met per month."

"Because I thought we'd get to know each other better," Victory said. "Keep any more nasty surprises from popping up. Instead, we're all getting sick of each other's faces."

Toria laughed. "Sorry, Mama, but suck it up. The summer has barely started." She set the finished salad in the middle of the table and pulled place settings from a drawer. "More coffee?"

"No, thank you," Victory said. "Asaron is fetching dinner from the cellar. Or he should be. I sent him ages ago."

"Sorry, my fault," Kane said, as he strode into the kitchen with Asaron close behind. "I waylaid him to pick his brain about contracting issues."

Asaron held up two glass bottles. "Dinner is served." He set one in front of Victory and claimed his own seat at the table. He still wore pajama pants and a worn T-shirt. Being home in Limani meant Asaron was on vacation, and he'd still have been asleep if not for Toria and Kane joining the family for dinner.

Without prompting, Toria touched a finger to the top of each bottle, and with a twist of power, heated the liquid inside to body temperature. Apparently some people experienced queasiness at the sight of blood. But Toria's family had never hid their true natures from her, and blood had been a presence in her life since childhood.

Victory's sire Asaron could have claimed the Master title, but he didn't live in the city full-time. Instead, it was his base of operations between mercenary contracts in the Roman colonies to the south. He called Limani his vacation home.

"Contracting issues?" Mikelos raised his eyebrows as he placed serving dishes on the table. Though Victory and Asaron would sip from the bottles for their meal, the daywalker still ate food like a regular human. "You have a lead on a job?"

"Oh, good," Victory said. "Not to press, but I wasn't sure how much of a vacation you two really expected after graduation."

The five settled around the table to eat. "Well, the lease on our apartment runs out at the end of the summer," Kane said. "We plan to put our things in storage before we headed out."

"Our barn is your barn," Mikelos said, referencing the repurposed building that served as the manor's garage space. "Just tweak the climate control charms, and everything should be fine."

"Thanks, Dad," Toria said, sharing a humorous look with Kane. She had set those charms herself ages ago.

"No Syri tonight?" Victory asked.

"No, she had an overnight shift at the vet clinic last night, and we haven't seen her all day," Toria said. "She doesn't actually live with us, you know."

"But it's odd to see you both without her these days," Mikelos said. "Usually where you go, so goes her nation."

"Not today," Kane said. "And I don't think she was interested in hearing us talk about this trip anymore."

"You're decided?" Asaron said. He and Toria's parents focused expectant gazes on the warrior-mage pair.

Moment of truth. Would they take this matter as seriously as she and Kane did? For all Toria knew, this cycle of less mages occurred naturally, and her long-lived family would brush off their concerns.

"Well," Kane said. "It's not that simple. That's why I asked you about contracts."

Asaron and Victory exchanged bemused looks. "We can certainly help with that," Asaron said.

"Is it possible to hire yourself for a contract?" Toria asked. "We've run into something that needs to be investigated, and we might be in the perfect position to do so." She and Kane outlined their experiences the past two days, from the encounter with Dana Sjolander at the funeral to the meeting with Misty Lukis at the mage school.

Kane wrapped up the report. "Is this normal? Are we blowing something out of proportion?"

"If something was getting blown out of proportion," Mikelos said, "you'd be the one chasing down Toria to drag her back to reality." He caught the cherry tomato Toria tossed at him and popped it in his mouth.

"No, this is decidedly not normal," Victory said. "I'm going to join in on the concern. This explains why the school stopped hitting me up for donations once you graduated. There must not have been enough students to still require the additional funds."

"But as to your original question," Asaron said. "That's more complicated. Once you're full status, you can do whatever you want. Take jobs or don't take jobs, it's your livelihood to do with as you please."

"I wish the battlefield promotions had been permanent," Kane said. This was not the first time he had voiced this complaint, and his voice lacked heat.

"That was more about combat skills," Asaron said.

"The traditional eighteen months as a journeyman isn't about combat as much as it's about learning how to make mercenary work your life," Victory said. "Anyone can learn to swing a sword. A mercenary has to learn to live by it. And that includes hiring yourself out to the highest bidder and learning where your boundaries for those bids are."

Toria knew her mother spoke from years of experience. She and Asaron deserved their extensive reputation. They could afford to be picky about the work they chose and who would get the privilege of hiring them to do it.

She and Kane...could not. They were nobodies. Yes, they were the only warrior-mage pair in Limani and the surrounding colonies. They would get work based on that cachet alone. But they were unproven. And to be honest, they needed to find a way to support themselves that didn't involve still getting an allowance at twenty-one years old. She had justified the town-car and apartment rent and stipend as her parents allowing them their independence while still supporting them through their college educations.

Now time to see if they could fly on their own. Going off on a mad quest, even if it seemed important, would not be true adulthood.

Victory placed a gentle hand on one of Toria's. "I'm not saying you shouldn't pursue this," she said. "But that it's not the point of being a journeyman. Remember—the eighteen months doesn't begin until you sign your first contract and register it with a Guildhall."

Toria felt a tendril of power brush her mind and sensed agreement. Kane knew how she felt, because he likely had the same thoughts.

"Okay," Kane said. "Contract first, find where all the mages are going second. If the first contract pays well enough."

Toria presented her mother with the most innocent smile she could manage. "So, Master of the City," she said. "Does the Limani city council want to hire someone to find out where all their mages have gone?"

Mikelos laughed. "Good luck with that one."

Toria hid her disappointment with a sip of cranberry juice. Kane squeezed her hand under the table.

"Back to the original question," Asaron said. "Where are you going?"

"The Grand Strand," Kane said, in the same instance that Toria said, "Europa!"

"I can see we still have some progress to make," Asaron said. "Who needs another drink?"

#

Victory was sweet about it, but in the end, Toria realized she and Kane would still have to do their journeyman stint the old-fashioned way. The best they could do was keep their ears open and check in on the local magical scene wherever they traveled. Though her mother had spoken with the current elected head of the city council, Lucia Stein had agreed that it wouldn't be the best way for them to start their travels.

But the eighteen months would be over the sooner they started, and lazing about all summer appealed to neither of them. Kane had called Maximillian Asher, the head of Limani's Mercenary Guild, and told him to expect them the next morning. When they got home after dinner, the pair had enjoyed a final evening of beer and mindless movies on the couch. Today they would pack up the apartment after meeting with Max.

They swung by a local liquor store on the way to the Guildhall to snag a collection of empty boxes from the recycling bin in the rear. After filling the back of the town-car, they drove to Limani's Mercenary Guildhall, located on the edge of town toward Victory's manor house. The Guildhall served as the headquarters of Limani's local mercenary force, which doubled as Limani's military in times of need. It also housed a training center and meeting space, along with housing available for mercenaries passing through the city. Max also maintained an office and apartment there.

Syri met them at the entrance to the Guildhall, sitting on the front steps and basking in the morning sun. It was barely the end of June, and Toria already tired of the humidity. Syri didn't even sweat under her leather jacket. She stood and fell into step on Toria's other side as the three made their way to Max's office. "No luck with Victory?"

"Not really," Toria said. "What are you doing here?" Syri hadn't shown up the previous evening either, which was weird. For the past two years, the elven girl had spent three nights out of five at their apartment, either crashing on the futon in their living room or curling up in one of their beds.

They entered the anteroom of Max's office, and Kane waved to the retired merc who worked as Max's aide-de-camp. "Good morning, Liliah. Max is expecting us."

"Good to see you kids," Liliah said. "I'll let him know you're here. Grab a seat." She stood and poked her head into Max's office. If Toria hadn't known they were there, she never would have realized the older woman walked on two prosthetic legs.

Toria perched on the edge of one of the hard wooden chairs. Max discouraged visitors who didn't have appointments by having the least comfortable seats in the building outside his office. "So?" She poked Syri in the arm.

Syri shrugged. "Zerandan strongly suggested that I be here this morning."

Kane cocked his head. "How did Zerandan know we'd be here?"

"I've known him my whole life," Syri said, "and I will never understand my esteemed elder. But he's never steered me wrong. If there's a reason for me to be at this meeting, I guess we'll find out." She slouched in her own chair, going boneless in that way only elves and cats could in uncomfortable spots. "I'm still not going with you guys, though. I have vacation saved up, and the beach is calling my name."

Kane laughed. "We know, we know. Wear sunscreen." He patted Syri's porcelain thigh, a sharp contrast to his darker skin.

"Sunscreen," Syri said, the disdain evident in her voice. "That's what shields are for."

Saving Toria from the recurring argument that skin cancer threatened elves as much as anybody else, Max pushed open his office door. "Kids! Come on in. Sorry we kept you waiting."

The trio stood, and Toria mouthed "We?" to Kane as they passed Liliah's desk and entered Max's office. The spacious room embraced her with its familiarity. She and Kane had spent many hours here discussing military tactics and history with Max, surrounded by wall-to-wall bookshelves and overlooking the Guildhall's gym through a glass wall that stretched from floor to ceiling.

Max led them to the two couches facing each other in the center of the room, much more comfortable than the wooden chairs outside. Syri's great-great-uncle, the ancient elf Zerandan, sat in one, hand resting on his simple wooden cane. Toria knew the cane was an affectation, and his close-cropped blond hair, an unusual style choice among elves, threw her as always. Max settled next to him, looking much too casual in jeans and a T-shirt compared with Zerandan's impeccable suit.

"Greetings, Zerandan," Kane said. Toria echoed the words, and their mutual surprise echoed through their bond. Syri bent to kiss her uncle's cheek before she joined Toria and Kane on the facing sofa. Her expression was more shuttered.

"So." Max clapped his hands together. "Vacation over?"

"Vacation over," Toria said. "We're going to start packing up the apartment today. We need help making the final decision." Politeness held her tongue from asking outright, despite her curiosity.

"South to the Roman Colonies or across the ocean to Europa." Kane gave an eloquent shrug. "I want to get hired to kill beasties on the edge of the Wasteland. Toria wants to find bodyguard work for spoiled nobility. Eventually we have to come to a compromise."

"The perk of being a warrior-mage pair," Max said. His dry tone was arid as a desert.

"Yep," Toria said. "Phenomenal power! Best friend for life! And the complete inability to ever again make a decision on your own." Her hand found Kane's and squeezed. She'd never trade him for anything. "Anyway. We need your opinion on which focus might be more lucrative for journeymen. Kane thinks it'll be monster hunting, but I think the novelty of being warrior-mages will get us a lot of bodyguard opportunities for rich people who care more about appearances than initial ability."

"Those are both valid arguments," Max said. "And ordinarily I would be happy to talk you through both options to help you decide. But I think you two should hear what Zerandan has to say first."

"I do believe I have a solution to your problem," Zerandan said. "And that is why I asked Master Asher if I could be present for this meeting when Syrisinia told me about it." Syri's full name rolled off Zerandan's tongue as only elven names could to one of their own.

"Yes, sir?" Kane straightened on the couch.

"If Master Asher is not averse to letting you two take your first contract while you are still in Limani," Zerandan said. "I wish to hire you both."

"Nothing in the regs says you can't take your first job in your home territory. I certainly have no problem with it." Max gestured for Zerandan to continue.

"This should also settle your debate for you," Zerandan said. "Syrisinia informed me that there was concern over the fate of the human mage school here in Limani. I would like to hire you to investigate the decline in the mage population. If you accept the contract, I will arrange for you to have a meeting with the head of the larger mage school in New Angouleme."

Well. That did settle a few things. Toria sent an inquisitive mental push in Kane's direction, and he responded with a wide grin. New Angouleme was not to the south or across the ocean—instead, it was the capital to the British colonies to the north. They had decided not to immediately pursue contracts there because of the British cultural and political aversion to vampires, and neither Toria nor Kane took prejudice well after the short-lived Humanist movement in Limani two years ago.

But Zerandan had handed them the exact contract they wanted. They couldn't get much luckier than that.

"That would be amazing, sir," Kane said.

His grip on her hand had become too tight in his excitement. Toria wriggled it loose. "You must have known this was an issue before Syri told you, right?"

Zerandan favored her with a grave nod. "I was also approached to teach at the mage school, but elven magic, while not incompatible with human power as you know by your experience with my niece, is not conducive to training young humans to wield their gifts effectively."

"You didn't tell anyone that Toria and I would take over teaching, did you?" Kane asked.

"Of course not," Zerandan said. "That idea came about from other angles, and I would also not expect you two to take up those reins at this point in your lives. But I am concerned about the lack of mages in Limani. I hope that the mages in New Angouleme will be better informed on whether this is a natural downturn in population." He paused. "Syrisinia will be accompanying you."

"What!" Syri, heretofore silent on Toria's other side, all but leapt out of her seat. "Absolutely not, Uncle. I'm no mercenary."

Zerandan's kind voice was firm. "I wish you to go as my representative."

Toria smothered a laugh at her friend's dismay. "But I had beach plans," Syri said, sagging back down on the couch.

"If I recall my geography correctly, New Angouleme is a city on an island," Zerandan said, his tone brokering no argument.

Kane reached over Toria to pat Syri's shoulder, choking back a laugh. "I don't think you have a choice on this, love."

"If Master Asher will please retrieve the papers," Zerandan said. "I believe we have a contract to draw up."

"Congratulations, kids," Max said as he left the couch to rummage in his desk. "Day one of your journeyman stint starts right now."

\#

"No. Absolutely not."

Kane's frustrated tone carried through the apartment to the back bedroom. She loaded a few more books into a box in Kane's room, taped it closed, and hauled it with her when she got to her feet. Carrying it into the main room, she found Kane standing before Syri, arms crossed, dismay coloring his expression.

When Toria set down her box with the others ready to be moved to the manor, she saw why. Next to Syri sat two large trunks.

The elven girl also had her arms crossed in defiance. "Why the hell not?"

"Do you not understand the meaning of 'packing light'?" Kane said. "We are not taking all this stuff with us!"

"But I need it!"

"It's all clothes!"

"How do you know?"

Toria broke in. "Syri, is it actually all clothes?"

Syri uncrossed her arms, but wouldn't meet Toria's gaze. "Not exactly."

Kane grabbed a handwritten list off the kitchen counter. "Here."

He handed it over, and Syri perused it. "What's this?"

"What you're allowed to bring," Toria said. She nudged one of the trunks with her foot. Yep, probably stuffed to the brim. "Max and Mama helped us put this together a few months ago, when we were still undecided about where to go."

"We're going to New Angouleme by train," Syri said. "We can taxi to a hotel. I've made this trip before. It's civilized. We don't have to hand-carry everything."

"But we don't know where we might end up after that," Toria said. "Better safe than have to worry about what to leave behind in New Angouleme."

"Tell you what," Kane said. "Leave the trunks there. Help me finish this up, and I'll go back home with you and help you repack."

While Toria finished boxing up their personal belongings, which mostly consisted of Kane's book collection and her chemistry supplies, her partner was in charge of restoring the hardwood floor in the main room to its original pristine condition. They had three days to pack up. They were scheduled to depart Limani on the next transport barge north, and train tickets from Calverton to New Angouleme had been purchased.

They both already had their travel packs sorted and propped by the front door, and now it was a matter of readying the rest of their things for storage at the manor.

Since Kane would get distracted perusing his old books, Toria had accepted that task. Besides, he was the only one who could refinish the floor, and she had already helped him roll up the carpet and set it aside.

The carpet had hidden their working circle, drawn in paint and magic and spotted with drips of wax. While neither of them was prone to ritual, sometimes a magic circle was either required or useful. Toria would never forget sitting with Syri and making contact with Kane after his abduction. From that moment on, Syri's peculiar brand of elven magic had been entwined with their own magical abilities. It was a bit more difficult, but she could link minds with each of them as well as Toria and Kane could with each other.

But ritual circles were not things to leave lying around. Kane would use his connection with all things earth to remind the old wooden boards what they used to be. With Syri lending her own energy, the task would be done in half the time.

Syri gave one longing look at both trunks. "Okay. What do you need?"

Toria left them sitting cross-legged within the circle. A tickle of magic twisted up her spine as they set to work. With a mental flick, she tossed Kane a strand of her own energy, and she felt him braid it together with his own with the ease of long practice.

She had more books to pack.

#

"No. Absolutely not."

Toria turned around and tried to wipe the guilty expression from her face. As she feared, it was Kane's turn to despair over her packing abilities.

After packing everything into the barn behind the house, Toria had ducked out to visit Victory's training room and peruse the collection of weaponry along the walls while Kane and Syri finished their late lunch.

Kane pointed at the two extra swords, three knives (one almost long enough to count as a sword), and two firearms Toria had laid out on a bench. "We are not taking those."

"They're backups!"

"We don't need them! We're not bringing the supplies to make more ammo for the guns. Purchasing it will make us unnecessary targets."

Well, he had a point. Since manufacturing new firearms was not possible, local gossip always spread like wildfire if anyone bought ammunition. "You'll change your tune if you misplace your sword." Toria folded her own arms across her chest and faced off with him.

"Oh, man," Syri said. She leaned against the doorframe with a wide smile. "And I thought I had a problem."

"We are not going to lose our swords," Kane said. "You have a complex."

"I have legitimate concerns," Toria said. "You remember what happened."

26

"We got your rapier back," Kane said, injecting patience into his voice. "You never lost the saber, and Max replaced the gladius from what the Romans left behind."

"I'm pretty sure you do actually have a complex," Syri said. "But I might have to agree with Kane on this one."

"You're not even bringing any weapons," Toria said. Not willing to voice her agreement with them, she nonetheless replaced the pieces she'd picked out.

"Not true," Syri said. "I might not make a habit of wandering around Limani armed, but I did pack my knives."

That made Toria feel better, for a much different reason. She wasn't one hundred percent sure why Zerandan insisted Syri accompany them on this quest, and while she knew Syri could more than take care of herself in a fight, it was nice to know she and Kane wouldn't have that distraction.

She would still snag that long-knife before they left in the morning, though. And maybe the palm pistol.

#

Today was the day.

Toria stood at the entrance to Limani's customs house with her father and Kane while Syri shared a quiet moment with Zerandan a few feet away. The heavy scent of the river permeated the air, and the summer foliage of the surrounding forest was lush. With her usual luck, the awful humidity had finally broken, and a cool breeze drifted from the river. Despite her excitement to be on their way, Limani was her home, and she soaked it in for these last few moments.

They all dressed casually for travel, jeans and T-shirts and boots, with the swords at their waists their only apparent armament. Toria had visited the British colonies only once before in her life, with Kane's parents before they passed away. At the time, she hadn't paid attention to such things, but she took Max at his word when he said that it was more common for people to walk about armed, especially mercenaries and the nobility. The rest of her gear was bundled in the packs that lined the side of the customs house behind her. At least Kane had talked Syri down to two packs as well.

She sipped from her water bottle, turning away from the bright summer sunlight. The party at the manor house last night had been epic. It wasn't an official tradition to wave mercenary journeymen on their way with massive hangovers, but it might as well be. Kane was fine, of course. Hangovers were one of the few things he could heal on himself but couldn't touch on other people, not even his partner. Max and some of Limani's other mercenaries in residence had shown up with a keg, and there hadn't been a drop left when she'd checked it out of curiosity that morning.

Victory and Asaron had matched Max drink for drink, which probably explained Max's absence from the docks that morning as well. It was the daylight, not hangovers, that prevented her mother and grandfather from seeing them off. However, Toria was pleased that Mikelos had joined them.

She slipped an arm around her father's waist and leaned into him. "I'll miss you, Dad."

"I'll miss you, too," he said. Holding her close and whispering in her ear, he added, "You'll be fine. In fact, you guys will be great." Mikelos reached over and tugged Kane into a hug as well, and when he released them, his eyes were suspiciously bright.

That echoed what Victory had said to her last night, when she pulled her into the relative quiet of the library and away from the rest of the partygoers before either of them became more inebriated.

"You'll be amazing, daughter," Victory said, clasping both of Toria's hands in hers. "You and Kane both. Together you'll be unstoppable."

"Any final words of advice?" Toria blinked away a sudden spate of threatening tears. This wasn't supposed to be a sad moment. This was supposed to be the beginning of the rest of her life.

"Trust each other," Victory said. "You and Kane will be better partners than even Asaron and I ever were. And that's saying a lot."

That startled a giggle out of Toria. "So modest!"

Victory matched her wide smile, as always never hesitating to show vampiric fang around her daughter. "We'll talk when they write songs about you."

Syri and Zerandan joined them in the shade of the customs house. "I think in order to compete with Victory and Asaron, you two would pretty much have to save the world."

"Something to the effect," Mikelos said.

The customs house master, Rhaavi, came out of the front office, pulling on a cap over his shaved head. "Heard over the radio that the barge is almost here. You kids ready to go?"

"Ready as we'll ever be," Kane said.

Zerandan placed a hand on Syri's shoulder. "Daywalker, if I might have a moment with the young ones?"

Mikelos nodded, then followed Rhaavi back inside.

"Yes, sir?" Toria said. She and Kane fell into position, bracing Syri's left and right sides, respectively. She had the feeling that she should get used to that. Zerandan hadn't written protecting Syri into their contract, but Toria didn't think he'd be too pleased if anything happened to his niece. And while Syri was not a civilian per se, it was a good habit to get into if they wanted to pursue bodyguard contracts in the future.

"I have not contracted the two of you to perform this mission out of pity," Zerandan said. "While I was aware of the ongoing debate of where to seek your fortunes, I did not offer this quest as a solution. I have tasked all three of you with seeking the reason behind Limani's lack of mages because this is important, and because I feel that you will be the best to seek the answer."

"Thank you, sir," Toria said. She got the feeling that Zerandan wasn't telling them the whole story, but that was okay. She and Kane had gotten what they wanted—a contract to formalize the beginning to their journeyman travels. A contract that actually interested them.

"I realize Syri does not understand why I have asked her to accompany you," Zerandan said. "But have faith that I do not ask lightly."

"I know, Uncle," Syri said, stepping forward to place a hand on Zerandan's where it rested on his cane. "And I wouldn't have agreed to come if I didn't realize it meant so much to you. And if Toria and Kane weren't such good friends."

"Remember that you are all important to each other, and you will need each other in the days to come."

Before Zerandan could elaborate further, the barge appeared around the river bend, and Mikelos and Rhaavi emerged from the customs house again.

"Time to go," Toria said. It wasn't the most noble of sendoffs, but she didn't pull away when her father wrapped her in a hug once more. The "daddy's little girl" clichés could write themselves.

Mikelos squeezed her tight. "Just don't forget to write."

#

Toria stood at the railing at the deck's edge, keeping out of the way of the crewmembers performing final checks that the containers of trade goods they'd taken on in Limani were secure. This wasn't a passenger vessel. The large ferry only made the rounds between Calverton and the Grand Strand every two weeks. That would have made a more comfortable ride, especially for Kane, who lasted less than ten minutes away from shore before throwing up over the side of the ship. Earth mages handled being away from land about as well as storm mages dealt with being underground. Toria shivered in sympathy.

But the crew was used to the occasional travelers who didn't mind roughing it. One of the officers had been kind enough to offer his tiny cabin to store their gear for the day-long trip, and when he noticed the pallor evident even with Kane's dark skin, he insisted that Kane use the bunk as well. It was a measure of how much Kane trusted Syri that he had allowed her to put him to sleep for the duration of the voyage.

The trip from Limani to Calverton would span less than a day, so there had been no reason to wait for the more comfortable passenger ferry. They had tickets for the train the rest of the way north in the following morning.

Syri joined Toria at the railing, resting her arms in a matching pose.

"Kane okay?"

The elven girl nodded. "His brain wanted relief, so getting him under was hardly an effort. The second officer assured me that there would be enough time to wake him after we docked in Calverton, since they'll need time to load and unload cargo. We can wait until the ship isn't moving under his feet anymore."

"Good. Thanks for that."

Syri nodded once, and they lapsed into silence. Once down the Agios River, the barge sailed north up the Tranosari Bay, which widened until they could no longer see the shore to either side. Calverton, the southern capital of the British colonies, was a major trading port with the Romans colonies to the south.

It was official. They were on their way.

"So," Toria said. "Still no idea why Zerandan insisted you come with us?"

"No fucking clue," Syri said.

Toria saw a passing crewmember jerk in surprise at Syri's strong language. At this point, Syri's cursing didn't faze her. "There's no culture of young elves being pushed out of the nest, as it were, is there?"

"Not really," Syri said. "We all leave eventually, but I think that's mostly because we get sick of each other. But I'm not even from Limani. My mother followed Zerandan there shortly after I was born in Lenapenn. She left for Europa when I was still pretty young. I stuck around because I was in the middle of my degree at Jarimis University at the time."

"And now?"

"Well, now I'm stuck with you two." Syri nudged Toria in the arm with an elbow. "But really, I like the city. I like my job. I'm lucky my boss was okay with a sabbatical of undetermined length."

While Toria and Kane planned to make careers out of mercenary work, Syri had been content with her part-time position as a tech at Limani's veterinary office that catered to household pets, with occasional shifts over at the clinic dedicated to larger animals. She wasn't one of the elves with a talent for communicating with animals, but the mental component to her magic made it easier to soothe and even sedate them when doing so chemically might be unsafe.

Toria had lost count of how many times she'd come home to find a litter of kittens or puppies (and once, memorably, ferrets) tumbling about the apartment. Many all-night study sessions had been interspersed with hand-feeding baby animals.

They fell into comfortable silence again. Now was the time to poke at the metaphorical elephant. "You think Zerandan knows more about the situation with the mages than he's letting on?"

"Oh, thank gods, I thought it was only me." Syri sagged against the railing in comical relief. "I didn't want to say anything because I didn't want to freak you guys out."

"Yeah, not just you," Toria said. "Max and I chatted about it for a few minutes last night, but I got dragged away." She gave a mental wince at the memory of that round of shots. Her headache still hadn't faded all the way. "He has no idea either."

"I feel like he would have told us if it was something to really be concerned about," Syri said. "But at the same time, why would he have hired you two for this crazy quest if there wasn't something to be worried about?"

"Well, we'll check in with New Angouleme's mercs when we get to the city," Toria said. "Ask around there for any rumors. And we have the letter of introduction from Zerandan to the head of the mage school."

"Are you worried about the reception you'll get in the British colonies?" Syri asked.

"Not really." Toria shrugged. "We're not vampires, and it's not a crime to be related to one. Shouldn't be an issue."

So far, her first day as on official mercenary was less than thrilling. Toria fingered the hilt of her rapier and stared out over the water. Kane was even sleeping through it, but if the alternative was him in misery, that was more than fine with her.

"Come on," Syri said. "Almost lunchtime. Let's go see what the crew of this barge considers food."

"Welcome to living rough," Toria said. "Get used to it."

"Whatever," Syri said, though there was no vehemence in her voice. The two left the railing and threaded their way through shipping containers toward the crew quarters at the rear of the ship. "Remember that I could be sitting on a beach sipping a delicious alcoholic fruit drink instead."

"I'll buy you a flask of rum in Calverton tonight." Toria nodded her thanks at the crewmember who held the door open for them. They stepped over the raised lintel and aimed for the mess.

"Find me a pineapple to go with it, and you've got a deal," Syri said.

#

The barge docked in Calverton on schedule that afternoon. Syri woke Kane, and the three piled off the ship with their gear. Calverton had a different vibe than Limani: it was a much larger city, and shipping was a significant facet of its economy. The docks bustled with people, and the city proper sprang up immediately beyond. Cranes towered above office buildings and warehouses.

The tallest building in Limani stood at five stories, a fancy office building with residential lofts. Toria tried not to gape like a provincial, but she caught Kane stretching his neck back to appreciate the view as well.

"Come on, let's get through customs," Syri said. This was nothing new to her, and she led them through the crowd.

Max had been right about one thing already, and Toria was sure it wouldn't be the last. Open weapons were much more evident here, from dockworkers with knives at their belts to a businessman who wore a rapier similar to Toria's own blade. It wasn't that the British colonies were a more violent place, just a different culture. Dueling was still legal, and Toria knew she would be much less likely to challenge the elegant lady they passed with the well-worn compound longbow strapped to her back as if it wasn't even there.

The customs house was larger, too, and a security guard at the entrance directed them toward the short line of other incoming visitors. Within a few minutes, a clerk called the the three of them up to the counter to present their papers.

The customs officer examined their green leather-bound Limani passports, peered at each of them through gold-rimmed spectacles, and compared what he saw with their passports again.

"Reason for being in the colonies?" he asked, still studying the names in each booklet.

"Traveling to the mage school in New Angouleme, sir," Kane said. "We have train tickets for tomorrow morning."

"Mhm." He looked up at them again and removed his glasses. "Two humans traveling with an elf. But the humans have elven names?"

Of all the things for the customs officer to fixate on—two warrior-mages, journeymen mercenaries—their names had not been high on Toria's list. She knew her full first name, Torialanthas, was a mouthful, and Kane's surname wasn't common either. She wasn't keen on lying to a city official, but she knew bringing up her vampiric adopted mother was a terrible idea if she didn't want to arouse suspicion. Lying to a public official was not an auspicious way to start her mercenary career, but Toria figured it wouldn't be the last time. "I was fostered by elves, sir."

"And Nalamas was my great-grandfather," Kane said. "Also fostered by elves." That, at least, was the truth.

"Mhm." Without further comment, he stamped their passports and waved forward the next person in line.

The three traded curious glances as they left the customs house and headed away from the docks. "Shall we call a cab?" Toria asked. Within the past few months, Max had made her and Kane memorize the addresses of the Guildhalls in every major city, both on this continent and the old one. Even as journeymen, they had the right to rent spartan rooms in the barracks rather than pay for more expensive lodgings.

"No, wait," Syri said. "I've got a better idea." She snagged a passing dock worker, and asked whether a specific hotel was still in business. She lit up upon receiving an affirmative answer, then set off in a purposeful direction, Toria and Kane trailing behind.

Not more than a few blocks away, tucked between an office building and a large warehouse, was a quaint hotel set back from the road behind a garden. Its architecture indicated that it pre-dated the Last War, with a large veranda and decorative columns bracing the front entrance. A stone sign at the front drive read simply "Calvert Hall."

The doorman nodded at Syri as they passed through the entrance, large double-doors left open to the breeze that held the vague odor of harbor water. A shimmer of energy caressed Toria's exposed skin as they entered the lobby, and the brackish smell disappeared, replaced by a refreshing citrus scent.

"How pricy is this place, Syri?" Kane eyed the gilt-framed paintings on the surrounding plaster walls, portraits of Calverton businessmen and old-fashioned sailing ships in the harbor.

"Not pricy at all, for us," Syri said. They followed her to the desk, where she greeted the clerk. "Ceres! How's your father these days?"

The elven woman lit up as they approached. She left her position behind the desk to wrap Syri in a hug. "Syri! We had no idea you were coming to town!" She held Syri at arm's length to look her up and down, and the two made a striking pair. Syri in her jeans and leather jacket versus the stylish woman in a cream silk business suit. Ceres' black skin was multiple shades darker than even Kane's, in sharp contrast to her typically elven emerald eyes and pale blond hair.

"I wasn't even sure this place still existed," Syri said. "Didn't occur to me until on the boat up here. I take it the main suite is unavailable?"

"Sorry, some businessmen from Lenapenn are in town for a conference and had it booked months ahead of time," Ceres said. "But there are a couple other good rooms available. Let me check where to put you three." She returned to her position behind the desk and tapped away at the computer. "This must be the infamous warrior-mage pair that everyone has heard about?"

"Oh, I'm sorry," Syri said. "Torilanthas Connor, Toria, and Kane Nalamas, Kane. This is Cereskarensa, Ceres." She gave the casual elven introduction, rather than making the effort to trace everyone's convoluted familial connections as she would have in a more formal setting. "Third cousin, twice removed? Something like that."

"Our fathers were good friends," Ceres said. "But I haven't seen you in almost ten years! I hate to ask whether the gossip is true, but there's an awful lot of gossip." She plucked three keys from the rack on the wall behind her and distributed one to each of them. "And the fee is waived, of course. Papa's not due back from Fort Caroline until this weekend. He'll be devastated that he missed you."

"We appreciate it, thank you," Toria said. She turned her attention to Syri. "Gossip, eh?"

Syri waved a dismissive hand in her direction. "Elves talk, that's all they're good for. Don't worry about it." She looked at her key. "Blue suite?"

"Yep," Ceres said. "Need help with your bags?"

"No, thank you," Kane said.

"You have to have dinner here, of course," Ceres said. "The dining room will be open in an hour."

"You'll join us?" Syri said. "We'll drop our packs in the room and chill in the bar until you're free."

The desk telephone chose that moment to ring, and Ceres mouthed her acknowledgment before answering it. The three picked up their packs and headed to the elevator in the back of the lobby.

The hotel suite was small but luxurious. Toria plotted with Kane how to keep Syri with them for the next eighteen months if this was the level of accommodations they could expect wherever they travelled. Syri rolled her eyes at them, and they traipsed back downstairs to the hotel dining room and lounge that overlooked a lovely back lawn. If it weren't for the brick buildings on all three sides, it was almost as if they weren't in the middle of a city's bustling downtown district.

In lieu of searching for pineapples, Toria had the bartender concoct Syri the most outrageous fruit cocktail she could manage. The three settled in for some people-watching as they waited for Ceres to join them for dinner.

Syri and Kane chatted about the next morning's train trip, but Toria stared around the fancy lounge. It wasn't that she was unused to such surroundings, not with her elite parentage, but it was odd to be in such an environment without the patronage of Victory or Mikelos. Of course, her and Kane's status as warrior-mages would open similar doors in their travels, but she would still need some time before she stopped looking for her mother over her shoulder.

The three looked a bit out of place in their casual travel garb while surrounded by business professionals. Most were human, but Toria threw on her magesight for a few seconds and noticed a cluster of werewolves in a back corner. Rather than colorful auras, most werecreatures showed their other forms in a shadowy overlay, along with a vague sensation that indicated their age and relative power. The hotel's dining staff gave these four much deference, and Toria remembered that all werewolves in the colonies were essentially British nobility, regardless of their status.

The Roman Empire had once rulled Britannia, as it had most of the continent of Europa, until the four main werewolf clans of Albion had joined forces. These days, the two empires operated under a delicate set of treaties, such as using Limani as a neutral zone between both sets of colonies on the New Continent. However, vampires were still anathema in all lands under British rule, since vampires ruled Roma during the time of expansion and still held much influence in the current senate.

Toria waved to Ceres when the elven woman entered the dining room, but instead, Ceres approached the seated werewolves first. She couldn't overhear the conversation, but by Ceres' body language, it was clear that even elves showed the wolves respect in British holdings. A far cry from the equality for which Limani was famous.

After a final short bow, Ceres made her way to their table. "Sorry I'm later than expected," she said, settling into the table's empty seat. "I already stopped by the kitchen, and Cook is preparing something special for us. I hope you all like crab? A Calverton specialty." The business suit was gone, replaced with refined a blouse and slacks. Now Toria felt even more underdressed.

"Sounds great," Kane said, with a light touch to Toria's knee under the table. Her anxiety must have bled through their link. He had always been much surer of himself in formal settings. That was probably another one of the reasons why he got more dates than she did.

"Everything okay?" Toria asked, cocking her head toward the wolves.

Ceres waved a hand. "Oh, no problems. Just checking on some guests." She leaned closer over the table, whispering, "They're the ones staying in the penthouse suite."

Ah, the fancy businessmen from up north that Ceres had mentioned earlier. Made sense.

Syri and Ceres soon lost Kane and Toria as the women caught up on years' worth of gossip, and the conversation turned to friends and family across the land. But the crab cakes served for dinner were as delicious as promised, and the warrior-mages were content to sit back and let the voices wash over them, interjecting here and there with anecdotes from life in Limani.

Dessert had been served, caramel ice cream flavored with a popular local spice, when two of the werewolves approached their table, one gray-haired and distinguished and the second much younger, but with a family resemblance. Ceres rose to her feet, and the other three followed a beat later.

"Lord Hurst," Ceres said. "May I help you?"

"Please pardon my interruption," the elder said, smoothing the front of his pinstripe three-piece suit. "I hope I can trouble you for an introduction. If I'm not mistaken, this young couple are the warrior-mages of Limani?"

"Yes, sir," Ceres said. "May I introduce Toria Connor and Kane Nalamas. This is Lord Caspian Hurst, and his son, Evan Hurst."

Toria racked her brain about how to handle a formal introduction with bonafide British nobility. Victory's etiquette lessons had been long ago. Lord Hurst took her hand but did not shake it, so Toria bobbled a short curtsy, awkward as it was in jeans. Kane fared much better with a short bow. "It is an honor to meet you, sir," Toria said.

"The pleasure is mine, my dear," Lord Hurst said. "Please, resume your dessert. Thank you for indulging an old man his curiosity." After a short bow of his own, he made his way back to his corner booth. His son stared at them for a beat longer before turning to follow his father in silence.

They all returned to their seats. "That was odd," Syri said. "The kid okay?"

Ceres peeked at the werewolves over her shoulder, ensuring they were ensconced back in their booth, before she responded. "Of course they already knew who you were. They wanted to check out the vampire's kids." She waved away the looks of surprise on her companion's faces. "Trust me, everyone from Lenapenn to Calverton is well aware of Victory and Asaron as the closest vampires to our borders."

"I hope they don't think we're some sort of threat," Kane said.

"Probably not," Ceres said. "And I certainly have no aversion to vampires. But you know how the British are."

"We're certainly learning," Toria said, scraping the bottom of her bowl of ice cream.

#

The three were on their way again early the next morning, after a hearty breakfast in Calvert House's dining room. Ceres wasn't on duty early, but the night before, she had arranged for a taxi to meet them in front of the hotel and transport them to the train station. Somehow, Toria was not surprised when an unmarked stylish town-car arrived to collect them rather than one of the yellow cabs they'd passed on the way to the hotel the previous afternoon.

The ride to the train station passed quickly as they all stared out at the passing city. The station was located near the docks they had arrived at, farther down the harbor. It was the southernmost end of the line for the modern railway system built less than ten years before, after the success of the same electric system in the isles of Britannia.

The driver waved away all efforts to compensate him, insisting that Ceres had even taken care of the tip. Toria and Syri waited with the packs while Kane ducked inside the station to collect their reserved tickets from the main office.

Syri hid a yawn behind her hand, which prompted the same involuntary response from Toria.

"How can you be tired already?" Toria asked.

"That breakfast was huge," Syri said. "Now I'm crashing."

"You can sleep on the train."

"I've got a better idea." Syri dropped her second pack next to Kane's on the sidewalk. "Be right back." She darted across the street and disappeared into a coffee shop that catered to patrons of the train station.

"Toria Connor."

Startled, Toria turned on her heel. Though he wore more casual clothing, she recognized the man in front of her from the Calvert House. "Lord Evan Hurst," she said. "Good morning."

He did not return her courtesy. "Where's your partner?" The werewolf's stony gaze did not waver. He crossed his arms, emphasizing supernaturally enhanced muscles even more.

Honesty never hurt anyone. "He's inside, fetching our tickets." With a flash of magesight, Toria spotted more werewolves lurking up the block, their invisible furry exteriors overlaying two more overmuscled men. That couldn't be coincidence. As if it had grown too heavy for her to bear any longer, Toria dropped her pack next to the others. She held back from placing a hand on the hilt of her rapier, though. No need to borrow trouble. "Are you also travelling this morning?"

"No," Evan said. "My father sent me to find out what you are hiding."

Toria blinked in genuine surprise. "Hiding? What would we be hiding?"

"The real reason behind your trip to our lands," he said. "Espionage."

"Yeah, you've lost me," she said. "We're on contract to a friend in Limani. We just officially became mercenary journeymen. No intention of spying, sorry. Besides, it's not as if we're the only people from Limani to ever visit Calverton."

"But you're the only ones who count vampires in your lineage."

Oh. So that's what this was about. "I apologize again," Toria said. "But my mother has nothing to do with this trip. Feel free to drop her a line and ask. I can even give you her direct number."

Evan's eyes flashed from hazel to amber, his wolf growing closer to the surface. "I do not consort with vampires."

Power caressed Toria's skin, and she felt her shields grow stronger as they merged with Kane's. Her partner loomed up behind her. "Bigotry doesn't suit you, Lord Hurst."

Toria noted that the two werewolves up the street drifted closer to them. But they didn't have time for a fight—they had a train to catch. "I apologize for the confusion, sir," she said, "but I promise you that we really are here on behalf of our patron, the elf Zerandan. Not representing Limani, and certainly not representing my mother." Now she did lay a gentle hand on the hilt of her rapier. "Please give our respects to your father. If he has any further concern, we will be staying at the Mercenary Guildhall in New Angouleme for the foreseeable future." Perhaps her willingness to share their whereabouts would allay the werewolves' fears.

Evan backed away a few steps. "See that you stay out of trouble in New Angouleme. The wolves of our capital will not be so forgiving." At that, he turned on his heel and stormed away. With a snap of his fingers, the other two werewolves Toria had been tracking fell into step behind him.

Now Toria faced her partner. He held his bared scimitar low. "What the hell was that about?" Kane asked.

"No idea," Toria said.

Syri appeared at their side, balancing a travel tray holding three paper cups, and peered up the street in the direction they were looking. The scent of coffee and chocolate permeated the air around her. "What'd I miss?"

#

They boarded the train without further incident, claiming a private compartment for themselves and loading their packs in the netting above the padded bench seats Toria kept her magesight on, but though she saw a few werewolves in the gaggle of people boarding the train with them, none gave the trio a second glance. She let it fade halfway once they settled in their compartment with the door shut.

Kane inhaled his latte, then gave Toria's mocha yearning looks from the opposite bench. She cradled the drink close. "My caffeine."

Syri had finished her latte even faster than Kane. She stretched herself out on the bench with her head in Kane's lap and her eyes closed. "Technically, my coffee. I bought it."

"Thank you, darling," Toria said.

"Anything for you, my love," Syri said, twitching the fingers of her left hand in a dismissive gesture. "Anyone want to tell me what that was all about back there?"

Toria recounted her impromptu meeting with the younger werewolf lord, following up the short tale with, "Are we seriously going to have to watch our backs in New Angouleme?"

Syri cracked an eye open at Toria. "I doubt it. Sounded more like the young Lord Hurst was doing more posturing than actual threatening."

"I didn't get the impression that his father was being anything other than cordial when he approached us last night," Kane said. "But we'll keep our eyes open, just in case."

With a barely perceptible lurch, the train started moving. They heard none of the loud clacking over train tracks Toria remembered from old vids, only a smooth electric hum. She could see the same thoughts crossing Kane's face, and she grinned at him. "We're living in the future!"

"I'm sure Asaron would have something to say about how spoiled we are." Kane threaded his fingers through Syri's hair, but she batted his hand away.

Toria contemplated stretching out over her own bench, but she didn't have the advantage of Syri's petite height. "What's the plan when we get to New Angouleme? This ride is only four hours long. We'll still have most of the day."

Kane shrugged one shoulder. "Check into the local Guildhall. See if they have barracks available and whether they'll let Syri crash with us. Go to the mage school and poke around?"

"We won't really have to poke around," Toria said. She reached over her head and patted one of her packs. "We have the letter of introduction from Zerandan, so we can go straight to the top."

"Sounds good," Kane said. They lapsed into silence for a bit, enjoying the gentle sway of the train carriage and the quiet murmur of voices spilling over from the next compartment.

Despite the caffeine, the motion of the train and her large breakfast lulled Toria into relaxation. Her magesight had receded into the relative background of her vision, and she let her eyes unfocus further, until the sparkle of her violet prismatic shields, the fluid emerald of Kane's, and rainbow hues of Syri's filled her field of view. She relaxed sideways against the window of the train, propping her leg up on the bench next to her. "Prime, not prime?"

"I'm not playing your ridiculous number game," Kane said. "You cheat."

"It's not cheating to know the rules of how numbers work," Toria said.

"Just really nerdy," Syri said.

"You both suck." Toria let them off the hook, knowing it had been a long shot. Her vision narrowed to a slit, until the colors of their magical shields and elven aura filled her entire view.

A sudden flash of pure white light crossed her vision. Toria flinched back, knocking the back of her skull against the window, and threw a forearm across her face with a yelp of pain. When she blinked spots away, she found Kane and Syri sitting straight up, eyeing her with concern from the other side of the compartment.

"What the hell did you do?" Syri asked.

"Nothing!" Toria scrubbed her face with her hands. "It was really bright."

"I didn't see anything," Kane said.

"I had magesight on," Toria said. "Something must have passed right outside our compartment. I've never seen anything like it."

"That was it?" Syri said. "Just something—bright?"

"Yep," Toria said. She flicked the mental switch to the off position, and the world faded back to dull reality. She wasn't eager to repeat that experience if the mysterious light came back from the opposite direction.

"An aura or a shield?" Kane said.

"Not sure," Toria said. "It was a split second. It might not have even been a person, but something they carried."

"Hold on, what's that?" Syri reached to the floor of the cabin and picked up a slip of paper. She unfolded it and flipped it over and back again, but both sides were empty.

Toria plucked it from her and examined either side. A blank scrap of white paper, ripped from a notebook. "Must have been left here by the previous passengers and we just now noticed it."

"Well, keep your magesight off," Kane said, "but we'll all keep our eyes open. Something with that much power is bound to be noticeable."

With a dramatic sigh, Syri slumped back against the bench. "No nap for me, then."

"Nope, sorry," Toria said. She shoved the scrap of paper into her jeans pocket. No sense in littering. "So…prime, not prime?"

#

A few hours later, the view as they approached New Angouleme pulled them away from their debate of whether two friends back in Limani were indeed hooking up or not. Though fields of wheat and corn still surrounded them, skyscrapers were visible in the distance as the tracks looped south of the city. The silver- and bronze-hued structures dominated the small island that made up the city proper, and the tops of the suspension bridge the train would use to cross also peeked above the fields.

"That's…wow," Toria said. With no one else around, she felt freer to gape than she had in Calverton. Of course, the buildings in Calverton now seemed like nothing special in comparison.

41

Kane was also plastered to the window. "How is that even possible? Magic?"

"Nope," Syri said. She wasn't as impressed, and Toria was reminded that Syri had been well-traveled before settling in Limani to attend college. Even if it hadn't been during Toria's lifetime, Syri had visited New Angouleme before, and the sight would be nothing new to her.

"Pure physics and engineering," Toria said. She'd seen pictures, but they paled in comparison to the real thing.

"Wow is right," Kane said.

Toria and Kane remained entranced by the approaching city for the last half hour of the trip. Farmland made way for suburbs of townhouses and apartment buildings, and once they crossed the river, they entered the city proper. Toria had seen maps, and except for a few large parks, the entire island teemed with humanity. The population of Limani could fit in a few of the towering buildings.

They gathered their packs as the train pulled into the station. Syri touched Kane's hand as he lifted down her packs. "Hey, are you okay?"

"Yeah, I'm fine."

Toria heard the hesitation in his voice. She studied her partner's face. They'd been living in each other's pockets for over a decade, and he couldn't hide the pallor behind his dark skin. "Seriously, what's wrong?" She stepped in front of the train compartment's door before he could open it.

"I'm…not sure," Kane said. "Once we crossed the bridge, my stomach started churning. It's probably nothing."

"Do you need anything?" Toria dropped one pack from her shoulder onto the bench behind her. "I can dig out the med kit."

"No, no, it'll be okay," Kane said.

"Promise you'll say something if it gets worse?" Syri said.

"I promise," Kane said. "Let's get out of here."

#

If Toria had thought the docks at Calverton were busy, they had nothing on the central train station of New Angouleme. The trains had entered tunnels at the city limits, and when they came up the escalator, it was as if they'd appeared downtown by magic. Kane had to grab her arm to pull her along when she stopped in the main hall to stare at the mural on the ceiling.

"The stars are wrong." She couldn't hide the plaintive note in her voice.

"Who knows why the Brits do what they do," Kane said. "You're holding up traffic."

When they exited the building, the noise was almost overwhelming. Traffic, construction noise, and the sheer number of voices swirled around them. Buildings towered above, and if it hadn't been near noon, the streets would have been cast in shadow. Instead, sunlight gleamed off metal and concrete. And what was that smell? Too many people crammed into too close a space.

This time, Kane stopped in the middle of the sidewalk, and a passing businessman cursed tourists under his breath. But Kane wasn't distracted by the chaos. His packs fell at his feet and he wrapped his arms around his stomach. "Hold up."

Toria wheeled around and also dropped her packs at the look on her partner's face. Now his skin was ashen. She grasped his upper arms and flinched at the sensations that coursed through the contact. Now she felt what Kane felt—the air smelled rancid, and the ground beneath their feet roiled with toxins. The natural feeling of earth was buried, covered in layers of manmade material.

Both of them sagged in relief when Syri reached up to place her hands behind their necks and the overwhelming miasma faded. "Shield. Now."

With a mental twist, Toria pulled up her walls to almost combat levels. Kane did the same less than a heartbeat later. The horrible feelings didn't disappear completely, but the shields muted them to a more manageable level.

Syri stepped back. "Better?"

They both nodded. "What the hell was that?" Kane asked.

"I should have known this would happen," Syri said. "New Angouleme is an old city, built up over the centuries. There's a reason there aren't many earth mages here."

"I don't blame them." The color was back in his face, so Toria didn't stop him when he stooped to pick up their packs. "Okay, now we're really blocking traffic."

People had never stopped streaming past them during their private little drama. If Toria hadn't already known, this showed how different Limani was, where people would have paused to make sure they were okay.

Kane handed each of them their packs before picking up his own. "Okay. Let's get settled in before we visit the mage school. Know anyone who runs fancy hotels in New Angouleme?" he asked Syri.

Syri rolled her eyes, but the fact that Kane could joke made Toria feel better. Keeping their shields at this strength would be draining after a while, but hopefully only this heart of the city messed with Kane's earth sense to such a strong degree.

Syri hailed a cab, and they shoved their packs in the trunk before piling into the town-car. Toria gave the driver the address to the local Mercenary Guildhall. Without batting an eyelash, the young woman merged into the jostling, honking mess that was New Angouleme traffic.

Another way Limani was different. The local cab drivers made it their business to converse with—gossip with, interrogate—their passengers, but this driver ignored them while bopping along to the music emanating from her front dash. Toria didn't recognize the band, but she didn't find the perky beat too terrible.

Less than thirty harrowing minutes later, most of it stuck at one intersection, they left the shadow of the towering skyscrapers and their speed picked up. Now they passed by smaller businesses and private townhouses, down tree-lined streets. Every block held a vacant lot that featured gardens or a tiny park. Toria placed two fingers on Kane's bare wrist and lowered her shields a fraction. Nothing. At her mental nudge, Kane let his own combat shields fall away, and she felt the relief that crossed his face shiver down her own spine. They would be better prepared next time they ventured downtown.

The driver pulled to a stop before a sprawling mess of buildings that occupied an entire city block. The Guildhall of New Angouleme appeared to have grown organically over the years, enveloping its neighbors as it expanded. There was no signage, simply an unobtrusive bronze plaque by the double doors standing open to let in the warm summer breeze. It bore the crossed broadsword and longbow mark of the British Mercenary Guild. They were in the right place.

Toria paid the cab driver and thanked her as Kane unloaded their packs. Syri stared up at the building, her expression unreadable. Toria nudged her with an elbow. "You okay?"

"They going to let a punk like me in there?"

"You're with us," Toria said. "They better."

The three trooped up the granite steps, shoulder to shoulder, and entered a grand foyer that seemed dim after the bright sunlight. A darkened enormous crystal chandelier hung from the ceiling, but wall sconces that cast shadows over the marble floor provided the room's lighting. "Fancy," Kane said under his breath, and Toria couldn't help but agree. Limani's Guildhall was smaller and much more utilitarian. But since New Angouleme had almost ten times the population, and a proportionally larger number of local mercenaries, Toria supposed their annual dues had to go somewhere.

"Can I help you?" A stern voice from their left called their attention to a large reception desk. An older man stood behind it, his hands clasped behind his back.

Despite their distance, he appeared to be looking down his nose at them. Even his crisp suit emanated minor disdain.

Toria plastered on her sweetest smile. "Good afternoon. We are visiting New Angouleme on contract and wanted to inquire about renting a room in the barracks for a few nights." She pulled her Guild badge and identification card out of her wallet and laid them on the desk. The placard in front of the computer read "Scott Graham." Must be their charming new friend.

Rather than reaching for her ID, Graham cleared his throat. Kane also handed over his badge and card, and Syri presented her passport. He peered at the Guild documents and flipped through Syri's passport. "She is not Guild?" he asked Toria. Apparently not being a member of the Mercenary Guild meant Syri was also a nonentity to this gentleman.

"She's a friend," Kane said. "Traveling with us as part of our contract."

"There are regulations."

"We have no problems sharing a room," Toria said. This had become more of a production than anticipated.

Graham compared the two Guild identification cards, then looked back up at them, a hint of surprise warring with suspicion in his eyes. "Journeymen?"

"Yes, sir," Kane said.

"Aren't you a little...old?"

So that was the problem. "Not at all, sir," Toria said. "We joined the Guild at sixteen. But we delayed our journeyman stint until after we finished college." They had faced that stigma in the past, mostly from other mercenaries passing through Limani. But Limani citizens who passed up the quality of education that Jarimis University offered were fools, and Victory and Mikelos did not raise fools.

"I see. Let me see what is available." Graham placed the cards on the desk in front of him, then typed notes into his computer.

What a difference from the Limani Guildhall, which had no fancy hall, no receptionist. Just a large common room, where any lounging mercs were more likely to help haul your bags to a free room and scrounge up a beer than to interrogate you.

It was only their second day gone, but Toria felt the stirrings of homesickness. Kane slipped his hand into hers under the counter, and she squeezed back in thanks. Home was where her partner was.

Graham distracted her from her pensiveness when he pushed their IDs and Syri's passport back to them. "We have one room available with two beds. Will that suffice?" His gaze was not quite disdainful.

Kane's turn to be charming. "Thank you, sir," he said. "That will be perfect."

"Very well," Graham said. "You have missed luncheon, but the mess schedule is available in your room." Their dues to Limani's Guildhall covered their stay here. Every month, the Guildhalls across five continents settled accounts for traveling mercenaries. One of the perks of being a Guildmember was guaranteed shelter in most major cities.

Graham only handed them one key, but Toria wasn't inclined to complain at this point. He also pointed them down a corridor toward the barracks section of the compound. They pulled their packs onto their shoulders—Toria crossed mental fingers that it was for the last time that day—and they traipsed through the New Angouleme Guildhall.

Even a simple service hallway to the barracks was tasteful, with polished hardwood floors and random artwork tucked into corners. They soon found their room, which was neatly appointed. Sunlight streamed through a large window that overlooked a courtyard garden. If Graham had given them the worst in the house, it was still a clean room with two beds tucked against opposite walls. They would work out sleeping arrangements later. It wasn't as if the three hadn't shared beds with each other on multiple occasions since Syri became attached to them.

"Fancy," Syri said, dropping onto one of the beds and bouncing a bit. "Max needs to step up his game."

"Max has a more limited budget," Kane said. "And Limani's mercs prefer a stocked bar over lavish decor."

"We have our priorities in order," Toria said. "I'm starved. Let's find lunch, then the mage school. We've got work to do."

Kane found a map of the city in the desk under the window, and they plotted a route to the mage school. If the Guildhall took up an entire city block, the mage school occupied an entire estate with attached large park. But it was less than two miles away, and they could easily walk it and acquire food on the way.

"Gear up," Kane said. "The easy part's done."

#

They didn't don battle armor for an audience with the master of one of the biggest mage schools on the New Continent, but they showered quickly in the room's tiny private bath and changed out of their travel clothes. It never hurt to make a good impression.

Toria accepted possession of the key after they locked up the room, and they retraced their steps back to the front of the Guildhall. Syri waved at Graham as they passed through the foyer, but the older merc ignored them in favor of his computer. This did not surprise Toria, though she still didn't think being older journeymen was cause for this level of disrespect.

Nope, they certainly weren't in Limani anymore.

They purchased sausages in buns at a food cart and ate as they strolled, rather than finding a cafe to sit down. Syri informed them that such a practice was common in the city, and it was cheaper than anything on the menu posted by the door of one restaurant they passed. The cost of living in this city was also much higher than back home—the British colonial tax system at work. But the sausages were savory and filling, especially when chased with a large bottle of sparkling water shared between the three of them.

After passing one last block of townhouses, they found themselves at the entrance of a park. Ivy-covered walls stretched in either direction, and the wrought iron fence stood open. Much like the New Angouleme Guildhall, a golden plaque attached to the wall next to the gate subtly declared the premises to be the "New Angouleme Center for Magical Education."

The gatehouse stood empty. With a shrug to her companions, Toria started up the paved road. Magic shivered over her as she passed through the gates. Even though they felt like passive identification shields, they were the most powerful Toria had ever touched. Activating her magesight, Toria halted on the path in awe.

"Whoa." Kane's breathless exclamation behind her meant he must have done the same.

A rainbow shimmer hung in the air before her, coating every tree, flower, and blade of grass in the manicured gardens around them with iridescent sparkles. Kane's connection to the earth must show him an even more spectacular vision, but the arching colors alone impressed Toria. This wasn't the work of one or even a dozen mages maintaining shields around the grounds of the school. This was the result of decades of the school's mages infusing extra power into a set of shields tied to the school itself. If New Angouleme was ever threatened by a rogue nuclear weapon the way Limani had been two years before, Toria suspected that this area could escape unscathed. Though the surrounding city would become uninhabitable, rendering the location a poor one for any "center for magical education."

"Okay, kids," Syri said. "Stop being distracted by the pretty colors."

With a reluctant mental twitch, Toria closed away her magesight. "How do you even know what we're looking at?"

"Because you both only get those rapturous expressions when you're playing with complex magic or sparring with each other," Syri said. "And because even I can feel the power in this place, which means it has to be epic."

With a visible shake, Kane blinked at Toria and Syri with a sheepish grin. "It was definitely shiny."

They wended down the path again, through more gardens and grottos, toward the stone structure that emerged from the trees. "A castle?" Toria said. "Really?"

"It's only pretentious if you don't know the history," Syri said. "It was originally intended to be a museum of artifacts from the British Empire, but the builders ran out of money. The local mages were looking to expand the school so they took it over."

"How economical," Kane said. He still stared around at random plants in the surrounding gardens. Toria hooked her hand in his elbow and prodded him forward at a faster pace.

Perhaps because of the opulent surroundings, Toria expected doorkeepers at the grand front entrance. However, similar to Limani's mage school, New Angouleme's front door opened to a lounge area, though much larger and lavish. It seemed that everyone in New Angouleme preferred silk where cotton would do. Or at least the mages and the mercs did.

Unlike Limani's mage school, however, this reception desk was manned. "May I help you?"

The quiet voice startled Toria, and she felt Syri twitch next to her.

The petite woman standing behind the desk stood shorter than Syri, and she appeared to fade into the background even while Toria stared straight at her. Neutral hair, somewhere between light brown and dirty blond. Beige business suit. Pale skin, but not the porcelain of an elf's. Washed-out blue eyes that appeared glazed over—perhaps she had a vision impairment? Something seemed off about the woman, overall.

On a hunch, Toria blinked on her magesight. Next to her, Syri whispered, "Simulacrum." That made sense. What appeared to be a woman had no aura, only a pale gray shimmer visible above her exposed skin. The simulacrum's form had originated as clay, and achieved limited sentience through high quantities of magic. With a slight shudder, Toria closed off her magesight again. Creepy.

As if they hadn't just been ogling her, the woman asked again, "May I help you?" The smile on her face never wavered as they approached her with caution.

"Um, good afternoon," Toria said. "My name is Torialanthas Connor, with my partners Kane Nalamas and Syrisinia. We are here as representatives of Zerandan of Limani. We have a letter of introduction to meet with Master Sherman Burrows at his convenience." They weren't on a strict deadline after all, and it never hurt to be as polite as possible when requesting the attention of one of the most powerful mages of the British Empire.

Syri withdrew the letter in question from an inside pocket of her leather jacket and slid it across the desk to the simulacrum. They had spent a lot of time on the petitioner's side of desks over the last two days. Max was right—much like war, mercenary work would be ninety-nine percent waiting and one percent sheer terror.

The woman picked up the letter, and Toria hid another flinch. Her hands looked fine, except for the lack of fingernails. The movement of her limbs appeared natural, with the barest hint of jerkiness that would not have been obvious had Toria not been looking for it. The sheer amount of power needed to maintain this simulacrum to run a reception desk impressed her even more than the ambient energy outside had. That was the result of decades of magical students and residents. This was an intentional use of power for a rather benign purpose.

The simulacrum scanned the text of the letter once before refolding it and passing it back to Syri. She cocked her head to the side and stared in between Syri and Kane's bodies at the far wall. Before Toria could ask whether she needed any other information from them, the woman said, "Master Burrows will send a representative to meet with you soon. Please help yourself to a beverage and have a seat in the waiting area." She must have a magical connection with someone else here in the school to be able to make such a proclamation.

All three of them backed away from the desk a few steps before turning to the lounge area. Silk over cotton indeed. Luxurious couches and chairs formed three separate seating areas, and a beverage bar lined the far wall. Across from them, a fire crackled in a grand fireplace. The room was cool despite the summer weather outside, and as Toria approached it, she realized the fire was pure illusion. She dropped onto a couch, keeping a weather-eye on the simulacrum. She ignored them, staring straight ahead at nothing. Eerie.

Kane sat next to her after he finished investigating the bar area. He pressed a glass of water into her hand. The cool glass had already formed condensation, but when she peeked back over her shoulder, she saw that the glass pitcher on the counter contained no ice.

Perhaps it was the way she and Kane had been trained, but such flagrant uses of energy for convenience rather than purpose set her nerves on edge. Master

Procella and the other teachers of Limani's mage school had favored economy of power and self-reliance. Her biggest cheat was setting candles alight with mind alone, but most of that impulse stemmed from how long it had taken her to master that particular cantrip.

Syri finished examining the New Angouleme cityscapes that decorated the walls on either side of the fireplace. She drew a finger across the mantle as if inspecting for dust, then wandered over and stole Toria's glass. She settled back into the sofa across from them, almost swallowed by the plush cushions.

"Prime, not prime?" Toria ducked away from the blow Kane mimed in her direction. "Joking, joking. So. Fancy mage school, or fanciest mage school ever?"

"It's certainly not what I was expecting," Syri said. "I've only ever visited Limani's and the one in the Roman colonies to the south. This is definitely a notch above both."

Kane nodded. "I wonder if this is all to impress nonmagical visitors, or if the whole place is like this?"

One of the double doors on the other end of the lobby swung open, and a young man a few years older than Toria and Kane maundered in. The three of them rose to their feet to meet him. He must have heard Kane, because as he approached, he said, "Mostly just the public areas to impress guests and parents. The rest is much more casual." Image supported words, because he sported jeans and a fitted T-shirt. However, despite his informal attire, he was the most gorgeous man Toria had ever seen in her life.

Dark blue eyes over arched cheekbones were set in dusky olive skin, and his close-cropped black hair was styled as neatly as his goatee. He stopped before the three of them, cocked a hand on a hip, and favored each of them with a smile. Toria could feel the instant attraction she'd felt for the stranger reflecting back as Kane had the same idea.

But there was something about that smile...

With a gentle nudge of her mind, Toria poked at the illusion that surrounded the man. It fell away in a dust of sparkles, leaving a man with the same clothing and dusky skin, but with plain brown eyes. What he lacked in magically induced sexual appeal he made up for with his striking hair, which now fell in dreadlocks over his shoulder. Some of the ropes were dyed the same blue as his illusionary eyes.

But Toria recognized this man. The hair was different, and he was much older, but the cocky look rang familiar. "Archer?"

Archer Sophin, former student of Limani's mage school during Toria's apprentice days, grinned back at her. "Hey, Tor. Long time no see."

With a squeal, Toria threw her arms around Archer. "What the hell are you doing here?"

He laughed and squeezed her back. "Making a nuisance of myself, mostly, since I'm not teaching any classes during summer term. But look at you, all grown up." He stepped back and held Toria out at arm's length.

"You're one to talk," Toria said, looking up a few inches to meet Archer's eyes. "What the hell is up with your hair? And why the ridiculous illusion?"

"Hey, I worked hard on that illusion," Archer said, his expression feigning indignation. "The hair isn't exactly dress code around here, that's why I hide it. No one ever cracks the illusion that fast, though." He released Toria and looked beyond her to Kane. "And you must be why. Limani's infamous warrior-mage pair."

"I'm not sure we're exactly infamous," Kane said, stepping forward to shake Archer's hand. "Kane Nalamas. And this is our friend Syri."

Archer shook Syri's hand as well. "I guess infamous isn't the best term. But when you're the only warrior-mages on this continent, stories are going to travel."

"Archer was a student in Limani while I was still an apprentice," Toria said, answering Kane's mental nudge for more information. "His family moved away before you and I bonded." Since Kane's magical ability hadn't manifested until after the warrior-mage bond occurred, he'd never met the older student.

"Tor used to follow me around like a puppy," Archer said, winking at her.

"You were a menace who made fun of me constantly." Toria bumped shoulders with him, and ignored the way Kane tensed when she got near the other mage. "Don't go rewriting history to make yourself look clever."

Syri was also unimpressed by his antics. She had stayed a step behind Kane during the introductions, and kept her arms folded across her chest. "Are you here to escort us to Master Burrows?"

"Alas, no." Archer seemed oblivious to her cold tone. "But I heard your names come down the wire and had to run up to see my old friend. Someone else should be up shortly."

As if on cue, another person entered the lobby. "Master Sophin," she said, with a snap to her voice. "Hair."

With another wink to Toria, Archer donned his illusionary self once more. Now that she knew it was mere mirage, the overt sexuality the illusion oozed distracted her less. "My apologies, Master Wick." He stepped to the side to let the gray-haired woman approach their group. Despite the hair, there was nothing elderly about her. There was steel in her spine, to match the sharp lines of her professional attire. "Allow me to introduce—"

"I know who they are," Master Wick said. "I am here to escort them to Master Burrows. I believe you have a tutoring session to attend to?"

With a short bow, Archer backed away from her. "I'm sure I can wrangle some poor summer student's time for an hour or so. Catch you later, Tor." He disappeared back the way he came.

Toria waved, but dropped her hand under Wick's frosty gaze. "Thank you for your time, ma'am," she said, offering politeness as a peace offering.

"It is not my time you should be thanking me for wasting," she said. "Save it for Master Burrows. You can attend him during his afternoon tea." Without waiting for a response, she turned on her heel and hurried toward the door.

After a beat, the three scrambled to follow her. Toria was getting whiplash from the differing welcomes they were experiencing.

True to Archer's claim, once they left the expansive lobby, the school was much more utilitarian. Smooth stone walls lined the passageway, and they passed various classrooms and offices on their winding tour of the school. Master Wick did not seem inclined to play guide, so Toria refrained from asking about the beautiful stained glass windows she spotted in some of the rooms, each showing different representations of elemental magic. Maybe they could get Archer to give them a proper visit later.

Without a word, Master Wick stopped in front of a plain wooden door. After a single rap of her knuckles, she pushed it open. "Master Burrows' study. He will see you now." Instead of escorting them inside, she returned the way they had come at a brisk clip.

With a shrug toward Wick's retreating back, Kane pushed the door the rest of the way open and stepped inside. Toria and Syri followed close on his heels. "Master Burrows?" he asked.

"Come in, come in. I see Lana got you here safely." The friendly voice emanated from an older gentleman sitting in an armchair before another illusory fire. Three other overstuffed seats spread around a low table featuring a high tea service. Master Burrows wore a plain white button-up with sleeves rolled to the elbows, in sharp contrast to skin even darker than Kane's. His graying hair was buzzed close to his scalp, and the smile lines around his warm brown eyes reassured Toria. "Please, do sit with me."

Kane sat across from Master Burrows, and Toria slipped around the room to the far chair. The unnecessary use of energy for the fake fire behind her seat still bothered her a bit, but she had to admit that it made the study cheery. A cluttered desk sat underneath a high window, and overflowing bookshelves lined the walls around them. A colorful tapestry with the compass rose of the magical elements hung above the mantle, and Toria dragged her attention away from it to focus on the most powerful mage in the British colonies.

He certainly wasn't what she had expected.

"No introductions are necessary," Master Burrows said. "Zerandan alerted me that his niece was coming, and of course I know the names of Limani's warrior-mages. May I offer you some tea?"

What followed were some of the most surreal moments of Toria's life, when said most powerful mage in the British colonies served tea and cookies and chatted with them about their trip up from Limani. He even commiserated with Kane as a fellow earth mage over the hazards of water travel, standing to pluck a slim volume on shielding from a bookshelf and insisting that Kane keep it. "You might not be my student, but I am always a teacher first." Settling back in his seat, tea cup cradled in his hands, he said, "To what do I owe the pleasure of this visit to break up a dull summer afternoon?"

Toria assumed that Kane's mental nudge and Syri's sudden interest in another cookie was her cue to speak up. "The mage school in Limani is closing because there are too few students and no mages available to teach them. Kane and I are on contract from Zerandan to investigate whether this problem is limited to Limani or whether the British colonies are also experiencing a downturn in the mage population."

Master Burrows leaned forward to place his empty cup on the low table between them. He settled back in his chair and steepled his fingers under his chin. "I see," he said.

"Any insight you have would be greatly appreciated," Kane said.

Master Burrows nodded. "I understand. Smart of Zerandan to use his connections to send you to me. Right to the source, as it were. He was one of my teachers, you know. Many, many years ago, of course." He busied himself preparing a second cup of tea. "Miss Syri, what interest does your uncle have in this matter?"

Syri blinked once in surprise, but she gulped down her sip of tea. "I believe his interest stems from the fact that mages are a healthy part of any society, and that a lack of mages to train the next generation is a serious issue. Untrained mages are dangerous, regardless of whether they are human or elf."

"This is true," Master Burrows said. "And the reason that Zerandan sent Limani's warrior-mages to ask me a question he could have written a letter?"

"Ah, I think that was more of a favor to us," Kane said. "Or else Toria and I would never have figured out where to start our journeymen mercenary careers."

"How kind of him," Master Burrows said. "Well, I'm sorry to disappoint you all, but this school has had no shortage of students in all the years that I have been the head of teaching. I feel it is safe to say that this problem is indeed local to Limani, and I'm not sure what further help I can be to you."

They made a bit more small talk, with Master Burrows encouraging Syri to send his regards to Zerandan, but it was soon clear the audience had ended. He showed them to the door, and Master Wick waited outside in the hallway. In silence, she led them out the way they came, leaving them in the lobby once more. Toria wouldn't get that chance to admire the stained glass after all.

She waved to the receptionist as they walked through the lobby, but the simulacrum did not acknowledge her presence. Kane pushed through the front door and led them into the late afternoon sunshine.

They paused at the top of the granite steps. "Well," Syri said. "That was a bust."

"All due respect to Master Burrows, but he's full of shit." Archer leaned against the stone wall a few feet away from the door. His illusion was gone, and now only a pair of black sunglasses hid his face.

"Archer?" Toria asked. "And how would you know what we met with him about?"

"Because no one can keep a secret around here," he said. "And the only thing scarier than the lack of mages in this city is how desperately everyone wants to keep it a secret from the rest of the world."

"I'm not sure if I should feel better that it's not just Limani," Kane said, "or be even more worried."

"Oh, you should definitely be worried," Archer said. "Let's go. We're having dinner at my club. We need to talk."

#

Archer led them out of the school grounds and to a taxi already waiting for them. Syri started to speak once the town-car got moving, but from the front passenger seat, Archer lifted a hand for silence. "Let's not get into it now," he said. "Trust me."

The ride was only a few blocks back toward downtown, hardly worth the trouble of driving, but Archer handed the driver a generous handful of bills when he deposited them in front of a large brownstone indistinguishable from the other venerable homes on the block. "Thanks, Yann. Tell your brother I said hi." The driver tipped an imaginary cap and drove off down the quiet street.

"This way, kids," Archer said, taking one step up toward the house. "Get ready for the best steak you've ever had in your life."

As Toria and Kane followed him, but Syri crossed her arms and donned her most haughty elven expression. "I barely know you."

"But Tor knows me," he said.

"That was a long time ago, buddy," Toria said. "If I recall correctly, you completely reneged on our deal to whisk me away to glamorous New Angouleme after high school."

"Ah, but that deal was made before you left me for the likes of Nalamas here," Archer said. "Definitely an upgrade. Well done, Tor."

Kane ignored Archer's appraising gaze. "You never let anyone call you that," he said.

Toria shrugged. "I gave up telling him that after he proved less likely to fill my book bag with seawater if I let him get away with it." Seeing Archer again after so many years had brought back all sorts of memories. But while she was willing to go along with the other mage for now, she knew that people were capable of changing over the course of time. The man Archer was now might be a different person from her childhood friend.

It was apparent that the standoff between Syri and Archer wouldn't be done away with that easily. "Archer, tell Syri what we're doing here," Toria said.

"I was serious about the steak," Archer said. He twitched his fingers and a silver plaque appeared next to the door. *Liquid Gold* was written in stylish script. "It's an exclusive club, and I happen to be a member. Please let me buy you dinner so we can talk in a place that I know is secure?"

Syri turned her pointed look to Toria and Kane. It never hurt to at least humor Syri's paranoia, so Toria activated her magesight and scanned the building. Basic shielding and wards, all with the mental flavor of water mages, surrounded the building and the two adjoining. No sign of anything nefarious. "It's fine, Syri," Toria said. "Trust me?" She held out her hand.

Syri held out for another beat before accepting her hand. Toria pulled her up the stairs after Archer and Kane, ignoring the quiet, "I trust *you*," that came under Syri's breath behind her.

Dark wood paneled the foyer of the brownstone, and a tuxedo-clad butler shut the door behind them. "Master Sophin," he said.

"Alexei, is the private room available for dinner?" Archer asked.

"I do believe it has not been reserved," the butler said. "I shall escort you there myself."

As the group followed along behind, Toria spotted chic meeting rooms, a smoking lounge, and a billiards room. It was like something out of the last century. "Are we dressed well enough for dinner here?" she asked Archer.

"I could show up naked and they'd take me in," Archer said. "Don't worry about it. You're my guests, and this is the safest place in the city while I'm here."

The butler ushered them into a private dining room, and Archer gestured for them to have seats. He held a whispered conversation with the butler at the door, and Toria studied the decor rather than give in to the urge to eavesdrop. The lack of windows should have made it feel claustrophobic, but large seascape murals decorated two of the walls, featuring the famous white seaside cliffs of southern Britannia.

Another tuxedoed waiter entered the room to fill their water glasses and clear away the two extra place settings of delicate silverware. The butler followed him out, and Archer shut the room's door. With a click that Toria felt more than heard, magical shields closed around them, cradling the room in a feeling of security.

"Alexei can give us about five minutes before the kitchen gets antsy," Archer said. "But this is perfect for what we need right now."

"What the hell is going on, Archer?" Toria asked. She propped her elbows on the table and leaned forward. "Why all the secrecy?"

"Because I can't guarantee that our words won't get back to Burrows anywhere else in the city except here," he said.

"And where exactly are we?" Syri said. "Safe for you might not be safe for us."

"Liquid Gold is a secret society of water mages and their families that has dated back almost two hundred years," Archer said. "Water is the foundation of life, after all."

Though his face remained calm, Toria felt Kane's affront over their link. Instead, Kane said, "I've heard of these societies, but Limani doesn't seem to have any in the city."

Archer waved a hand and slouched back in his chair. "That's because Limani is too big on the openness and democracy thing. This is much more old-world."

"And why are we concerned with this conversation getting back to Master Burrows?" Toria asked.

"The two questions are actually kind of related," Archer said. "Liquid Gold is protective of me because I'm one of three water mages left in the city. And because Burrows will do anything to keep up the pretense that the New Angouleme Center for Magical Education—" He sniffed in disdain at the name. "—has more than six students currently enrolled."

"Only six?" Kane raised both eyebrows. "Who's powering everything you've got going on over there? All the excess energy in the gardens?"

Syri laughed with little humor. "And that creepy simulacrum?"

"Power stockpiled over the years when there were plenty of mages," Archer said. "We're supposed to meditate a certain number of hours of week." He toasted them with his glass and took a delicate sip. "I pretend to. I'm not giving them any of my power when I'm essentially being held hostage."

"Well, this gets better and better," Kane said. "If you're being held hostage, how are you here?"

"Liquid Gold has a certain amount of pull, politically," Archer said. "Burrows won't make waves if I come here for dinner occasionally. But I haven't slept in my rooms here in almost two years."

"He seemed like such a nice old gentleman." Toria reeled at all the news Archer had thrown at them, so sarcasm seemed like a safe default.

"Yeah, Zerandan looks harmless, too," Syri said. "And I'm starting to think he knew exactly what he was sending us into."

"So the decrease in mages isn't local to Limani," Toria said. "And it hit New Angouleme even earlier, if you take population percentages into account. Now the question is, what are we supposed to do about it?"

"Whatever it is, count me in," Archer said. "I don't fancy spending the rest of my life as a walking battery." He waggled his eyebrows at Kane, who ignored him. "I had plans."

"Should we call home to report this?" Kane kept his attention focused on Toria and Syri. His face was calm, but he couldn't hide the aura of irritation toward Archer that Toria could sense.

"Not a decision that we need to make tonight, I think," Toria said. She pushed a wave of affection at her partner, and he gave her a slow blink in thanks. "I believe Archer promised us an amazing dinner."

"That I can do," Archer said. "And it would also not be out of character for me to take you three club-hopping in the most fashionable city on the New Continent. Just don't be surprised if I get hauled back to the school by dawn." As if on cue, they heard a knock. "Come in, Alexei!"

The butler pushed open the door, letting in a waft of fresh air. Toria hadn't realized how stuffy the room had gotten with the tension of their conversation. Behind him stood two of the waiters, each carrying two covered trays. Alexei poured red wine in their goblets as the waiters presented the meals.

Toria murmured a short thanks to her waiter, and Alexei led them out again. She picked up her fork and used it to poke at her filet. The steak was a touch shy of rare, the way she liked it. "You know, I was raised on stories of the hardships of mercenary life," she said. "At the knee of the Guildmaster of Limani himself, no less. And yet we've had two gourmet meals in two days and slept in a first-class hotel last night. Maybe Max pulled a con to make us think mercenary life was terrible." She savored a bite of meat. Archer was right. This was probably the most amazing steak she'd ever had in her life.

Kane laughed. "I'm pretty sure we're going to pay this back many times over by the time our eighteen months are up."

"Remind me to go home before that time comes," Syri said. "I'll stick with the gourmet meals, thanks."

"And here I thought little Toria the storm mage prodigy was going to live out her life as the princess of Limani," Archer said, his voice teasing. "Whatever made you choose this road?"

Toria gestured her fork to Kane. "This guy. Sort of."

"Oh, don't blame me," Kane said. "I knew you were following in your mother's footsteps from day one. Bonding with me and jumping ahead years in your training was just a convenient excuse."

"And how does Syri fit into all this?" Archer asked. At their surprised looks, he shrugged. "Don't tell me you can't see with magesight how you three are linked."

"That's a bit more complicated," Syri said.

"You heard about the troubles Limani had with the Romans about two years ago?" Toria asked.

Archer nodded. "Everybody heard about that. Thanks for not getting invaded, by the way. We like our neutral zone."

"No problem," Kane said, his voice dry. "Good to know I got kidnapped and tortured for a few days for the good of the British Empire."

Over the rest of the delicious meal, they shared with Archer the details of their involvement in the situation with the Roman almost-invasion. It pleased Toria to see that Archer wasn't just digging to get under Kane's skin with more flirting, but that he showed genuine interest from a magical theory perspective.

Even Syri seemed to get over her spiky defensiveness toward him as she answered Archer's questions about linking to Kane through Toria with more patience than Toria would have expected.

"Dessert?" Syri looked hopeful as she pushed away her plate.

"Better than dessert," Archer said. "Let's go dancing."

#

As they left Liquid Gold and piled into the waiting town-car, Toria thought she saw someone lurking at the end of the block, leaning against a wall outside a pool of streetlight. She pointed him out as they drove by, and Archer surprised her by rolling down his window in the front passenger seat and waving at the man.

"My shadow, compliments of Burrows," he said. "When I don't show up back at the school within ten minutes, they'll do a location spell and track me down wherever I am."

"If they can find you so easily, why do they make you stay at the school?" Syri asked.

"Living battery, remember?" Archer gave a mocking laugh. "But don't worry about that tonight. Let's have some fun instead."

Toria and Kane exchanged looks over Syri's head. Either he didn't want to discuss it in front of their driver, or he didn't want to discuss it at all. But they were on a mission, and the situation in New Angouleme was part of it whether Archer wanted to face facts or not. He seemed more than willing to tell them what was going on in the city, but Toria couldn't be sure that he would stand against Master Burrows if it came down to it. A nightclub was an incongruous place to hold a strategy meeting, but Toria knew for a fact that Victory's old club back home in Limani, the Twilight Mists, had been used for stranger purposes.

Pressure built on her skin as the town-car drove deeper into the city, buildings rising higher and higher above the street, and Toria summoned her shields around her as a precaution. She sensed Kane doing the same. One thing was certain—once they'd learned all they could in New Angouleme, they wouldn't stay much longer. Good thing the Guildhall was far enough away from the city center. Maintaining combat-level shielding while asleep did not make for a restful night.

The town-car drove them to an area of the city that couldn't seem to decide whether it was a trendy nightclub district or a collection of odd-shaped warehouses. Perhaps it was both, and the nightclubs were taking over. They followed Archer out of the town-car when it dropped them off on a corner, the driver hesitant to drive into the crowds that spilled from the sidewalks and into the middle of the street. Toria would have felt underdressed, but the mix of crowd was eclectic in a way that the nighttime district of Limani was not.

She wrapped the fingers of her left hand around the elbow that Kane offered her, and they followed Syri and Archer down the sidewalk. The dim streetlights paled in comparison to the neon signs and bright lights that lit the entrances to every club and restaurant. Some enterprising food vendors had set up on a few corners, and Toria savored the smell of spices that drifted in the evening breeze. The scent of water underlay it, so they must be in a section of city near the river. If she hadn't still been full from the amazing dinner at Liquid Gold, she would have dragged Kane to the nearest cart for a snack. Their appetites would probably be back after dancing, and the night was yet young.

Archer returned waves and shouts of greeting from various people they passed. He must escape down here on a regular basis, which Toria couldn't blame him for if the alternative was staying at the mage school day in and day out. After about a block and a half, he turned them toward the club with the longest line waiting outside the door. But of course he bypassed the crowd and beelined for the entrance. Blocky neon script above the door read "The Red Eye."

"Evening, Master Sophin," the doorman said, with short bow. The man was tall and lanky, but held himself in such a way that Toria would not want to cross him, especially if her only goal was to get inside the club.

"Good evening, Tom," Archer said. "Four of us tonight, please."

"Go on in," Tom said, unhooking the velvet rope blocking the entrance. "I'm sure one of your usual tables is open."

They followed Archer past Tom, ignoring the catcalls and boos from the people still waiting in line. Outside the club, the beat of the music was a dull echo, lost in the bass beats emanating from the surrounding clubs and the roar of the crowd. Inside, it reverberated through Toria's boots and curled through her bones. She noted that Syri, a few steps in front of her, already tapped her fingers against her leg in time to the music. The hallway was bright, lit with industrial lamps left over from the club's warehousing days. Blood-red carpeting absorbed the light that reflected off the black-painted walls.

Archer led them past the coat and weapons check in the front hallway, nodding at a second bouncer. The man, halfway between muscular and heavyset, glanced at the swords at Toria's and Kane's waists before nodding back at Archer. He let them pass without comment. The hallway had no other exits and aimed them to a set of double doors that Archer pushed through. The music volume rose even higher.

The interior layout was a lot like another nightclub Toria was familiar with—the Twilight Mists, the club her mother used to own back home in Limani. It too had been converted from a warehouse space. But where the Mists embraced its industrial image, the Red Eye took class to another level. Dark wood mixed with steel and glass, and delicate chandeliers hung from the ceiling girders. Seating at the Mists was a variety of furniture that favored comfortable over matching. The Red Eye had been designed with a single look in mind, but Toria couldn't imagine spending hours lounging on the ultra-modern couches that lined the room.

And the people. As Archer led them through the crowd toward a back corner, once again exchanging greetings from all around, Toria felt conspicuous in her more casual clothing when everyone around her sported their evening best. But no one questioned Archer's entourage, and she found herself returning her own share of welcoming smiles that were more curious than judgmental.

Soon they situated in an alcove that had been empty despite the standing-room only nature of the rest of the club. Within moments of them settling on couches much more comfortable than they had looked at first glance, a waiter appeared for their drink orders, then disappeared into the crowd in the direction of the bar that spanned an entire wall.

"This is where you hang out, huh?" Syri asked, lounging back in the couch's embrace and propping her boots up on the coffee table between them.

"One of a few places, yes." Archer sat next to her, in a similar state of apparent relaxation. Toria and Kane perched across from them.

"Not bad," Syri said. "I can see the appeal."

She had to appreciate, with sensitive elven ears, how the acoustics in their alcove made conversation possible while the music blared over the dance floor. Toria was happy they didn't have to shout to talk.

The waiter returned with their drinks, and Toria sipped her white wine. It was a much better quality than she would have expected from even a nightclub as posh as this, and she noted Archer's patronage had a hand in it. A flutter of pleasure at the other end of their link said that his draft beer equally impressed Kane.

Every few minutes, as if on some unspoken schedule, a random person would approach them to greet Archer. In quick succession, he introduced them to the nightclub's owner, the general manager, and the chief of security. After, the people who approached included a local restaurateur, the leading lady of a show premiering soon in the theater district, a police detective on her night off, and a man who flirted shamelessly with Toria but was nothing more than a local socialite.

After she finished her fruity mixed drink, Syri abandoned them for the dance floor. The socialite wandered after her once he realized that he would get nowhere with Toria. The next man who approached the alcove was in direct contrast to the previous visitors. Instead of deferring to Archer regarding what level of interaction the water mage was willing to provide, the stranger dropped into Syri's empty spot and draped an arm over Archer's shoulders. "You must be the warrior-mages."

Even without her magesight active, Toria could tell he had werewolf written all over him. He sat with preternatural stillness, except for the fingers toying with the back of Archer's neck, and his amber gaze darted from Toria to Kane and back again, not subtle in the way he eyed their weapons. She could see the power coiled in his muscles, which stretched against his black jeans and dark ribbed shirt. It was obvious who Archer had modeled his pretty-boy illusion after.

"Toria Connor and Kane Nalamas," Archer said. His posture didn't welcome the werewolf's physical attention, but he didn't remove the arm. "Meet Henry Delacour, Earl of Calaitum. My very former boyfriend. What are you doing here, Hal?"

"Allison recieved a message from that idiot Evan Hurst and asked me to check up on the warrior-mages," Henry said. "Seems to think they're vampire spies or such nonsense. Are you?"

"Not today," Kane said, lifting his beer in toast.

"Good enough for me," Henry said. He held up an imaginary glass. "Welcome to New Angouleme, don't get into any trouble, and watch out for my aunt." He pecked Archer on the cheek and disappeared back into the dancing crowd.

"Ex-boyfriend?" Toria asked. There's no way Archer's illusionary self would imitate an ex if the mage didn't still have feelings for the man.

Archer shrugged. "He's an only son. Needs to pass on the family line. I can't be his kept man as long as Burrows has his roots in me." He finished off his wine in one long pull and set the empty glass next to Syri's. "Besides, I didn't know another handsome man would find his way into my life. But if you'll pardon me, I believe I've had enough socializing for one night. I'll go see if Syri is in need of a dancing partner."

Without more than a nod to Kane, Archer swept into the crowd. Toria turned to her partner. His skin hid a flush, but she had known him long enough to read the embarrassment plastered on his face. She nudged her shoulder against his, careful not to jostle his beer. "I think someone likes you."

"It's pretty obvious someone likes me," Kane said. "And if Archer means any of it, I'll eat my hat."

"I'm not sure we packed any hats," Toria said. A thought occurred to her. "Hell, you haven't had a date in over a year."

"Neither have you." Kane softened his retort by curling his empty hand around hers.

He had a valid point. "Yeah, well, it's hard," Toria said.

"How is it hard? You're smart, powerful, and beautiful. And your potential dating pool is bigger." That last wasn't said as harsh criticism, just Kane pointing out the obvious.

"We've been busy with school." But Toria couldn't hide a lie from her partner, not when it echoed down their link.

"Seriously." Kane shifted on the couch to face her. "You really haven't been on a date in over a year. And we were busy, sure, but we had some social life."

"Because everyone who we haven't known since we were children thinks we're a couple, idiot." Toria nudged amusement down their link. "Living together with my parents was one thing. But we've shared an apartment all through college. We're always together. It seems obvious to us, but it tends to give the wrong impression to strangers." She gestured in the general direction of the dance floor. "But not one stranger, apparently."

"You heard him," Kane said. "Archer'd rather be a kept man to that earl. A handsome earl, I'll grant him that, but still not even a real relationship."

Toria favored Kane with her most exaggerated disbelieving look, eyebrow arched to its fullest extent. "I imagine Archer would much rather be in a proper relationship, which is why he keeps flirting with you."

"He's been flirting with you, too." Now her partner scraped the bottom of the barrel. "Hell, he's been flirting with Syri, and Syri has made it clear she doesn't trust a hair on his head."

"The hair is a bit outrageous." Toria ignored Kane's noise of exasperation. He was being stubborn. Maybe a nightclub in New Angouleme wasn't best time or place to have this conversation, but it had been a long time in coming. "I should be jealous, you know," she said.

"Of what?" Kane slumped back into the cushions, twisting his empty pint glass between his hands.

"Archer made all sorts of pretty promises before he moved away that he would come back and marry me," Toria said. "Of course, he was all of eleven years old, so I suppose a boy's tastes can change."

"Not that much."

Archer's voice directly in her ear startled Toria, and Kane jumped next to her. The source of the voice weaved out of the crowd, a mischievous smile dancing on his face. "Sorry, I do have these seats bugged. I didn't intend to eavesdrop, but my name triggered the spell."

Like a pushy cat, he dropped down between Toria and Kane on the couch, forcing them to move aside or be sat on. He draped an arm over each of their shoulders, then pecked each of them on the cheek in turn.

Toria could feel the tension vibrating from Kane even through Archer.

"I am sorry, my dearest Torialanthas," Archer said. "For not following through on my promise to come back for you." A touch of seriousness leaked into his voice, though Toria could tell he tried to be flippant. "But once I 'graduated' from the mage school here, it was made clear that leaving wasn't an option. But enough about my love life! You two should see the elf trying to con our Syri out of a kiss."

Toria enjoyed the mental image of Syri smacking Archer if she ever heard him refer to her that way in person. "Syri takes her dancing seriously," she said. "No time for kissing allowed—"

Even without her magesight activated, it was hard to miss the brilliant flash of white light that erupted from the middle of the dance floor. The music continued unabated, but the entire tone of the room changed as dancers stopped mid-motion and backed away to the edges of the open space. The strongest of magic could be seen by even the nonmagical, and that flash had been intense.

Archer leapt to his feet and dove into the crowd toward the light, with Kane and Toria close on his heels. They wound their way through the gaping bystanders to find Syri in the middle of the cleared space. She stared down at a man sprawled on his back—an elf, indicated by the pointed eartips that stuck through unruly blond curls. Fury stiffened her back and her fists balled at her side.

This would not have been Syri's reaction to an unwanted advance. Something more must have happened. Toria and Kane moved to either side of Syri, prepared to draw steel. Archer stood above the elf, his magic shields shimmering around him like the darkest depths of the ocean.

The chief of the Red Eye's security burst through the clustered patrons on the other side of the dance floor, but backed down when he saw Archer. Toria wouldn't have wanted to interfere at that point either. The elf moved, as if to scramble to his feet, but Archer placed a heel on his shoulder. He shouldn't have looked threatening with his ridiculous blue dreadlocks, but body language said a lot.

"Syri." The music had finally stopped, and Archer's voice echoed through the cavernous space. "What happened?"

She still vibrated with anger, and Toria placed two fingers on the girl's wrist. She couldn't push emotions at Syri the way she could with Kane, but that touch was all that was needed. Syri knew they had her back. "He insulted me. Called me a broken elf, whatever the hell that means. When I tried to ignore him, he grabbed my arm. His touch burned, so I pushed him back. Sorry for the light show."

Toria looked down at Syri's bare arms at this report and saw a brilliant red mark, as if the man had wrapped his hand around her upper arm. She had never heard of the touch of one elf harming another, so some form of offensive magic must have been at work. Syri activating her own shields must have caused the flare of light.

Archer stepped away, releasing the elf. He looked to be in his mid-twenties, which put him at least a century or two older than Syri. When he tossed his curls out of his eyes, dark green irises glinted in the club's low light.

"Rattigan," Archer said. The security chief came forward. "Please eject this man and put him on the black list. I will meet with the owner and manager if they have any objections."

"Yes, Master Sophin." He and Archer hauled the elf to his feet, and Rattigan dragged him toward the exit. The other patrons cleared a path, shuffling away in fear. The low rumble of conversation began as whispers spread throughout the club.

The elf looked back and held his ground before they had cleared the dance space. Rattigan tried to haul him away, but he didn't budge. Toria could see his fury even from the distance that separated them.

"Her kind doesn't belong here! The broken have no place in this city," he said, pitching his voice to be heard above the restless crowd. Rattigan tugged once more, and the elf allowed himself to be pulled away.

Archer clapped his hands once. "Okay, kids. Show's over. Music!" At his command, the interrupted music began as if it had never stopped. The dancers in the farther reaches of the club resumed their dancing and socializing, but those around their group still stared in curiosity. In a moment of perfect harmony, Toria and Archer took each of Syri's hands and led her back to their alcove. Kane followed behind. Toria could feel the steel in his gaze on the back of her neck, daring anyone to impede their progress.

They settled Syri onto one of the couches. Kane stood in the entryway, arms crossed, facing out. Any curious bystanders found another area of the club to loiter. Syri was shivering now, in delayed reaction to the attack. But her eyes were cold, and Toria knew from long association that she was replaying every microsecond of the encounter, searing the elf's face into her memory. Toria sat next to her, tucking a free arm around Syri's shoulders.

Archer plucked Toria's empty wine glass from the table and traced a finger around the rim. Toria's exposed skin tightened as Archer drew humidity out of the ambient air and coalesced it into water. This was an exclusive water mage talent, but Toria knew he was more concerned for Syri than about showing off—otherwise he probably would have made sure Kane paid more attention to his trick. Syri wrapped both hands around the bowl of the glass with a nod of thanks, and her shivers faded as she sipped the water. It must have tasted a bit like the wine residue left in the glass, and it was a measure of her distress that she didn't make a face. Syri hated white wine.

As their novelty as the show of the evening faded, Kane left his post for a seat on the opposite couch. Archer still hovered over Syri, and Kane gripped his elbow. Big surprise—Archer didn't resist being pulled down next to Kane. Toria bottled her amusement when Archer sat closer on the couch than necessary. She considered it a win when Kane didn't shift away. The roar of the music and crowd had faded a bit, so Kane must have used the time to set up a privacy barrier. Toria didn't even need to activate magesight to reach out and feel the construct of her partner's shield. With a flick of power, she turned the shields opaque. Other magic users would see a shimmering wall, hiding the alcove from sight. Nonmagic users would still see the alcove, but their attention would slide away, unable to focus on the occupants inside.

"What the hell was that?" Kane asked. His voice was far from accusatory, but he obviously worried about their partner-in-crime as well.

"No fucking clue," Syri said. "You heard him. He's a crazy man who thinks something is wrong with me."

"Trust me, there is nothing wrong with you," Archer said. Syri narrowed her eyes at him, but she did not argue the compliment.

Syri was stressed if she was even warming up to Archer. Toria squeezed her shoulders.

"How did he leave that handprint on you?" Kane leaned over and drew Syri's arm toward him to inspect it. The mark no longer blazed, but faded into Syri's skin. It wasn't a real burn, but something more magical in nature. Elven healing wasn't significantly better than human for it to be fading so fast.

"Also, no fucking clue," Syri said. "He was yelling at me, I told him to fuck off, and when I turned away, he grabbed me. Hurt like hell, which is why I lashed out."

"He called you 'broken,'" Toria said. "Have you ever heard that before?"

Syri was silent, and she tugged her hand out of Kane's. "Once." She was drawing in on herself, but Toria wouldn't let her pull away, even as she stared unseeing into the distance. If this was a sore subject, Syri would tell them at her own pace, or not at all. "Can we get out of here?" Syri asked. "I'm exhausted."

It appeared the answer was not at all. "Of course," Toria said. "It's been a long day. Let's get back to the Guildhall."

Archer made a show of looking at his wrist, despite the lack of watch adorning it. "Time for me to get back, too, before my personal escort comes for me." He stood and retrieved Syri's leather jacket from where it draped over the back of the couch, holding it up so that she could slide into it. She didn't even flinch when the material brushed over the mark on her arm.

Kane flicked his fingers toward the alcove entrance, and his privacy shield collapsed in on itself. Toria felt a wave of energy pulse through her as the flow of her own contribution to the shield fed back to her. From all appearances, the club was back to normal, and their drama would be a footnote in The Red Eye's evening. Archer led them out of the club, but people only waved to him rather than approaching. They left through the same hallway they had entered and passed Tom the doorman, still manning his post. Though the evening had drawn late, the line of people waiting for entrance had grown rather than diminished. The rest of the district was also as crowded with people as it had been earlier.

Toria looked back to wave at Tom, and he flashed a smile at her as he pulled aside the velvet rope to let two waiting women into the club. She stumbled on Syri's heels in front of her. "What—?"

Syri had frozen in the middle of the sidewalk. "Do you hear that?"

The men also paused, and they ignored the flow of the raucous crowd around them. Archer gave a dismissive wave to someone who greeted him, but his entire attention was focused on Syri.

"For the millionth time," Kane said, "your hearing is a bit better than ours. What's going on?"

Now Syri turned in a circle, looking up and down the street, trying to pinpoint whatever called to her. "Someone's screaming in elven. She's being attacked!" Syri sprinted across the street, dodging a town-car that swerved to avoid her with a screech of tires. Metal flashed in her hands. She'd drawn the silver knives from inside her leather jacket.

No time to think about what they rushed into. Toria wasn't about to let Syri throw herself into danger without backup. Trusting Kane to be right behind her, Toria also hurled herself between two passersby, throwing an apology over her shoulder and ignoring their calls of alarm as she drew her rapier. The town-car Syri had evaded sat askew in the middle of the street while the driver shouted invectives out his window toward the alley down which the elven girl had disappeared. Toria slid across the hood of the town-car and dashed to the other side of the street.

Now the driver shouted at her about the town-car's paint job, but Toria had reached the sidewalk on the other side of the street. She darted around a trio of women wearing too little clothing and too much high heel. More trills of mixed fear and excitement at her sword. But Syri was nowhere in sight.

A quick glance down the sidewalk to either side of her showed no signs of a scuffle. She stretched up on tiptoe, but that didn't help much. People had knotted around her, gaping at the crazy woman with the sword, closing off her view. Where the hell had Syri disappeared?

But now Kane had reached her side, and he had the advantage of height. "In the alley, go!" He dodged a leather-clad couple and dashed around a corner Toria hadn't noticed. He held his scimitar down, close to his legs, but the textured wootz steel flashed in the neon lights of the club signs.

Archer snagged her empty hand as he passed, hauling her behind him in the direction Kane had gone. He wasn't visibly armed, but Toria felt the tingle of power gathering where their palms touched. The water mage might not have the martial training she and Kane did, but master mages were far from helpless.

The alley between two clubs was rather narrow, and Archer and Toria leapt over piles of indistinct refuse. Kane's dim form was a few feet in front of them, with his sword now held higher in a defensive position. Toria edged in front of Archer, also bringing her blade to bear. She felt unfamiliar shields weaving around her, tinged with the scent of ocean breeze rather than summer-warmed grass, and tried not to blast them away. They'd have a talk about power etiquette after they figured out what the hell Syri was up to.

She didn't hear the calls for help Syri had. She hoped the victim had run off, rather than the alternative.

Kane disappeared around another corner, and now the clang of blade against blade echoed down the alleyway. Toria paused at the corner rather than following Kane in blind, bringing up an arm to block Archer from passing her. She peeked around the edge of the brick building.

A grimy lightbulb over the back exit of a club was the only light source that lit the small courtyard surrounded by warehouse exteriors. Silver blades flashed as Kane exchanged blows with two lithe men in dark clothes. Both elves, judging by their long cornsilk hair and fluid movements.

Two more elves, a man and a woman, gripped each of Syri's arms against a wall beyond where Kane fought. She screamed and struggled to no avail, and Toria spotted Syri's knives discarded at her kicking feet.

This wasn't a rescue. This was an ambush.

Time to think tactics. To think like Victory. Her shields were already at combat strength to keep out the sickening aura of the city around her, but Toria poured more energy into them. Every bit would help. "Help Kane," Toria said to Archer. Without waiting for his response, she launched herself around the corner into the courtyard, dodged the blade that one of Kane's attackers flashed toward her. She turned to the side in time to body-slam the man pinning Syri's right arm.

Elves might be slim, but they were packed with muscle. It felt like running into the side of a truck. But Toria had the element of surprise, and she and the man crashed to the cement in a heap of limbs. A sickening sizzle of flesh reached her ears and nose. The steel of her rapier must have met elven flesh—she'd been more concerned with not falling on her own blade and less with not injuring Syri's captor. The man beneath her grunted in pain and shoved Toria off him.

The muscle was more than show. Toria slid halfway across the courtyard, keeping a grip on her rapier more through luck than anything else. But she ended up right behind one of the elves attacking Kane. Throwing her arm to the side, it was the work of less than a second to slice the man's closest calf. He collapsed to his injured side with a scream of pain and the smell of more burnt flesh, but landed across Toria's legs. The back of his skull slammed against the concrete. He twitched for a second, then laid still. Toria was pinned.

Kane still traded deft blows with his other attacker, and Archer was nowhere to be seen. Had he even joined the fight? Syri grappled with the elven woman, but the first man Toria had attacked aimed for her. He held an injured arm close to his side, his sleeve sliced open and dripping with blood where he must have tangled with Toria's rapier in their fall. He stooped to pick up one of Syri's discarded long-knives with his good hand.

Toria tried to kick the downed elf off her legs, but the limp body was heavy and uncooperative. A flash of pain lanced up her right leg, and she knew she'd turned her ankle wrong while struggling. Even if she got free, would she be able to stand, much less fight?

Silver fur flashed across the courtyard toward the advancing elf. With a snarl, a wolf crashed into him, knocking him away from Toria. Syri's knife flew out of his hand, straight toward Toria. She tensed her entire body, ignoring the flare of pain from her injured leg, and sent a pulse of energy through her shields. The dim courtyard brightened as the knife bounced off her shields that flashed in vivid violet prisms. With one last heave, Toria shoved the unconscious elf away and staggered to her feet. Her ankle held, but her center of balance was off.

Wolf faced off against elf. He'd managed to snag Syri's other knife, and he brandished it at the growling wolf. A werewolf, obviously, given the large size, intelligence, and urban surroundings. Archer's boyfriend, the earl? Didn't matter as long as he was on their side.

"A little help!"

Kane's shout echoed through the courtyard, and Toria whirled. Both his original attacker and the female elf, who had drawn some sort of short sword, had backed him into a corner. The combat had drawn on for too long. Through their years of sparring and knowing her partner's fighting style as well as her own, his every move telegraphed that his speed was slowing.

Wait, where was Syri?

Kane blocked the woman's blow, but the man's longer blade slipped through his defenses. Kane cried out in pain as the sword sliced his ribs. A dark bloodstain blossomed on his shirt.

They were only a few feet away but she would take too long to get there before the elves overwhelmed Kane. Toria raised both her rapier and her empty hand, fingers outstretched, and pushed another pulse of power outward. This was quick and dirty, but she couldn't save reserves for a fight that needed to end now.

Energy lanced down the edge of her rapier and out the tips of her fingers. The bright heat seared her vision. Bolts of lightning crashed through the courtyard toward the two elves fighting Kane. He brought his scimitar up in time to block the woman as she was launched into him from behind. The male elf hit the wall next to Kane with a sickening crunch she could hear even over the crackle of energy that coursed between them.

But the woman still struggled with Kane, and though she'd dropped her weapon, now she was inside the reach of his sword. Toria drained power from her shields, ignoring the nausea that crept into her stomach as her defenses against New Angouleme's tainted aura were stripped away. She pushed another wave of out of her empty hand, this time of pure kinetic energy, more reminiscent of crashing thunder clouds than of lightning. She couldn't risk a transfer of electricity shocking and injuring Kane as well.

The blast also knocked the woman into the wall next to Kane, and she collapsed to the ground. With Kane out of immediate danger, Toria whirled to check on the fight that had raged on the other side of the courtyard.

The werewolf stood over what remained of the elf, blood staining his muzzle and down his silver-furred chest. He braced all four of his paws to hold up his body, which heaved with exhaustion. Toria brought up her rapier, but there was no violence in his pale amber gaze. She dropped the tip of her sword an inch and asked, "Earl Delacour?"

The wolf dipped his snout once and sat back on his haunches and let his tongue loll out. Now the panting werewolf looked more like a large friendly dog, despite the blood. The adrenaline surge was fading, and Toria's right ankle now refused to bear any of her weight.

"Toria. Where's Syri? And who's our friend?"

She looked back to see Kane leaning against the wall, matching herself and the werewolf for exhaustion. His scimitar drooped in limp fingers. Elven bodies surrounded them, dead or unconscious, but their friend was not one of them. "Archer's boyfriend came to our rescue," Toria said. "I lost track of Syri in the fight. And Archer was right behind me, but…" Her voice trailed off. For all his pretty words, and despite the power he'd been building as he followed her down the alley, the water mage had vanished as thoroughly as Syri.

Delacour's ears pricked forward a second before Toria heard her named called out. Speaking of errant water mages. Archer appeared around the corner at a run, sliding and falling to his knees in a spot of wet blood and what might be entrails from Delacour's victim. "Run! Now!"

The words took a second to make their way through the tired fog of Toria's brain. That second was long enough for a flechette to appear in the side of Archer's neck. Delacour snarled and leapt to Archer's side as the mage collapsed.

Ouch. That stung. Toria clapped her hand to her own neck at the sharp insect prick she felt there. But the pressure drove the dart farther into her skin. She was tired from combat and too much power usage, but the exhaustion that now dragged at her limbs and clouded the edge of her vision was unnatural.

Toria reached for Kane, but her vision dimmed and she fell to the bloody concrete. Her partner's voice calling her name echoed in her ears as her eyes closed on the sight of a dead elf's leg, inches from her face.

#

Syri couldn't breathe. Cloth covered her face, sucking close when she inhaled.

She lashed out. But strong hands gripped each limb, carrying her, and they tightened painfully at her struggles.

She forced herself limp and focused on breathing. In. Out. The fabric was thick and smelled of rancid dried sweat. But she was in no danger of suffocating as long as she didn't panic and hyperventilate. Syri strained her hearing, but what covered her face and head had to be more than simple cloth. Nothing penetrated, not even the footsteps of those who carried her.

Her forward momentum stopped, and she swayed in midair. At an unheard order, the hands released as one and she crashed to a hard surface. Her head bounced, and she saw stars in the darkness. "Fuck!"

A booted foot slammed into her ribs, and she pulled in her arms and legs to protect her torso. But when no further attack came, she scrambled to her feet and ripped off the hood. Sensation crashed over her. She snapped her eyes shut at the bright strobing light and clapped her hands to her ears to deafen the white noise that threatened to overwhelm her.

It was too much. She dropped to her knees as invisible fingers dug into her back, her arms, her neck, everywhere. The sickening sweetness of vanilla and the rankest of sewage fought for attention in her nose. She screamed and fell to the floor, curling into the fetal position.

When unconsciousness claimed her, Syri embraced it as a mercy and followed it into blessed dark silence.

#

"Toria. Toria. Wake up, Toria."

The combination of Kane's voice and the tendril of power he kept poking at her penetrated the fog enveloping her brain. When she opened her eyes, Kane's face was inches away from her own. "What the hell, Kane?" Her body twitched at the phantom sensation of hands on her arms and legs, but her partner was the only one near.

"Thank god," he said, sitting back. "I got worried when you didn't wake up around the same time I did. My larger size must have metabolized the drugs faster."

Memory flooded back, and Toria brought her hand to the side of her neck. The dart was gone, but she felt a tiny scab where it must have penetrated her skin. "No, seriously, what the hell?" Toria pushed herself to a sitting position, but the change in elevation sent her head swimming. She groaned and almost fell back again, but Kane nudged her legs apart and pushed her head down between her knees.

"Breathe," he said. "We're safe for now. I think."

Her brain stopped trying to climb out of her skull after a few deep breaths. Now Toria looked around. Someone had stripped her to the jeans and the camisole she'd worn under her thicker T-shirt. No belt, no wallet, no hold-out dagger strapped to her ankle. Neither sword was evident, but that was no surprise. They'd even removed her socks. Kane sat next to her on a cot bolted into the side of a plaster-walled cell, in a similar state of half-dress.

An empty cot lined the opposite wall, only a few feet way. Mussed sheets showed where Kane must have awoken. Indistinct light suffused the room, emanating from the four corners. Toria knew half a dozen charms that could create magical light, so that was not much of a clue. The only exit was a steel door with a slit near the bottom. The floor was plain concrete. But the cots had mattresses and pillows, and the sheets felt of cotton when Toria ran her fingers down them. This was either the nicest prison cell in existence, or a hotel room with a terrible interior decorator. At least the plaster kept out the damp. She gave an involuntary shiver. They were probably underground. She shoved down the vague sense of claustrophobia that thought inspired in her.

Considering the events that had led them there, Toria figured it was a prison cell. Then the rest of her memories caught up to her. Not a single twinge of pain from her knee, and she snapped her focus to examine Kane's side.

He placed his hand over the blood-stained rent in his shirt. "Healed. Not by me. Must have happened when we were out. What do you remember?"

"We'd taken out the elves," Toria said. She stood, testing her weight on her leg. It felt as if it had never been injured. "I was checking on the wolf. I think you and I talked? And then Archer showed up. Told us to run. I saw him get darted, and he collapsed. Then I got hit. Everything is fuzzy."

Kane leaned against the wall, lacing his fingers over his stomach. "I remember hearing Archer screaming my name, but I never even saw him. I barely remember talking to you, nothing after seeing two electrocuted elves hitting the wall on either side of me. The wolf was on our side?"

"I'm a little concerned about the drug affecting our memory," Toria said. She sat back on the cot next to Kane, pressing her shoulder to his. "But I think the wolf was Henry Delacour, Archer's earl." Kane made an indistinct noise low in his throat, and Toria nudged his shoulder with her own. "This is the definition of the time not to be jealous. I'm pretty sure he saved our asses. I'd have one of Syri's knives in my stomach if not for him." She paused. "I think it was Syri's knife."

"Do you remember seeing Syri there?" Kane asked.

"I think?" Toria said. "They had her against the wall, but we were fighting them…" Her voice trailed off as she tried to dig through memories that were hard to pin down. Her stomach rumbled. Hunger would not make it easier to focus. How long had they been out?

"I remember seeing her against the wall," Kane said. "But hell, I don't even really remember seeing Archer, and you do."

They were going in circles. Time to try a new approach. "If she was taken, too," Toria said, "why isn't see locked up with us?"

"Why would she be?" Kane said. "We're not stating the obvious." He gestured to the nearest corner, at the pale light that shimmered from the white plaster. "We're at the mage school."

"Yeah. We probably are," Toria said. Their shields were only at basic levels, but she didn't feel the miasma of the city creeping down her neck. They'd either been removed from the urban area, or they were within the protected confines of the New Angouleme Center for Magical Education. Archer had never implied that the New Angouleme masters who kept him one step short of captive were idiots. If she'd woken in a cell without Kane, she'd have already tried to blast her way out and find her way back to him. She shivered at the much clearer memory of being cut off from him when he'd been held captive two years ago. Syri's restraining influence was one of the few reasons she hadn't gotten herself killed going after her partner.

But letting them wake up together was another story. The immediate panic wasn't there, so they would be more inclined to wait out the situation before doing anything rash. Hell hath no fury like a warrior-mage pair separated.

Little did their mysterious captors—and by mysterious, it was probably Master Burrows—know, but Syri might as well be part of their pairing when it came to their dedication to her.

Words were unnecessary. Toria and Kane reached for each other at the same time, twining the fingers of their closest hands together. While her knee was healed, Toria's energy reserves were still low from throwing power around in that courtyard. But now Kane's body was an extension of her own. His sliced ribs had been healed, and his body was still a giant ache from the prolonged combat against multiple attackers. However, his fight had been physical in nature, and his energy levels were still high.

As one, they merged their shields together. Toria blinked once, and the world around her, limited though it might be to a twelve by twelve cell, shimmered into greater existence with her magesight. Kane's clouds of verdant energy bolstered her fading violet prisms. She blinked again, and the shields faded out of her immediate focus.

They studied the room. The magical light source was still generic and nondescript, as far as magical creations went. It didn't strike Toria as being from any particular elemental school of magic. She would have recognized the more primordial storm power, but it wasn't that either. She cocked an eyebrow at Kane, but felt a touch of negative trinkle down their link. Not earth magic either. Even if they had identified the source, they didn't know any of New Angouleme's mages well enough to identify the caster. For all they knew, the way power was hoarded around here, the spell had been set decades ago and the mage responsible was long dead.

"I'll take the door," Kane said.

Toria squeezed his hand and set her attention the walls. Once she faded out the magical light the same way she had their shields, shimmering lines of power appeared. The plaster had been a later addition. Beneath it stood stone walls etched with magical runes and symbols, from at least three magical traditions Toria recognized offhand and a few more she didn't. Ah, that made sense. The plaster was probably added to prevent prisoners from altering the runes to suit their own purposes. It was at least a few inches thick. Her fingernails would be bloody stubs before she made it far enough down to get to the runes. Their escape wouldn't lie that way.

Smart captors were contrary to those in the adventure novels she had grown up with. At least Victory and Asaron had never censored their stories for her. This was much more in line with an actual prison cell. Even if the nice sheets and not-terrible mattress covering the cot beneath them threw her for a bit of a loop.

Tension drained out of Kane's shoulder from where it pressed against hers. "Anything?" she asked.

"Nope," Kane said. "Solid steel. Might be runes on the outside of the door, but nothing we can tap into. Deadbolt accessible from the outside. You?"

"Runes under the plaster, but it's too thick to get to," Tori said. "I recognized some, but not all. Quite an eclectic mix of magical traditions they've got going on here."

"Same with the door. Makes you wonder what they've had to keep contained in the past," Kane said.

"Nothing as scary as us, obviously," Toria said.

"Obviously." They clinked imaginary glasses with their free hands. "What's that?" He poked at Toria's leg.

She looked down. A sliver of paper peeked out the top of her hip pocket, shimmering with faint light. It was the scrap of paper she'd shoved away after finding it on the floor of the train. She drew it out and unfolded it. What had been a blank paper ripped down one edge now showed glowing elven runes decorating one side. Light traced the runes in rainbow hues. "Can you read it?" Toria asked. She could identify some alchemical symbols from her chemistry classes, but Kane had taken at least one class on elven literature.

"Hardly," Kane said. He jabbed a finger at one of the three symbols at the top. "But we did learn our names, and that's mine. Or Nalamas, at least. Kane doesn't really translate. The one to the right might be Torialanthas."

"The first rune might be Syrisinia," Toria said. "That flash of light on the train. It was a lot like the flash Syri created at the club when that guy harassed her. An elf left this specifically for us."

"And without Syri, we can't read it," Kane said. "I'm an idiot."

"You're not the one who just left it in her pocket," Toria said. "We can be idiots together. After we get out of here and find Syri. And our swords."

"Don't you dare obsess over that, too." Kane's irritation oozed through their link. "That is angst I don't need right now."

"Got it," Toria said. "No angst. But I don't think we're getting out of this cell until someone lets us out."

"Well, they have to feed us eventually," Kane said.

"We hope," Toria said. They relaxed against the wall again. "Prime, not prime?"

"*No.*"

#

Toria didn't know how much time had passed. At least a few hours. She even heard Kane's stomach rumbling in protest now. She couldn't get him to agree to a number game, and he smacked her arm when she suggested "I Spy." When she'd brought up the topic of Archer, Kane had given her a withering glare and shut his eyes.

She had to admit that she wasn't a great cellmate.

The plaster wall wasn't comfortable to lean against, so Kane had reclined on the cot. It wasn't wide, and Toria was stretched along his side, squished between him and the wall. Using his shoulder as a pillow and with her top arm and leg draped over him, Toria could pretend it was a Saturday night back at the apartment, after Kane fell asleep watching television but she wasn't ready to go to bed yet.

Well, she could almost pretend. The plaster wall was even less comfortable than their cheap futon.

A scraping noise sounded from the cell's door. Toria lifted her arm and leg off of Kane in time for him to roll off the cot. He landed on the floor in a crouch. Toria shoved herself up and darted to the other side the cell. Since the door would swing outward, she couldn't hide behind it and ambush whoever entered, but at least she and Kane could flank them. She raised her fists and balanced on the balls of her bare feet. Kane was still in his crouch, ready to tackle, as another grating lock twisted open and the deadbolt slid home.

A crackle of energy descended over the cell, freezing her into place. Based on sense of panic she felt, Kane found himself in a similar situation. Damn mages.

The door swung open, and Master Burrows sauntered in. While his attire was similar to what he'd worn during the previous meeting, gone was the genial attitude he'd shown them. He stood just inside the cell with his arms crossed over his chest. He glowered at Kane before turning the harsh look on Toria. "What the hell did you two punks think you were going to do?" he asked. "Attack me?"

Toria could breathe, but she couldn't speak. It felt as if her teeth were wired shut. A muscle twitched at the corner of Kane's jaw.

Burrows pressed two fingers to the point between his eyes. "I knew you would be more trouble than you're worth, but Lana seems to think your power will be worth it." He circled Kane, examining him. "I must admit to a certain curiosity regarding the potential of in a warrior-mage pair. There hasn't been one in New Angouleme in over fifty years."

He approached Toria and gave her the same once-over. There was nothing sexual in his gaze, but the hunger unnerved her. She had seen Asaron use the threat of eating someone to make a prisoner talk once, back when she and Kane had accompanied him on a job while they were still in high school. He'd wanted to show them the reality and danger inherent in mercenary work, so they had accompanied him on a series of bounty hunter jobs. But where Asaron's vampiric hunger was more animalistic, the look in Burrows' eyes was all too human.

He nodded once, coming to some sort of mental decision, and stepped away from her. "I will inform Master Wick that we will perform the ritual tonight," he said. "Don't expect dinner. We've learned from experience that physical deprivation breaks down many mental barriers as well. Depending on how the ritual goes, and how well you cooperate, we might allow you to see Archer soon."

Burrows turned and exited the cell. He paused when he reached for the door, looking back in at them. "Oh, you must be wondering about your family. We will send word to Limani in a few weeks that you have given up this silly mercenary nonsense and have decided to settle in New Angouleme to further your magical education. It's foolish to risk such a unique skill set by throwing yourself in danger. You'll both have bright futures here."

The door clanged shut, and energy swirled through the cell. Toria had relaxed into the magical bonds, and when the captivity spell released, she collapsed backward onto the floor. Kane, on the other hand, must have been straining against the spell, and he launched himself at the closed door.

"They'll never believe you, you son of a bitch!" Kane pounded his fist against the door. "Our family knows us too well!"

Toria picked herself up off the floor and stepped toward Kane. He sagged against the door, and she placed a hand on his shoulder, squeezing once. "Our family does know us too well. We won't disappear here."

"Victory and Asaron can't exactly come to the rescue," Kane said, his voice muffled against the door. "British territory and all."

"Dad will drag Max out of retirement and come up here himself." Unbidden came the mental image of Mikelos bashing his way into the cell with a violin, with a grumbling Max close on his heels. She pushed the thought through their link and felt Kane suppress a flicker of amusement. She pulled Kane away from the door and put her hands on either side of his neck, pulling his forehead down to meet hers. "We're not going to rot in here."

With their link still open, Toria caught a flash of the interior of a Roman military tent. Kane's fists tightened at his side, and Toria knew that the scars on the insides of his wrists still pulled. Being a captive again, even used as a source of power rather than food, must be bringing back all sorts of unpleasant associations.

"We have to make it until we can see Archer," Kane said. "He's managed to survive here, and they've given him a certain amount of freedom. We can use that to our advantage."

Toria placed a finger over Kane's lips. "We have to assume that the walls have ears."

He pulled her into his arms, squeezing tight. She returned the embrace. "We're not going to rot in here," Kane said, repeating her earlier statement.

As a mantra, it wasn't a bad one to have.

#

The light in the cell never changed, and it was hard to judge the passing of time. The growling of her stomach had subsided, and Toria had passed from hungry to nauseated under the layer of exhaustion.

She and Kane had shared one of the cots for a little bit, but she'd abandoned him for her own once she felt too cramped. They didn't need conversation to pass the time, but the silence was getting to her.

Without warning, Toria felt the sweep of magic through the cell. The subtle crack was familiar, and her limbs tightened with the immobilization spell again. Since Kane was curled up, facing the wall and possibly asleep, Toria had no idea whether it was only her. The locks on the door churned again, and her partner didn't move. So he was stuck, too. They were helpless.

This time, it was Master Wick who breezed into the cell. The older woman had exchanged her business suit for khakis and a collared shirt, but her manner was no less severe than the first time Toria had seen her. Two burly men with the look of hired muscle followed her into the cell. Wick pointed at Toria. "That one."

Despite the nausea, Toria struggled against the magical bonds holding her, but to no avail. She managed to make a breathy grunting noise through her locked teeth, but Kane didn't move.

The men hauled her off the cot and draped her over the shoulder of the larger of the two. Her limbs dangled like a puppet with cut strings. Blood rushed to her head, and with her lungs compressed, Toria worried that she might pass out before they got too far. Lank hair fell around her face. All she could see was the floor of the cell and the back of this strange man's legs.

"Follow me."

At Wick's order, the man carried Toria out. The magic inherent to the school hit her with a rush, and she almost gagged on the gasp of relief that couldn't escape her mouth. Apparently the magical runes under the plaster kept extra power out as well as them in. The second man pushed the door shut after them. She couldn't catch a final glimpse of Kane before the concrete floor made way for utilitarian tile. Since they hadn't seen much of the mage school the day before, this awkward viewpoint made reconnaissance impossible with no concept of a starting point. The growing pressure in her sinuses didn't help much. If she puked while still under the effects of this captivity spell, she really hoped that someone would notice before she choked to death. What an inglorious way to go.

The three crowded into an elevator, and the back of Toria's skull conked against the metal wall. "Careful!" Wick said, her voice sharp.

"Sorry, ma'am." Her handler sounded contrite, and he shuffled away from the wall by a few inches.

The elevator ride didn't last long, but they were rising. The cell was in the basement, then. When they left, Toria's floor view changed to marble. A few twists and turns later, Toria heard another door open, one much simpler than the steel monstrosity back in the cell. A breeze caressed her face, and after a slate threshold, the interior marble made way for a gravel path.

They crossed some sort of grassy area, but Toria had no idea whether she was outside the mage school or in an interior courtyard. She heard another door, they crossed another slate threshold, and her view was once again marble floor. If she could get free, she might be able to make it back to Kane.

She strained against the spell. At this rate, she would pass out from exhaustion long before she made any headway against the enchantment. Without knowing what kind of spell it was, she had no idea how to begin countermeasures to unravel it. Sometimes she wished her strengths lay less in combat and more in the intricate nature of spellwork. Of course, her view would have been different during the fight last night.

The noise of another heavy door being hauled open reached her ears.

"Place her in the circle," Wick said. "On her back."

Toria felt the brush of a doorframe and gave an internal cringe at how close to a concussion she had come.

With a bewildering rush, the man carrying Toria swung her back over his shoulder and dropped her on the floor. The hard and cold marble floor. That would leave a bruise. He straightened her arms and legs, but her head still drooped to the side. At least now she could see some of the room.

Wick stood near an enormous steel door that opened inward. The second minion lurked outside. At a jerky gesture from Wick, minion number one joined him. She gestured with two fingers, and the door creaked closed.

Toria blinked through the wooziness as the blood rushed back out of her head. From her limited perspective, it appeared that the men had deposited her in a ritual circle created by tiles inlaid in the marble floor. Limani's mage school contained a similar workroom, but these tiles looked to be made of precious minerals rather than enameled metal.

Wick gestured again. With an audible crackle, the immobility spell disappeared.

Toria launched herself off the ground, ignoring the protests from her head, stomach, and aching tailbone. She could disable Wick before she could reset the immobility spell—

Toria bounced off the shielding set at the edge of the ritual circle as brilliant sapphire light flashed through the room. The shock launched her back, and she slid across the marble floor until she hit the shielding on the other side of the circle. This time the energy only flared a bit, shocking her and setting a static charge through her hair.

"Don't be an idiot, Connor," Wick said. "This will go much more smoothly if you cooperate with me."

Toria slumped over for a second, swallowing back the threatening dry heaves. Bracing both hands against the cool marble, she forced herself to her feet. It took her longer to catch her balance than she wanted to admit. Standing in the middle of the circle, Toria balled her hands at her sides—mostly to hide the fact that they shook from low blood sugar. "What the hell do you want from us?"

"What have they been teaching you in that hack little school in Limani?" she said. Wick leaned against the wall next to the closed door, crossing her arms, her expression unconcerned. "Have you even figured out why you're here?"

"Educate me, oh wise one," Toria said, hoping to get a rise out of the other woman.

Wick responded with the voice of one speaking to a child. "The power you sense around you is from the mages of this school donating a limited amount of their personal power, a bit each day. The reserves are the school itself, and all mages linked to the school have access to it when needed."

"But the mages are disappearing," Toria said. All the pieces were coming together. "That's why Burrows lied to us. You don't want the world to know that you're not as powerful as you once were. That's why you can't even risk letting Archer leave."

"We have come to an agreement with Master Sophin," Wick said. "He 'donates' the power he can, and we let him enjoy his little social freedoms. But he is well aware of the hold we have on him. He agreed to it, in fact."

"Why are you wasting so much power?" Toria asked. "I can't even imagine how much energy that simulacrum out front is draining every day."

"Appearances are everything, my dear," Wick said. "The New Angouleme Center for Magical Education is an elite institution. It only accepts half a dozen students at a time, at most, these days. Otherwise we would not be able to craft such excellent examples of magery."

"You mean there are only six students left in New Angouleme," Toria said. "Maybe in the whole British colonies. What are you afraid of?"

"It is not my responsibility to educate you in the matter of British politics," Wick said. "And we are wasting time. Sit."

Toria remained standing.

Wick sighed. "Sit, girl. This will go much easier for you if you cooperate."

Not letting the defiant glare leave her face, Toria sank to the floor, arranging her legs to sit tailor-style. She kept her hands tucked to her side. The trembling wouldn't stop. Her stomach roiled, but now it was more from anxiety than hunger.

This was a set spell, to drain her of power. She'd read about this before, and it had given her nightmares for a week. If Wick had done this before, then all the ritual needed was the caster to provide the final ingredient. All it needed was for someone to be in the circle.

How many other mages had they sucked dry in their quest for power? How many others had died already?

Toria pulled her shields around her, set to combat strength and more, using every dredge of energy she could pull from her reservoirs. Burrows had said this had never been attempted with a warrior-mage before. Would the spell only pull power from her, or would it travel through her link to affect Kane as well? Wick was with her, but no one was with Kane. If he felt her being drained, she couldn't stop him from funneling power to her. He could die in the process, and no one would know.

Without warning, Wick snapped her fingers. Toria's world went dark.

\#

Every nerve ending was on fire, but she couldn't move. An immense pressure pinned each limb and made every breath a struggle. Except the body existed in her mind alone, and once she accepted that, she was free.

Toria opened metaphorical eyes as she sat up in a body that was nothing more than a manifestation of her internal self. Darkness stretched in all directions beyond the halo of light illuminating her body-that-was-not-a-body.

Except the darkness existed in her mind alone, and once she accepted that, she could see.

She opened her metaphorical eyes again, stripping away another layer of self. But she wasn't paring herself down—an outside source had leeched on to her, and it drained her down to her essence. A steady pull, and a steady loss.

That explained the silk cords tied around her wrist and ankles. The few times she had practiced astral projection as part of her magical studies, her mental view of herself had worn casual dress, jeans and a worn T-shirt and comfortable ballet flats. This was something else. Now the jeans were ratty and the shirt torn, and when she looked down, the shoes disintegrated away. But the blue silk wrapped around her limbs remained vibrant. This was the leach.

Except the cords existed in her mind alone, and once she cut them—

In the space of a thought, Toria summoned a knife. A simple cooking knife that she had last seen in her father's kitchen. Mikelos smiled at her from where he chopped vegetables at the counter. She clamped down on the memory. She couldn't afford to be distracted.

With deft hands, Toria sliced the silk encircling each limb. She was stronger than Wick, and she would defeat this spell from the inside. But the hems of her imaginary jeans were unraveling, and her fingernails were brittle.

The silk cords were gone, but she still felt the drain. So it was to be more complicated than that. Toria tossed the useless knife away, and it disappeared into the darkness.

She ran frustrated hands through her hair. When she pulled them away, clumps of hair were caught in her fingers.

Toria screamed.

A hole opened beneath her feet. The light around her did not pierce its depth.

Except the hole existed in her mind alone, and once she accepted that, she would fly.

She fell.

#

Every nerve ending burned, but she couldn't move. An immense pressure weighted down each limb and made every breath a struggle. Except the body did not exist in her mind alone.

Something pinned her spread-eagle in the ritual circle. The cool marble pulled the heat from her skin, leaving every bone and muscle aching beneath the burning nerves. Her breath came in gasps. She was too spent to scream, but her throat burned. Had she been screaming before? How much time had passed?

Master Wick stood above her, feet straddling Toria's torso. A fine violet mist rose from Toria and gathered around Wick's outstretched hands.

Toria strained to move. Wick stood inside the circle, unprotected by physical shields. Even if Toria didn't have the strength to incapacitate her, if she could distract her, she could at least disrupt the ritual. The invisible force still held her. And she grew weaker by the second. Once she had nothing left to give, the power would drain from Kane. Alone in that cell.

Black spots crept at the edge of her vision.

She fell.

#

A hurricane screamed around her. Except this time it was real, with no escape.

Wind whipped at her hair, at her body, stealing her breath away. The maelstrom encircled her, tearing at the rags of her clothes. When she raised her arms to protect her face, she found that more of her hair was gone, leaving a few jagged clumps that even now fell away at her touch. She peeked through slit eyes at swirling azure, cerulean, cornflower, all representative colors of Wick's affinity for air.

Falling back on automatic defenses, Toria tried to shield against the whirlwind. But the winds were fierce, and the unrelenting gale sanded away at her delicate prisms. Within moments, her shields wore down to a smooth surface with gaping holes that let the wind right in. The forces buffeted her, making her stagger on her feet.

She crouched, trying to make herself as small as possible. She peered up into the hurricane, trying to see beyond the blue.

Victory beamed down at her, and fang flashed in her welcoming grin. She held out her hand.

But turquoise streaked Victory's deep auburn hair, and her eyes should have been a shade of midnight, not the light sky of early morning.

As Toria pulled her hand back, her mother's face warped into Wick's. The wide smile transformed into a snarl, and the rest of Wick's teeth elongated and sharpened, turning to gnashing blades.

The hurricane still screamed around her, but this time she found an escape. The metaphorical ground beneath Toria's feet disappeared as she staggered back.

She fell.

#

This time, when Toria awoke, she was alone in the ritual chamber. Wick was nowhere to be seen.

Her vision was hazy and she couldn't move, which meant Wick could still be somewhere in the room. She could feel her arms and legs, but from a distance. She focused everything she had on the index finger of her right hand, but it never left the cool tile beneath it.

A sharp stab of panic flared through her.

Hyperventilating wouldn't help. Toria inhaled deep in her chest and tried to calm herself. Distant memories of anatomy class drifted up in her mind. Depending on the level of paralysis, even maintaining that level of control over her breathing would be impossible. Either she was back under the immobility spell, or Wick had drained so much power that Toria literally didn't have the strength to lift a finger.

Was the ritual done? Was Wick finished with her?

Was Kane still alive?

It turned out she didn't even have enough power to send a pulse of emotion down their link. Either that, or Kane was dead. Toria suppressed the keening whimper that tried to pass her lips.

Even if Kane was dead, she was still alive. She still had to get out of here somehow.

She opened her eyes at a rustle of movement.

Wick stood above her once again. She gave a close-mouthed smile, but Toria shrank back from the hazy memory of sharpened teeth. "Good, you're still with me," Wick said. "It's true, warrior-mages have much more potential than Burrows and I could have hoped. We're not done yet." She held her hands out above Toria. Blue swirls of energy collected around them.

Oh gods, not again.

She fell.

#

She felt no pain.

Something had changed. Toria saw a city spread beneath her, lights twinkling in the night. A cool breeze caressed her skin, with a hint of winter's chill in the air. She recognized this vantage point. It was the roof of Limani's city council building.

She reached up a cautious hand and grasped a full handful of hair. But this time, when she ran her fingers through it, she found it much longer than the shoulder-length locks she had worn since high school.

Toria hadn't visited the roof of the council building in years. And the body she looked down at was barely recognizable. Her hips were too narrow, and she hadn't seen her this much of her feet over nonexistent breasts in years. And what the hell was she wearing? A long dress of green silk with heavy embroidered panels of silver and gold thread. An altered gown that had once belonged to Victory. She had been costumed as Roman nobility for an All Hallows Eve when she was twelve years old.

The All Hallows Eve when she met Kane.

Toria whirled on the roof and felt her face light up. There he was. Kane at twelve had been much shorter, much less muscled than he was now. Tight black curls sprang from his scalp, and she remembered the sprinkling of fuzz above his upper lip. He had always been taller than her, but now the difference was less.

His eyes narrowed, an incongruous look on a boy dressed as the hero of the latest space vid. "What are you laughing at?"

"It's good to see you," she said. "No matter the context." What a memory for Wick to have pulled out of her brain.

Kane stepped back, away from her. The frown on his face deepened. "Kids at school were right. You are a freak."

Wait. That wasn't how the conversation had happened. Kane had followed her onto the roof during the All Hallows Eve party, after she ditched the adults downstairs. Victory had made her come to this party specifically because she knew the new kid in town would be there. But their first conversation had been much more amicable. Probably because she had not come off as a crazy person during it.

Why had Wick brought her to this point? Tempting Toria with her mother was one thing, but why not show Kane as he was now?

Kane turned away to look over the rooftops of Limani's commercial district. He stepped closer toward the edge of the roof. They shouldn't have even been up here. It wasn't safe.

The time neared for the midnight fireworks from the mage school closer to the edge of town. Toria remembered feeling bitter that she hadn't been allowed to participate. Master Procella would only allow teenagers, citing things like maturity levels and insurance premiums. But that's why she'd come to the roof rather than jostle for space at the big picture window in the council room.

While she could feel the magic gathering in the air, Kane was oblivious. Both of his parents were mages, but he'd been born without the talent. Otherwise it would have started stirring when he hit the beginning of puberty. Until Kane's hand met hers, and the power between them exploded into the bond they had now.

Toria felt lightheaded as the blood drained from her face. That was why Wick had chosen this point. All this time, she had been afraid of Wick draining Kane through their bond. She had probably led the air mage right to this meeting. Wick still couldn't acces Kane's power, so she would recreate the bond in Toria's memories. "Oh my gods."

Kane looked over his shoulder at her. "What is wrong with you?" His voice broke midsentence, which should have made the withering disdain in his voice hilarious. Instead, he rolled his eyes and turned his back on her.

But his foot caught on the edge of the roof.

That had happened before. But then, Toria had stood at the edge of the roof next to him, pointing out the direction from which the fireworks would appear. She'd caught his arm, fireworks of a different sort had occurred, and the adult mages downstairs had poured onto the roof when they sensed the whirling energies above them. Limani's treasured warrior-mage pair had been born. Toria had found the other half of her soul.

This was what Wick waited for. For Toria to catch Kane again, activating the link between them.

All the pain from before was nothing. Not reaching out in this moment, even if it just existed in her mind, would be the most brutal, horrific thing Toria had ever done.

Kane stumbled. Fear and shock crossed his face as he listed backward. Nothing but air was between him and the concrete three stories below. He reached for her.

She stood her ground.

He fell.

#

"Wake up, love. Come on, time to get up now." A gentle hand stroked long fingers through her hair.

Kane's voice was in her ear. But that was impossible. Kane was dead. She hadn't saved him, and her best friend, her soulmate was gone forever. Without opening her eyes, she rolled onto her side and curled into the fetal position. Her entire body ached, and every movement was a tremendous effort. She was so tired.

She'd had enough of Wick's mental games. This was another ploy for her to have access to Kane. But she would keep fighting. The only way Wick would get to Kane was if she dragged him into the damn ritual chamber and performed the power drain spell on him. And Toria would die before she would let her partner go through this torture.

"I know you're awake. Come on, love." Kane's hand rested on the back of her neck, large and warm. The adult Kane that she remembered.

His younger self flashed in her mind. The fear on his face as he disappeared over the edge of the roof.

He squeezed her neck, a familiar gesture that was supposed to be comforting. He was touching her. A wave of love and affection passed through her as Kane pushed the emotion through their bond.

Their active bond. Maybe if she didn't acknowledge him, Wick couldn't take advantage of it.

The hand left her neck and she felt him move away. She curled up tighter and felt her back hit wall. The rest of her surroundings filtered into focus as she became aware of the soft fabric beneath her cheek. The air had a certain muffled quality. If this wasn't another illusion, she was back in the cell with Kane.

"Okay, now you're being silly. I've checked you over, and you're not physically injured. What's wrong?" Kane's voice had gone from gentle concern to mild frustration. "This isn't a wake up for school moment, this is a wake the hell up and tell your partner what's going on moment."

Toria cracked open one eye. Kane's face hovered inches away from her own, where he crouched on the floor next to the cot she laid on. It took way more effort than was warranted for such a simple use of her abilities, but she managed to summon magesight. She was reduced to no shields to speak of, but Kane was enveloped in his familiar vibrant emerald hues. The colors of a liquid forest surrounded him, and it was the most beautiful thing Toria had ever seen.

There was no way Wick could fake that, not without having an intimate knowledge of Kane's power. Not the way she now knew Toria's.

But that meant this was really Kane. With a sob, she threw her arms around his neck and clutched him tight, hanging off the cot.

88

"Whoa, it's okay," Kane said. He caught her in his own arms, supporting half her weight and holding her tight.

She couldn't stop the tears once they ran loose. She could move and she could breathe and she was back with Kane and he was alive and they were safe. Despite the awkward angle, Kane kept her close, and they clung to each other while she cried herself out. He kept up a steady stream of soothing noises in her ear and kept pushing love and comfort across to her.

With a last gasping heave, Toria managed to get back in control. She slid off the cot so that she sat sideways in Kane's lap on the concrete floor. But he kept his arms around her shoulders, pulling her in close to his chest. He didn't seem willing to let her go either. "How long was I gone?" she asked.

"I don't know," Kane said. "More than a few hours, but less than overnight? I couldn't move again when you were being taken, or when Burrows showed up a little afterward."

"What did he want?"

"To gloat, I think," Kane said. "It wasn't to check on me, because he already seemed to know what to expect. He babbled something about how Wick was getting closer, then left again. It wasn't a two-sided conversation."

"Oy," Toria said. "We are being held captive by caricatures."

"But you obviously experienced something," Kane said. "You were completely out of it when Wick brought you back. I got really worried when it took ages to wake you up. And your reaction when you did…" His voice trailed off.

She had to tell him, but she didn't know how she could. Not when talking about it would be almost reliving it. While she did have the occasional nightmare about the thwarted Roman invasion, she didn't have the posttraumatic stress symptoms that she knew some others did. What had happened to her tonight was different, though. Max had given her a frank talk on the realities of being a female mercenary when she first expressed an interest in following in her mother's footsteps, warning her that she didn't have the same strengths and protections that Victory did. And while it wasn't a physical rape, she hadn't expected to have to confront this issue on their first job. Raping her of her power, of her very mind, was still a trauma.

She tried to block it, but some of the impressions in her mind must have bled over. Kane's face grew ashen, but she pressed a finger to his lips before he could talk. "It was awful," she said. "Apparently Archer has been giving power willingly. If this is the alternative, I don't blame him."

"I'm sorry I couldn't stop it," Kane said.

He was struggling to come up with words. She didn't blame him. He filled the void by squeezing her tight. She tucked her face in the crook of his neck and breathed in the familiar scent of him. The rather ripe scent. She wrinkled her nose and pulled away. "You need a shower. Badly."

A bit of the tension in the room broke. Kane smiled at her, and an answering grin crossed her face in return. "You don't smell much better, lady. But you don't see me complaining." With a gentle shove, Kane pushed her off his lap. He used the cot to leverage himself to his feet, then reached down and hauled her up after him.

He grabbed her arm when she staggered from the blood rushing from her head. A quick flash of memory—real memory—showed herself grabbing a young Kane before he slipped off the council building roof. The squeezing of her heart was a physical pain. It would be a long time before she got over this experience.

Or maybe the squeezing was another symptom of hunger. She'd thought she was past that point, but her stomach let out an epic churning noise. Toria collapsed on the cot next to Kane. "We need food. Soon." She licked her dry lips and saw that Kane's were as chapped. "Water sooner."

"Nothing we can do about that now," Kane said. "Except conserve energy. I had an idea while you were gone, though."

"Oh?" Toria asked.

"We should try reaching out to Syri," he said. "Our magics are linked. We can at least find out whether she's alive, if not what her location is."

"That's pretty much the opposite of conserving energy," Toria said. "And I don't think I have any to fuel that sort of trick."

"But I do," Kane said. "And I'd rather put my power to better use before they come for me to steal it."

A chill ran up Toria's spine. Exhaustion made her control fuzzy, and Kane shot her a questioning look. It must have echoed over to him, and he didn't understand the context. "They're not coming for you," she said. "Not if I can stop it."

"You're still alive," Kane said. "I'll survive, too."

Toria kept her mouth shut. This wasn't a debate worth having or wasting energy on. "Fine. How are you going to contact Syri?"

"She managed to link us together when I was the one kidnapped," he said. "I'm pretty sure I can reverse engineer the process."

"She managed that by using elven magic," Toria said. "Her crazy mind-magic that she won't talk about. We don't have those abilities."

"But it's still worth trying," Kane said. He had grown rigid next to her in frustration, though he kept his voice calm.

Toria snagged one of his hands and held it between hers. "You're right, I'm sorry. It is absolutely worth trying. I'm not sure what help I'll be, but I'll be right here."

"Watch for now," Kane said. "I trust you'll help when and if you can." He leaned back against the plaster wall.

Toria activated her magesight, which once again needed more effort than it should have. Her shields were faded wisps next to his, but she linked to him where she could. Most of whatever Kane tried existed in his mind, but she saw tendrils of power extend from his shields. They appeared as leafy vines and stretched, kudzu-like, across the cell. Most disappeared through the walls, but one tendril wrapped around Toria's wrist and arm, keeping her close.

Last time, Syri had ransacked Toria's mind until she found the foundation of her connection with Kane. It had put her in contact with her missing partner, given them important intelligence about the Romans' invasion plot, and entrenched Syri in both of their minds. If anyone had the patience and skill to tease out that connection and follow it to the source, it was Kane.

With little ceremony, the room around Toria winked out of existence. Blackness engulfed her. Before she had time to panic, the image of a different location altogether swam into view. But now she looked with another's sight.

This time, it wasn't Kane's view of the inside of a Roman bivouac tent. It was the inside of a metal shipping container, lit from above with a flickering bare lightbulb covered in grime. Bits of refuse cluttered the floor of the container. But the bulb couldn't be bright enough to cast light in so many colors. The angles were too sharp, and everything had too many shadows.

Toria's first thought was more clinical and scientific. So that was what elven vision was like. The literature wasn't lying about them seeing more of the visible light spectrum.

But her next thought—*Syri!*

The image winked out, and Toria was afraid Kane had lost the connection. But it appeared again, and she realized that Syri must have made a slow blink.

As if from a great distance, Syri responded—*Torrr?* Even her mental voice was slurred. The image disappeared again in another slow blink. Something was very wrong.

Toria shoved as much love and comfort as she could down the link Kane had established, hoping it would reach Syri the same way it did with her partner. *We're coming for you, Sy—*

The vision winked out, and when it didn't return after another blink on Syri's end, Toria knew they had lost the connection. When Toria opened her own eyes, her magesight was gone. It resisted her attempt to resummon it, and either way, she knew that the energy tendrils Kane had sent out were gone.

"Anything?" Kane said. "I'm not sure that worked."

"It worked," Toria said, squeezing his hand. "Syri's alive. Trapped somewhere, and possibly drugged, but she's alive."

#

More time passed, but Toria had no idea how much. The hours ran into each other, blurring together in the unrelenting light of their magical cage. At some moment that could have been dawn or noon, the slit at the bottom of the steel door opened. Before either Toria or Kane could react, an unidentified figure shoved two plastic bottles of water into the cell before sliding the slit shut with a clang. They fell on the bottles, but before she could drink, Kane insisted on scanning the contents first. Even after he identified it as regular tap water, he forced her to take sips rather than guzzle down the whole bottle.

They were so dehydrated that the lack of toilet didn't matter. The water wouldn't go to waste in their parched bodies. More time passed, and they went back to lying on separate cots. Contacting Syri on an empty stomach had worn out Kane, and Toria had no reserves left.

Toria still had great plans to fight off Master Wick when she came for Kane. She just had no idea how she would manage it in her current state. She drifted in and out of conscious, but the unrelented light made anything more than a light doze difficult.

After more water, a decent meal, freedom from this cell, and a reunion with Syri, the next item on her wish list was a long, hot shower.

"Do you hear that?"

Toria lifted her head an inch off the cot and looked across the cell at Kane. "Hear what?"

The door to their cell creaked as the first deadbolt slid open. As one, they rolled off their cots and landed in crouches on either side of the door. Toria leaned against the wall, suppressing the nausea that rolled through her at the sudden movement. They had this planned. As long as the immobility spell wasn't cast, they could handle whoever came through that door. Toria would distract them—somehow. It might be by passing out at their feet. Kane would appear from behind the door and take them out—somehow. Judging from his own state over the last few hours, he might also pass out, but at least he might aim for landing on top of them.

Best escape plan ever.

The locks finished engaging, and the door swung open. Toria counted a few beats, but no one entered the cell. With cautious movement, she leaned forward and peeked around the doorframe.

A lone figure stood in the middle of the hallway, looking identical to the first time Toria had seen her. The simulacrum stared straight ahead, with her arms at her sides. The beige business suit was the same, as were the hairstyle and blank expression on her face.

Toria leaned farther out of the doorway, looking up and down the hallway. No one else was around. "We're good, Kane." She used the doorframe to pull herself to her feet.

Kane also looked around edge of the door. "What the hell?" He joined Toria in the doorway. The simulacrum still did not move.

"I think we're being set free?" Toria stepped forward, out of the cell. Still no reaction from the simulacrum. The world swam around her, and she grabbed for the wall.

Kane wrapped an arm around her torso, balancing and supporting her. "We're not turning it down. Which way?"

"Left," Toria said. "Elevator down the hall. Ground level was one floor up." They set out with one last look back. Their rescuer stared into the cell, not acknowledging them in any way. Still creepy as hell, but Toria wasn't about to complain at this point.

Despite how limited her previous view of the journey had been, they found the elevator right where she expected it. What she didn't expect was the security keypad that locked out control. However, there was a note taped to the wall right above it, with a five-digit number printed in neat copperplate. "Either their security measures are awful," she said, "or our escape is being orchestrated."

Kane punched the number into the keypad, and the elevator doors opened. "I'm not going to argue." He pulled her into the cargo elevator after him. "We are getting the hell out of here." The digital display inside the elevator read *B*, so Kane punched the next highest button for the first floor.

As before, the ride wasn't long. When the doors opened again, Master Wick stood on the other side. From the shocked expression on her face, she did not expect to see them out of their cell. Her two minions did not accompany her, as they had when she retrieved Toria from the cell the first time. That was all the information Toria needed.

Rage let her tap into a strength she didn't know she had left. With a snarl, she slipped from Kane's grasp and launched herself out of the elevator at Wick. The strength didn't also translate into dexterity. When she slammed into the air mage, the two of them fell in a heap of limbs.

Her assessment the evening before had been correct—most mages didn't expect physical attacks from other mages and thus did not guard against them. Wick was one of them. She crashed to the ground with Toria on top of her, letting out a high-pitched squeal of surprise that cut off when the back of her skull hit the marble floor with a sickening thud.

Toria pushed herself to her knees, straddling Wick in an awkward reversal of the energy draining ritual. But rather than try to recover any of the power Wick had stolen, it was more efficient and much more satisfying to draw her first back and pound it into Wick's face. Bone cracked, and blood spurted from the older woman's nose. She didn't even try to fight back. Toria punched again. And again.

When she pulled back her fist for another hit, Kane snagged it. "No."

Toria struggled in his grasp, but his grip was firm. "You don't know what she did to me."

"But I know she's already dead," he said.

Toria blinked. Wick's eyes were open and unseeing. Her nose was broken, and blood smeared the side of her face from Toria's hits. But blood pooled on the marble, soaking Wick's gray hair. "Oh gods." Kane still had her wrist, and she let him pull her to her feet. She staggered back, hitting the wall beside the elevator, where she slid down to the floor. The body didn't move.

Kane kneeled next to the body and checked the pulse point on Wick's neck. He shook his head, and wiped his bloody fingers on her blouse.

Toria should have felt something about this. She had killed before, and every time had been brutal. Someone her age shouldn't have such a high body count even before beginning her life as an official mercenary, but she hadn't lived a typical life. She looked at the bloodied knuckles of her right hand. This didn't feel like vengeance. This felt like nothing at all.

How could she feel remorse for killing someone who had raped her? Who had raped how many others?

Footsteps pounded down the marble hall. Toria looked up, but didn't move. They'd already taken out the most dangerous person in the New Angouleme Center for Magical Education through sheer bad luck. Nothing else the day could throw at them would be much of a challenge.

It should have been harder to kill someone that evil.

Kane dropped to a defensive stance before her. Archer slid around the corner, his dreadlocks flying.

"I've got them!" Archer sprinted down the hall toward them, drawing to a halt when he saw the body on the floor. Henry Delacour, in human form, was a few steps behind. "Oh gods," Archer said, in an unknowing echo of Toria's words.

"Well, that's one less obstacle," Henry said, his tone business-like.

Archer shook himself, dragging his attention away from Wick's body. He looked between Kane and Toria. "Fee got you out?"

"The simulacrum?" Kane asked. Archer gave a sharp nod. "Yes," Kane said. "She's back downstairs where we left her, I think."

"I didn't give her any orders beyond freeing you," Archer said. "What happened?" He and Kane hauled Toria to a standing position.

She didn't resist, and when Kane tucked her under his arm, she leaned into him. "I got mad," she said. That was all the explanation she had the inclination for, and if Archer knew what Wick was capable of, it should be all the explanation necessary.

"Not important," Henry said. "The ship leaves within the hour, and we need to be gone before Burrows gets back from his meeting with my cousins." He gave Wick's body a hard look. "No big loss anyway."

"You have an exit strategy?" Kane asked.

"This way," Archer said. "It's dinnertime, so the students are in the dining hall with the servants. Burrows is out for his meeting. Wick was our only concern, but not anymore." He lifted his shoulder, showing off the long rucksack slung over one shoulder. "I have your clothes and weapons here." He and Henry escorted them through the winding corridors.

"Why are you making your move now?" Toria found her voice as they bustled through the waiting area they had first seen in the mage school. Knowing they wouldn't have to search for the swords lifted a huge weight from her shoulders, especially if time was of the essence. "And how long has it been?"

"You were attacked a day and a half ago," Henry said. "It took me that long to get back in contact with Archer and make plans."

"Once they had you two," Archer said, "they locked me up tight. Hal and I have alternative means of communication."

They had emerged into the gardens now, and Toria wanted to stop and soak in the ambient energy floating through the air. But it felt tainted, now that she knew where a significant portion of it had come from. A feeling of death permeated the flow of power, giving the breeze that rustled their clothes a soapy, bitter aftertaste in the back of her throat. She shuddered, and Kane squeezed her shoulders.

"You mean money talks," Henry said. "Good, the town-car is here."

When they left the premises, Toria felt it easier to breathe. An extra-long black town-car sat in the street outside of the mage school's gates, electric engine running with a low purr. A uniformed chauffer stood next to the back door and pulled it open at their approach. He didn't blink at Toria and Kane's bare feet or the bloodstains on Toria's shirt from where she'd tried to wipe off the back of her hand. She ducked into the back of the town-car first and slid down the long bench seat along the side. The three men piled in behind her, Archer pulling in the rucksack after him.

Toria leaned back against the smooth leather of the seat as the chauffer drove the town-car. Kane settled next to her and wrapped an arm around her shoulders again, but she didn't protest at the clinginess. Her partner probably had his own issues to work through after the past two days.

She had no idea where they were going or why, but she was out of that place, and the woman who had hurt her was dead. She still had trouble forming a reaction to that. She should have paid more attention to all the literature on posttraumatic stress disorder distributed in Limani after the failed invasion. She tuned out Archer and Henry's low conversation in the cool, dim interior of the town-car. She was so tired.

"By the way," Henry said, pitching his voice a bit louder, "your gear is in the trunk. I had it picked up from the Guildhall."

Toria straightened. "How the hell did you manage that?"

Henry shrugged. "Money talks."

"Titles talk louder," Archer said. "But we wanted to avoid any unnecessary stops."

"You said we were going to the docks?" Kane asked. "Why?"

"Because I didn't go into that fight in the alley without backup," Henry said. "And my sources say that Syri was loaded on a ship bound for the Europa."

#

The ride through New Angouleme was quick and without incident. Toria didn't even try to peer out the tinted windows to catch a last view of the city's impressive skyline as they approached the shipping district on the river's edge. She was done with this city. Instead, she and Kane dozed after downing large bottles of water Henry scrounged up from the town-car's minibar.

"We're here, guys."

Toria's eyes snapped open at Archer's voice. She stretched in her seat. It would take more than a short nap for her to feel recovered. She still needed that warm meal and warmer shower.

She blinked in the afternoon summer sunlight when she emerged from the luxurious town-car. The scent of the river permeated the air, and they were far enough from the urban center that the oppressive feeling of the city was more of a tension at the back of her mind. She had no shields to speak of to block it out anyway. A tall cruise ship stretched stories above her at the edge of the massive dock, and bustling crew making final deliveries to the great vessel surrounded them. Tasteful script across the bow proclaimed its name to be *The Lunar Queen*, and Toria recognized the flags it flew as those of both the British Colonies and the northern empire across the sea.

Toria saw passengers boarding at the opposite end of the ship, but the town-car had deposited them at a more private entrance. The chauffer helped Henry unload their gear from the trunk, and Archer zipped open his rucksack. He pulled out two sheathed swords with the belts twisted down the lengths of the blades. "I believe these belong to you," he said.

Henry looked up from the trunk of the town-car. "You don't even give them their shoes first?"

"Archer understands priorities," Kane said. "Thank you, sir."

When he accepted the blades, Toria felt an electric tingle in her own hand where Kane and Archer must have touched. What an interesting development. Kane had throttled any hint of emotion when she gave a mental nudge as he passed over her rapier. Toria suppressed any trickle over her own amusement while she buckled her belt on. No need to embarrass either man right now.

Archer did find their socks and boots next. Kane stuffed his socks in his back pocket and shoved his feet in his boots without bothering to lace them, then helped Henry and Archer pile their packs on a cart to be transferred to the cruise ship. Toria noted that all of Syri's gear was with it, but took her time pulling on her own footwear. As she leaned against the side of the town-car to zip the boots up her calves, she sensed a figure emerge from the stacked cargo goods next to her.

Toria had her blade half-drawn when she realized the woman standing next to her was an elf. "Kane!" She backed away from the stranger, studying her pale face and trying to identify whether it was one of the elves they'd fought in nightclub district. But she'd never gotten a good look at the women in that fight, thanks to the dim light of the back alleyways. This elf had the typical green eyes and pointed features, but Toria thought she would have remembered the bright red hair, which was more of a rarity.

But the woman raised empty hands, and said, "I have no quarrel with you. I am not with the others."

Kane did draw his scimitar, heedless of the dockworkers around them gawking at the scene. He pointed the blade at the elven woman. "Who are you?"

"I am Brindisia, Brin," she said. She kept her hands raised, radiating harmlessness. "I must speak with Syrisinia. Is she with you?

"No," Kane said. "We don't know where she is."

"Did you not get my message on the train?"

Toria wasn't taking any chances. She stepped back, so that Kane and his weapon were closer to the elf than she was. "You're the one who left the oh-so-helpful note that we can't read?"

She didn't expect the look of anguish that crossed Brin's face. "You didn't get it to Syri?"

"We thought it was a blank scrap of paper!" Toria said. "A bright flash of light was a little too subtle, lady."

"I'm sorry," Brin said. "If Syri's not with you—"

"Your people took her," Toria said. "And we ran into a little trouble ourselves after."

"Not my people," Brin said. "I have nothing to do with those monsters. They have taken her to the old world for the sacrifice."

"The what?" Kane asked, alarm in his voice.

"Hey!" A voice shouted from across the docks, pulling Toria's attention away from Brin. Four bulky men tramped toward them.

"Oh, not now," Henry said. He stepped toward the newcomers. "I'll handle this." He snapped his fingers at the dockworkers around them who gaped at the show. "Get back to work! This ship is on a schedule."

A headache had formed behind Toria's eyes, from either hunger, exhaustion, or stress. It didn't help that she still operated on adrenaline alone, and soon that would not be enough to keep her functional. Henry's sources said Syri was bound for Europa, which the elves referred to as the "old world." If this boat was going there, she was getting on it. Maybe then she would have a chance to catch her breath.

The four men arrayed themselves before Henry, who stood with arms crossed and a bored expression on his face. "Can I help you, gentlemen?"

One of them stepped closer, intruding in Henry's personal space and looming over him. "What the hell are those two still doing here?" He pointed toward Toria and Kane.

Toria realized that Brin had disappeared during the distraction. Kane figured this out at the same time, and his face darkened. Damn elves. Brin's message had been cryptic, but anything referred to as a "sacrifice" couldn't be good. They were a day at most behind the ship Syri had left on, but had no idea what port in Europa she was being brought to. They didn't have time for this.

"My guests, the warrior-mages Toria Connor and Kane Nalamas, are boarding the *Lunar Queen* as soon as possible," Henry said. He didn't back away from the other man, but Toria could imagine his hackles rising. "I fail to see what you are concerned about, James."

"You were supposed to be keeping an eye on them, and they disappeared for two days," James said.

"They are mages," Henry said. "They were guests at the New Angouleme Center for Magical Education. Doing mage things, I imagine. I had no reason to track their activities more closely."

"They're vampire spies," was the retort, and the man spat on the ground.

"They are my guests," Henry said, a hint of a growl entering his words. "And they will be given the respect they are due."

"I will be speaking to your aunt about this," James said.

He inched back, but gave no other indication of submissiveness. Werewolf politics were weird. Now that the immediate danger was gone, the tension drained out of Toria. The world lurched, and she listed to the side. Kane caught her shoulder with his free hand.

"Do give her my regards when you do," Henry said. "Now, if you will excuse us?"

After a short bow that seemed to pain him as much as it did for Henry to return, James gestured to his compatriots. They followed him away from the docking area and disappeared from sight.

A man cleared his throat. A ship's officer stood beside the cart loaded with their luggage. "Your cabin is ready, sir."

"Thank you, Captain Dunn," Henry said. He clasped the captain's hand in greeting. "I will not be returning home today, but I do appreciate you letting my friend's occupy my family's quarters."

"Better they be used than stand empty, sir," Captain Dunn said. "We are honored to host guests of the Delacour family. Would you care to show them the way?"

"Absolutely," Henry said. "You go get her ready to depart. I'll make sure I'm off board before you leave." When he returned the captain's bow, it didn't look as forced. "This way." Henry held out an arm to Toria.

She stared at it for a moment, and Kane gave her a gentle push. She wrapped her fingers around Henry's forearm, and the two of them led Archer and Kane onboard the *Lunar Queen*.

#

Toria had been worried about them getting spoiled, between the sophisticated hotel in Calverton and the fancy Mercenary Guildhall of New Angouleme. But after the tiny cell she had occupied at the mage school, she had no complaints about the luxurious suite of rooms aboard the cruise ship that Henry dismissed as one of the more modest boats in the fleet owned by his family.

On the way to the cabin, Henry gave them a quick tour of the passenger section of the ship. While most of the *Lunar Queen* was cargo space reserved for firms that specialized in exotic and expensive goods, there was still room for a few hundred passengers and almost another hundred crew to serve them. They would be travelling in style for six nights to reach Calaitum, the seat of the Delacour holdings and the main port for their shipping assets.

Their "cabin" was really a two-bedroom apartment, complete with bathroom, living room, and kitchenette. Henry waved off the cooking area, informing them that they would take their meals in the dining room with the rest of their passengers, but that they could order food in whenever they preferred.

Toria had one eye on the fruit spread set out in the living room and another on the large shower she'd spotted through the ajar bathroom door.

"Keep an eye on them in Calaitum," Henry said to Archer, taking his hand and squeezing it.

"I will," Archer said.

"Wait, you're coming with us?" Kane asked.

That explained the extra baggage Toria hadn't recognized. The odd flutter of nervousness that ran through her stomach had to be from Kane. Well. This was going to get interesting, fast. Archer looked between Kane and Henry. He still held the werewolf's hand. This was going to get awkward fast, too.

Toria wasn't the only one in the room to realize that fact. Archer dropped Henry's hand, but said, "I'm going to see Hal off the ship and watch departure from up on deck. Why don't you two grab showers and have a bite to eat?"

Kane also eyed the fruit plate, filled with dainty morsels but not much sustenance. "That will not tide us over until dinner."

"I'll see what else I can scrounge up on my way back," Archer said.

It should have been uncomfortable, but somehow Toria found herself exchanging amused smiles with Henry. If Archer's statement at the club about the reality of Henry's marital situation was not exaggerated, then Henry had to be one of the most well-adjusted people Toria had ever met. She'd have to keep in touch with this guy.

Surprising even herself, Toria reached over and hugged Henry. "Thank you for everything," she said.

He squeezed her back, despite how offensive she must smell to his sensitive nose. "It is my pleasure," Henry said. "My family knows to expect your arrival. Archer has met them before. Be warned that my mother is…a bit of a character."

"You haven't met mine," Toria said, stepping away from him.

"Oh, but I've heard stories of yours," Henry said, exchanging a handshake with Kane. "We'll have to compare notes when next we meet. Be safe, and find your friend." With one last wave, he left the cabin, followed by Archer.

The second the door shut, Toria pointed at Kane. "We are sharing close quarters with Archer for the next week. Figure out what the hell you want, and stop making my insides feel confused." Before her partner to could respond, she staggered to the bathroom. "Dibs on the shower!"

The hot water felt luxurious, even if Toria did end up leaning against the cool tile of the shower stall while she scrubbed shampoo into her hair. Afterward, she wrapped herself in a towel almost as big as a blanket. She was incredibly tempted to crawl into one of the beds, but she knew that if she didn't eat a proper meal and get into a regular sleep cycle, she'd be more miserable later.

A peek into the first bedroom showed the unfamiliar luggage on the enormous king-sized bed. She found her bags on one of the smaller beds in the second room. Fresh clothes felt almost as good as the shower. The ship's dining room probably had a dress code for dinner, but the staff would have to deal with her limited wardrobe options.

Toria heard quiet talking in the suite's living room. Archer must be back. With any luck, he and Kane would find some way to get along without the sexual tension going through the roof. She didn't have the patience for that.

She rifled through the rest of her gear, making sure everything was accounted for. Clothes, toiletries, hidden cash, spare knives, all there. But when Toria checked the pocket hidden in the side of her bigger pack, something was missing—the palm pistol Kane had told her not to pack. The box of extra ammo was still there, but no gun. "Kane!"

"What?" Kane entered the bedroom at her call, a half-eaten sandwich in one hand. "Archer brought back sandwiches. If you hurry, I might save you one."

"Bigger problem right now, hon," she said. "Did you move the gun I brought to your pack?"

"No, because I told you not to bring it," Kane said.

"Well, I did," Toria said. "And now it's gone."

"Your mother is going to kill you," Kane said, around another bite of food.

"Even worse," Toria said, staring into the empty pocket. "I think it belonged to Asaron."

"Well, then he'll kill you," Kane said. "Come eat."

#

Toria had hoped that the larger ship would mitigate Kane's seasickness, but the wish had been in vain. The moment the cruise ship left sight of land, Kane vomited the three sandwiches he'd eaten. She couldn't convince him to come to dinner, so she spent the evening catching up with Archer without all the uncomfortable flirting getting in the way.

But Kane was sullen and resentful when she returned, and Toria felt awful for ditching him in his distress. He spent the night in the bathroom rather than in the comfortable second bed in Toria's room. His dry heaving woke her multiple times during the night, and this morning even her stomach felt queasy as his discomfort bled through their link.

"Food is evil," Kane said from his position on the bathroom floor, draped over the toilet bowl. "Get that away from me."

She set the bowl of oatmeal down on the floor and tried to press the glass of water into his hand. "Drink something, at least. You need to stay hydrated."

"Water is even more evil," Kane said, his voice hoarse and grating. He rested his temple on the edge of the toilet bowl. "How much longer is this trip?"

"Five more days until port," she said. "You can't be like this the entire time."

"I'm pretty sure I will be," Kane said. "Syri's not here to knock me out. Let me die in peace."

"Even Syri wouldn't keep you unconscious for five days," Toria said. "There's got to be something we can do."

A knock came on the doorframe, and Toria glanced over her shoulder. Archer stood in the doorway, trying and failing to be unobtrusive. "There might be something I can do. Water magic, and all."

Kane all but bared his teeth at Archer. "Water is what got me into this mess."

"I'm pretty sure that your connection with the earth is frayed, which is why you're feeling sick," Archer said. "The connection is dulled by the water beneath us, and the elements are acting in opposition. I can help."

"I don't need him mucking around in my brain," Kane said. If he could have shoved her away with the power of his mental irritation, he probably would have. "Leave me be."

"I don't know, hon," Toria said. "If Archer can help, you should let him."

But Kane had clammed up, so Toria waved Archer out of the bathroom. When the door clicked shut behind him, Toria whirled on Kane. "You are being a straight-up idiot now."

"Letting Syri muck in your head was what got her connected to us," Kane said, straightening up. The action didn't agree with him, and he gagged into the toilet. But there was nothing left in his body to expel, thankfully, because Toria could feel her gag reflex react in sympathy.

"Is that what this is about," Toria asked. "That's why you think Zerandan made her come with us?"

"If she wasn't with us, she wouldn't have been kidnapped!" Kane's roughened voice prevented a full-on yell, but Archer had to overhear them in the main room. At least they had the illusion of privacy.

"I'm pretty sure she got taken just for being in the British colonies," Toria said. "Because we missed Brin's crazy warning on the train."

That seemed to distract Kane from his own agony. "You think Zerandan set this up?"

Toria's knees ached on the tile floor. She settled back, leaning against the cupboard beneath the sink. "You try accusing Zerandan of putting Syri in danger. He'd swat you like a fly. Besides, the crazy New Angouleme mages would have kidnapped us anyway."

"But he's playing a longer game," Kane said.

She couldn't disagree, not when she and Syri had had a similar conversation on another boat in the not-to-distant past. Toria rubbed her hands over her face. "We don't know for sure," she said. "But we do know that we have to rescue Syri. And we can't do that if you die of stupidity before we even get to search for her again."

Kane didn't answer that, though he did snatch up the cup of water. Liquid sloshed over the side of the glass, but some of it ended up in his mouth. He gulped it down with a wince.

Five seconds later, he was back over the toilet, and the smell of bile permeated the bathroom. "Get out," Kane said.

"You're still being an idiot," Toria said. She pushed herself off the floor and left the bathroom, slamming the door behind her. But she shoved love and affection down their link as hard as she could. Let him gag on that.

#

Toria didn't look up from the book she'd borrowed from the ship's library when Archer entered the main area of the suite.

"Come have a drink with me," he said, leaning over the back of the sofa to read over her shoulder. "You're getting claustrophobic in here."

She'd skipped dinner in the dining room, and the sun's evening rays cast long shadows across the elegant suite. She might be pissed at Kane, but she didn't want to leave him alone. He'd stumbled into the bedroom a few hours ago. Toria had checked that he was breathing, and now he slept the sleep of the exhausted. "Thanks, I'm fine," Toria said. Abandoning Kane again was not an option, not when he was this ill.

Archer dropped onto the other couch with a dramatic sigh. "This is about Kane, isn't it?"

Toria set the book aside. "Of course it's about Kane. I'm not abandoning him two nights in a row."

"It's not exactly a big ship."

"It's the principle of the thing," Toria said. "You're not bonded. You wouldn't understand."

"Obviously," Archer said. "But I do know what partnership is."

The night before, their conversation had stayed in the past. Archer's family's move to New Angouleme and his training at the school there, before everything went to hell. He'd been one of the last students before Burrows and Wick took over. He couldn't say what happened to the other masters, but he'd fast learned that not asking too many questions would be better for his health. They hadn't talked about anything more serious than that, and Toria had steered the conversation away from Archer's love life. Now she couldn't resist the shot. "You mean like your partnership with dear Hal?"

Archer narrowed his eyes. "You don't know anything about that."

Kane's voice, which still sounded like gravel, emerged from the bedroom. "Go yell at each other somewhere else!"

Toria yelled back. "I'm not leaving you!"

"Archer, go get her drunk and leave me in peace!" The bedroom door slammed.

They sat in silence for a few beats. "The bars here are pretty nice," Archer said.

"They better be," Toria said, "because now you owe me a drink."

Rather than lead her to the dance floor toward the aft of the *Lunar Queen*, as Toria expected, Archer escorted her to a smaller lounge with a view out the front of the ship. Moonlight glinted off the water, and the room was smoky with the scent of cigars.

"I'm not dressed for this," Toria said under her breath. But the other patrons, still wearing evening garb from dinner, gave them little more than a passing glance. "And this doesn't really strike me as your scene."

"Everyone knows we're in the Delacours' suite," Archer said, pulling out a chair for Toria next to a large window. "We can wear whatever the hell we want. And do you hear that?"

Low classical music drifted in from invisible speakers, barely audible over the low conversations around them and clink of glassware from the bar. "Hear what?"

"Exactly," Archer said. "You can't yell at me here."

"I think you still think of me as a ten-year-old." Toria slouched in her seat.

"Don't act like one, and maybe I won't." Archer moved his foot away before Toria could kick him under the table. "That's not helping your case."

A waiter interrupted for their drink orders before the shenanigans could escalate. Toria was tempted to order her usual wine, but her thoughts were still half on Syri from that morning's conversation with Kane. Instead, she asked the waiter to bring the fruitiest, most obnoxious drink he could think of. Archer surprised her by asking for the same.

He shrugged. "Those usually have more alcohol. Kane told me to get you drunk."

"Getting me drunk is a terrible idea," Toria said. "You should never do what Kane tells you. He is a bad influence."

"He seems to have settled you down a bit," Archer said. "You were a hellion."

"So were you," Toria said. "Thank the gods I didn't bond with you instead."

"We'd eventually run into same problem," Archer said. He avoided her eyes in favor of staring out the window beside him.

"What do you mean?"

Archer shrugged. "Fate is a tricky thing. We'd eventually run into Kane somehow, and I'd be in his situation instead of the other way around."

"I'm not following," Toria said. "What situation?"

"He feels guilty for being attracted to me instead of to you." Archer looked surprised when Toria burst into peals of laughter. "What?"

The older couple at the nearest table gave her disapproving looks. Toria muffled her giggles in her hand. Apparently the Delacour name excused apparel, but not decorum. "The idea of Kane wanting me as anything other than a best friend," she said. "That is hilarious. You've been reading too many old stories." Toria thanked the waiter as he placed their drinks on the table.

Archer finished signing the receipt the waiter presented him and sipped his bright red cocktail before he responded. "In all the old tales, the stories of bonded mages are also epic stories of true love, regardless of whether they go down the warrior-mage path or not."

Toria also sampled her drink. It was fruity indeed, but she would need a lot more alcohol for this conversation. "I'll be right back." At the bar, she asked for four shots of spiced rum, putting them on Archer's tab. The expression on her face dissuaded the bartender from comment, and he poured four generous shots and even provided Toria with a tray to bring them back to the table. Now the fancy couple at the next table gave the drinks disgruntled looks. But they didn't try to stop her, so apparently shots were on the approved list of Delacour activities.

When she placed the tray in front of Archer, he said, "I don't actually like straight alcohol."

"Suck it up," Toria said. "I'm not drinking alone." She dropped back into her seat and picked up two of the glasses. She held one out to Archer, who took it from her hand with two fingers. Toria clinked the glasses together then drained the shot in one go, relishing in the smooth burn down her throat. That was expensive rum.

Archer managed half the shot before he put it down with a twisted face.

"You are bad at this," Toria said. She snagged his glass and gave the rest of his shot a good home. "You hang out in a nightclub."

"I hang out in a classy establishment," Archer said.

"I most definitely do not," Toria said, thinking of late nights at the Twilight Mists.

"Do we need to drink these, too?" Archer gestured to the remaining shots.

"Nope, those are for afterward," Toria said. "Finish your cocktail while we talk about this ridiculous notion you have."

"It's not ridiculous," Archer said. He nudged the tray with the remaining two shots closer to Toria's side of the table. "Warrior-mages are always true love. Even the few same-sex couples have hints of that in their legends."

"And you're familiar with these legends?" Toria knew where he was going with this. She'd done her share of research on those that had come before her.

"Sure," Archer said. "Word of you and Kane certainly reached us up in New Angouleme. I had a certain cachet with my peers because I knew you, if not him. I read up on it."

"Where the hell did you get the idea that we were in love?" The sheer ridiculousness of the idea boggled Toria's mind.

"Look at you two," Archer said. "It's obvious."

"Okay, someone has been remiss in your philosophical education," Toria said. "There are many different kinds of love. Kane is my best friend. He is my brother. He is the other half of my soul. He is not the love of my life."

"That whole soul comment usually indicates otherwise," Archer said, shrugging one shoulder and having another sip of his drink.

"Because he's in my head!" Toria threw her hands up in exasperation. At this point, the couple at the next table had their backs turned to her. That was probably best for their state of mind and sense of propriety. "I can feel him all the time. We can push emotions at each other if we're close enough. Sometimes I get his nightmares, and he gets mine. What does that have to do with romantic love?"

Archer sat silent for a moment, digesting this information. "You guys have never—" He gave a wavy hand gesture.

"Had sex?" Toria said, mimicking the movement of his hand. "Of course we have. We were sixteen and inundated with legendary expectations of great love, and Kane was freaking out because he had a crush on a boy in his math class and not on me. Sex doesn't have anything to do with romantic love either." Yep, the rum was more than setting in if she had gotten this personal. It was odd, having known Archer for so long, yet really only knowing him for three days. But if getting set straight about these crazy notions he had regarding her relationship with Kane cured some of the angst, she would spill all. The embarrassment could set in after she sobered up. "Remember all of your worst puberty issues and double them," she said. "That's what it's like growing up as part of a bonded pair."

"You are wise beyond your years," Archer said. "Or something." His cheeks were flushed. The alcohol must be hitting him, too.

"No, I have parents who are wise beyond their years," Toria said. "A father who has been in long-term relationships for the three centuries he's been alive. A mother who has been married four times. And a grandfather who loves to tell stories of what not to do. So, tell me about Henry."

Archer blinked at her sudden change of conversation. "What?"

"I'm not telling you my awkward sexual history without you having to be awkward, too," Toria said. "Spill. Or I'll make you drink more rum."

"Anything but that," Archer said. "There's not much to tell. I met Hal at The Red Eye when he first got to town a few years ago to supervise his family's holdings. We hooked up. We never really stopped hooking up."

"You are so in love with him," Toria said. "That's what all this is about. You, sir, are having angst because you like Hal *and* Kane."

"But I stand by what I said the other night," Archer said. "Hal has to pass on the family line. I will never be more than a kept man. I thought I was okay with that." He trailed off, and drew patterns in the ring of water left by his drink on the table. "And then I met Kane. And...wow."

"Yeah, he is pretty awesome," Toria said. "So you've given up on Henry?"

"I don't know," Archer said. "I could always set the good earl up with you."

"As pretty a solution that would be," Toria said, "I think me hooking up with a scion of British nobility would be frowned upon by his peers, considering my family ties."

"He doesn't care about the vampire thing," Archer said. "Hell, he didn't care about me not being a wolf. Now, if I were a werepanther, that would be a whole other issue."

"Well, I haven't given up on Kane finding true love," Toria said. "But that doesn't solve my issue." And now she'd said too much. She would blame the alcohol.

"And what issue could you possibly have?" Archer asked. "Your dating pool is wider."

Somehow, discussing the loss of her virginity was an easier topic than her immediate love life, or lack thereof. Toria pushed one of the remaining shots over to Archer, who groaned. "Nope," she said. "Man up and drink."

This time, Archer clinked his glass and tossed the entire shot back alongside her without protest. He chased it by draining the rest of his cocktail. "That is still disgusting."

"It's amazing," Toria said. "Be happy I'm not pouring vodka down your throat."

"I know something I'd like down my throat," Archer said, and slapped a hand across his mouth. "You've gotten me drunk. I never get drunk."

"My work here is done," Toria said, repressing laughter. Once she started, she'd never stop.

"Oh no, no, no," Archer said. "You have issues to discuss. Talk, woman."

"Well, you said it first," Toria said. "You thought I was in love with Kane, and vice versa. That's the issue. Who the hell is going to be in a relationship with someone who's basically already in a relationship?" After that exclamation, Toria lapsed into silence. Archer stared at her, so she stared out the window.

"You need the right person," Archer said. "So does Kane."

"And you're it?" Toria couldn't keep all of the sarcasm out of her voice.

"I don't know whether I am or not, but I think I might like to try," Archer said. "If you're willing to have me."

"Are you asking for my blessing to pursue my partner?" It was like a moment out of an old romance novel.

"Sure, why not?" Archer said. "You guys do kind of come as a package deal. And you both need someone who accepts that. If I can accept the fact that even if I stay with Hal, he'll still have to be married to someone else, I think I can handle a couple of dysfunctional warrior-mages."

His voice was so serious. Toria stared at him. She was possibly too drunk for this, but there was no help for it now. "Do you really think you can fix whatever's wrong with Kane?"

"I can damn well try," Archer said. "And I would try even if I wasn't kind of falling in love with the guy."

"You barely know him," Toria said.

"Tell that to my crazy heart," Archer said. He paused. "You should know that I almost said something else inappropriate there, but I restrained myself out of respect for Kane's current situation."

"Well, let's get him out of this situation," Toria said. "And you two can figure out all of your inappropriateness together."

#

When they stumbled back to their suite, they found Kane lying on one of the couches. Toria braced for resentment and anger to trickle into the back of her mind, even through the dullness that inebriation always caused in their link.

But Kane didn't seem to feel anything at all. "Have fun, kids?"

"Your partner is drunk." Archer moved Kane's legs and dropped onto the couch, then pulled the limbs back over him.

Toria braced for Kane to jerk away, but to her surprise, her partner let himself be manhandled. She dropped to the floor at the end of the couch and reached back to grab one of his hands.

"Yes, I am well aware," Kane said. "I'm usually there to play designated adult."

"I'm pretty sure she can take care of herself," Archer said.

"I'm pretty sure I can hear both of you," Toria said. She shut her eyes against the world. The gentle sway of the ship's movement through the ocean was more pronounced at night when it picked up speed. Or she was drunk. Or a combination of both.

"Ah, so Kane's the reason you haven't gotten laid recently," Archer said.

He was not bringing up that conversation now. "Nope, I'm pretty sure that was because of senior year of college kicking my ass," Toria said.

"College," Archer said. "How quaint."

"You didn't go?" Kane asked.

"Nope. I was offered a lucrative position in the Delacour shipping empire, placing protections on their vessels. Nepotism at its finest." Before Toria could ask why he wasn't doing that instead, Archer said, "Burrows and Wick convinced me that my talents were better suited to teaching."

"Didn't you tell Henry what was going on?" That had been bugging Toria for a while.

"Hal belongs to a powerful family, and that family belongs to one of the most powerful werewolf clans on both continents," Archer said. "But there are limits to that power."

Toria was too drunk to question Archer's life decisions. Time to change the subject. "Kane. Partner. Light of my life."

"I don't like where this is going," Kane said.

"Have you eaten today?" Toria released his hand and poked behind herself. Archer let out a whiff of air, as if Kane had kicked him, so her attempt at tickling must have aimed true. "Or drank anything?"

"Nope," Kane said. "Water is still evil."

"Aww, water loves you," Archer said. "You have to give it a chance."

Those statetments contained too much subtext for Toria to handle in her current mental state. "We have to fix you. You have to let Archer fix you."

"We talked about this already," Kane said.

"But I was less drunk then," Toria said. "And therefore less stubborn."

"Do these two things usually have correlation?" Archer asked.

"Surprisingly, yes," Kane said. "I'm feeling better. Just tired."

Toria captured his hand again and with all the subtlety of a…not subtle thing…dove into Kane's skin. He did sound better, but it was all a sham. His magic couldn't lie to hers. The paper-thin defenses he tried to throw up fell away from her in tatters. This wasn't the taint of a curse, or even the dullness of illness. Kane's magic was stretched too thin as it tried to seek connection with an earth that wasn't there. Traveling the river and bay on the way to Calverton had been nothing compared to this. No wonder he couldn't eat. That wasn't the sustenance that his body needed or wanted. And his statements about the evilness of water made sense now, too. The water below them was smothering him.

There had to be a way to fix this. And Archer said he could.

Kane would forgive her for this afterward.

With his hand still gripped in hers, Toria turned around to face Kane, kneeling on the carpet. She knew he was scared. Scared of being vulnerable. Scared of opening himself up to someone he barely knew. But if Toria could face those fears and let Syri into her head in order to reach Kane, Kane could do the same in order to save Syri.

"Archer," she said.

The water mage was a quick study. He had to be at least as drunk as she, but he read he read her intent and nodded once.

"Now," Toria said, and blew away what remained of Kane's shields.

Archer grasped the mental hand she threw toward him, linking his power with her own as though almost fifteen years hadn't passed since they practiced cantrips together as apprentices. The way his magic flowed in and through them was like diving into a cool pond on a hot summer's day. Wielding earth and storm took both strength and delicacy, but Archer's energy sought out every nook and cranny between them, weaving through and around their shields.

With deft mental hands, Archer pulled all of the wayward tendrils of Kane's power back home, cradling them in a nest of Toria's own energy. She watched in awe as he manipulated Kane to ground himself in her rather than in seeking true earth too far away. Archer had never even worked with warrior-mages before. If this was the type of magic he could do while drunk and improvising, Toria couldn't even imagine what sort of ritual workings he could pull off with research and preparation.

The fear and anger that pounded through Toria's skull receded as Kane also grew more impressed. When Archer withdrew, he left Kane's power safely nestled in a framework of Toria's sparking electrical energy, filling in any cracks with his own malleable power. It was a beautiful solution to an impossible problem.

Color had already returned to Kane's cheeks, and with a quick check of magesight, she saw that the glow of his energy was much steadier. She could kiss Archer. The drain on her power had sobered her some, but her inhibitions were still loose enough.

Actually…if the way Kane and Archer stared at each other was any indication, Kane had had an entirely different perspective on the magical working. Manipulating magic with Kane was like two halves of a brain working hand in hand. But the plots of entire romance novels revolved around two mages connecting with each on some deeper level while linking for some inane ritual.

Toria always found those plots contrived and unrealistic, written by housewives who had never met a mage in their lives.

And now Kane and Archer were holding hands, and Kane's grasp on her own hand had loosened. Sparks were flying, and if she stuck around any longer, that might stop being metaphorical.

It appeared those tropes were not as unrealistic as she once thought.

She scooted away from the couch, and Kane didn't even notice when she dropped his hand. "I'm going to, ah, go find a late snack. I'll bring you guys back something. In a few hours."

Kane's thumb stroked the back of Archer's hand, and he gave her a dismissive nod. Toria recognized the gentle purr echoing at the base of her skull. She'd better get out of here before the clothes came off and she got more of an eyeful than she needed.

Neither man noticed when she rose to her feet. She looked back once when she opened the cabin door. Archer had crawled up the length of the couch and braced himself over Kane. Toria slipped out the door and closed it behind her with a gentle click.

#

Back in Limani, when one of them brought home a date, the other was polite enough to clear out. That was more to avoid any awkwardness on the guest's

112

part than out of any uncomfortableness with each other. After living in each other's heads for almost a decade, they had no secrets and no embarrassment. And if Toria tended to find herself at Limani's Mercenary Guildhall, expending any residual sexual frustration on a punching bag or set of pells in the gym, that was her own business. Distance dulled strong feelings and emotions that bled through their link, and physical activity was a good distraction.

The *Lunar Queen* didn't have a punching bag in its limited gym.

The *Lunar Queen*, which had seemed enormous when she stood on the dock in New Angouleme, was also much too small a ship.

Not many guests or crew were up and about in the pre-dawn hours, but Toria found herself in an elevator with a man in a disheveled suit. He did not seem to have slept in his own cabin, so why give her that awkward smile?

Toria looked down, to make sure her clothing was not askew in some embarrassing way, and—oh.

She crossed her arms over her chest, blocking his view of her taut nipples visible through both bra and T-shirt, and glared at him. Creep. He was at least twice her age. That didn't stop him from tossing a wink at her over his shoulder when he exited the elevator on a deck of cabins.

The fact that her body was already having physical reactions to what Kane and Archer were up to cancelled her plans for a late-night snack in the twenty-four-hour café. Instead, she hit the elevator button for the top deck of the ship. The night air was chilled, and she grabbed two towels from the stand by the pool. No one on the ship swam this late.

The running track was one level up, but a maintenance crew scrubbed the deck. No luck there. She climbed a final flight of stairs. The breeze was rougher up here, but the "Sky Bar" was closed and the open-air patio was deserted.

Toria tossed the towels over one shoulder and reached for a deck chair. Her spine arched, and she let out an inadvertent gasp as invisible nails raked down her back.

Nope, this wasn't going to be the most uncomfortable night of her life at all.

She pulled the deck chair into a semi-hidden corner near the end of the bar, settling in after wrapping one of the towels around her shoulders. As she curled up in the chair and tucked the second towel around her feet, she cast a "you can't see me" aura around herself, based on one of Syri's tricks. Just in case.

At least Kane felt better.

Phantom teeth nibbled at the side of her neck, and Toria twitched.

It was going to be a long night.

#

Someone called Syri's name, far off through the foggy distance. Someone who represented safety, and home, and family.

Syri pushed through brambles and slogged through muddy streams, weaving her way through a dark, endless forest. If she could get through this valley, or over this rocky outcropping, or to the next peak, she would reach them.

She blinked once, and the forest disappeared. She was propped in the corner of a large metal box, lit by a single dingy lightbulb. But the forest was coming back, vines curling at the edge of consciousness, reaching to drag her back into the dark reaches of her mind.

Syri!

The voice was more familiar this time. A woman. It had the flat tonalities of a human voice, with none of the musical quality of an elven voice or the growling underlay of a werecreature. She knew this voice. She reached for a face to go with it, but the forest was there, closing off her view.

Now the forest was inside the metal container, two worlds crashing into each other. Syri dug through a thicket, trying to reach the woman. A figure disappeared around a tree trunk. Short brown hair, tied back in a purple bandana. A steel rapier at her side.

"Torrr?" Syri tried to call out, but the name stuck in her throat. Her foot was caught, trapped by a vine that curled around her ankle tighter with every tug. She reached into her leather jacket, but both of her knives were gone. Had she dropped them while stumbling through this endless forest?

The vine snapped, and she fell to the rocky ground with a crash. The back of her head jerked against the metal wall, and stars clouded her vision. Looming trees and metallic shadows merged in her vision. Something hard dug into her lower back, but it wasn't a rock. She rolled over, reaching for the lumpy object tucked into the waistband of her jeans.

A pistol rested in her hands. How useless. That wouldn't do anything against the vine knotted around her ankle. She shoved the pistol back where she found it.

She searched around herself for a sharp rock to cut the vine, since her knives had vanished. She had to find those, even if it meant retracing her steps. Maybe the woman knew where she had dropped them.

Syri patted the smooth ground around her. She could see twigs and rocks scattered around the forest floor. They were there. She could see them.

We're coming for you, Sy—

She waved the voice away. She didn't have time for this. The palms of her hands touched metal, and the rocks continued to evade her.

She really should find her knives.

#

As the sun finished rising over the ocean, the air warmed until Toria threw off the two towels to doze in the warm light. A few other sunbathers joined her on the sky deck but avoided her corner, thanks to the minor cantrip. She never fell all the way asleep, despite her lack of it the night before. Every time she did, her stranglehold on her bond with Kane loosened, and echoes of his shenanigans with Archer leaked through.

They must have ordered room service. Otherwise, she had no idea how they had that much energy for round two, much less round three.

Her own stomach growled, but not enough to prod her from her quiet nook and risk an embarrassing incident in public. But when half an hour had passed with no shadowy caresses down her body, Toria considered the idea of breakfast more. The dining room was closed by now, but the café might have some midmorning snacks around.

A chair scraped along the deck next to her. There were only two people on this ship who might possibly see through her protective spell. Kane dropped into the chair he'd moved next to her and tipped his face back to the sun.

"What a gorgeous view," he said. "Here." He tossed her a muffin.

Toria peeled away the wrapper, ignoring the spray of crumbs. "Thanks. Glad you're getting to enjoy it." It was hard to tell against his dark skin, but she could see the trail of bite marks that disappeared into the neck of his T-shirt. She squashed an irrational surge of resentment before it could cross over the link. She wasn't jealous, per se, and definitely not of Archer. But it had been a long time since she'd worn the content look on Kane's face. And not all of that contentment was from no longer feeling the aggravated seasickness he'd experienced since they left port.

She must not have squashed it all. Kane blinked through the sun at her. The contented expression vanished behind one of concern. "Are you okay?"

"Yes," she said, injecting as much affirmation into the word as possible. "Just tired. And hungry. And pretending that I'm not hungover. Is water still evil?"

"Water is far from evil," Kane said. He bounded out of his chair and over to the bar, where a staff member set up for the midmorning rush. Cruisers started their drinking early, Toria had noticed the previous day. After a quick exchange, Kane returned with a glass of ice water and handed it to Toria.

After she drained most of the liquid, Toria propped the cool glass against her forehead. Kane was back to enjoying the sun, but as if he sensed her attention in him, he reached out a hand. Toria held it in a loose grasp. "You're not pissed at me?" she asked.

"Oh, I am," Kane said. "But what's done is done. And I am feeling much better. What Archer did was amazing."

"Well, he is a few years older," Toria said. "And not distracted from studying magic by learning to swing a sword around."

"This is true," Kane said. "Eventually, we could have come up with something. If I hadn't died of dehydration first."

They sat in silence for a few minutes. Now that the bar was open, the deck attracted more people. But the other passengers still avoided their corner. Toria squeezed Kane's hand. "We stuck with Archer like we are with Syri?"

"Not quite," Kane said. "I spoke with Archer about it. He says the spell is set to collapse once we're close enough to shore and I don't need it anymore. This doesn't tie our minds together, not the way Syri's power did when you two found me."

"I will be mildly irritated if this was a complicated seduction attempt," Toria said.

Kane gave a sudden snort of laughter, loud enough to draw a curious glance from a nearby woman. She stared without seeing them, then continued chatting with her friend. "No, nothing of the sort," Kane said. "Archer was as surprised as me by the result. Not that either of us complained, mind…" His voice trailed off, and he seemed relieved when Toria toasted him with her empty cup.

"If you promise to feed him and walk him, you can keep him," Toria said. "Hell, one of us deserves a happy ending."

"What's that supposed to mean?" Kane asked.

"Forget it," Toria said. "I'm running on too little sleep for a coherent conversation."

"No," Kane said. "You're giving me a straight answer on this one."

"It's funny," Toria said. "Archer and I ended up having pretty much this exact same conversation last night. Hence the drunkenness."

"You don't have to be drunk to talk to me," Kane said.

He made it sound so easy. "It's just…you know why neither of us have dated much the past few years. We've been busy, sure, but you know that eventually everyone gets jealous of our connection to each other and can't handle how close we are, even though we make it abundantly clear that we are not in a romantic relationship. Archer gets it, because he knows how warrior-mages work. What are the odds of finding someone else?"

Kane absorbed her words. "We'll find someone for you. We're still young."

"We have a warped concept of what a lifespan is," Toria said. "Remember who raised us."

"Not important right now," Kane said. "Don't give up hope yet."

"I will endeavor not to," Toria said. "Now that we've got ourselves an Archer, what should we do now?"

"What we got on this damn boat to do in the first place," Kane said. "Find our Syri."

#

When they returned to their suite, Toria accepted the plate of breakfast food Archer handed her with a peck on his cheek. After inhaling the sausage biscuits and bowl of fruit, she passed out in her bed, not waking until Kane roused her for dinner. Toria pretended not to see the scratch marks on the back of his neck, but it was obvious what her partner had been up to that afternoon. At least the echoes didn't bleed through their link while she was asleep.

She would worry about them disturbing the neighbors, but sound suppressing spells were one of the easiest cantrips possible. It would still be an interesting rest of the voyage.

After dinner, they ended up back in the suite, and Toria and Kane shoved furniture around the living area while Archer looked on in bemusement. "You're not actually going to create a ritual circle here, are you?" he asked. "I don't imagine the Delacour family being too happy if we redecorated their private cabin. There are limits to our guest privilege."

"Nope," Toria said, pulling the cushions off one of the sofas and tossing them to Kane, who arranged them in a close triangle on the floor they'd cleared. "Just making room to be comfortable."

"Sit your ass down," Kane said. "We're going to find Syri. Be happy we're using cushions."

Archer opened his mouth but looked at Toria and closed it with a snap.

"Don't even think about it," Toria said. "I already know way more about your sex life than I really need to. I don't need terrible jokes about your ass on top of it." She held up a hand to Kane when he snorted in laughter. "Or details about sexual positions. Get your minds out of the gutter."

After the three sat on the cushions with hands grasped, Archer asked, "What now?"

"This morning, you were the one working the magic," Kane said. "Toria opened the gates, but we were passive participants. This will be different."

"You said you'd done research about the warrior-mage bond," Toria said. "Now you'll get to experience it firsthand. Open your eyes." Archer blinked once, and she assumed he'd activated his magesight. She did the same, smiling at the way all three of their shields tangled through the room. Crystalline violets provided the structure for fluid emerald, all surrounded by misty aquamarine, which sealed any loose gaps.

"Archer," Kane said, his voice echoing through the link.

Archer jerked in surprise, which intrigued Toria. He must also have heard the voice echo. "Yes?"

"Why is your aura blue when you're a water mage?" Kane asked. "I meant to ask earlier, but it ah, slipped my mind." A shiver of embarrassment circled through the three of them.

"Just a fluke," Archer said. "Parents were both air mages."

It was Toria's turn to be startled. "Were?"

"Yeah, they passed away soon after we moved to New Angouleme," Archer said. "Cancer and heart disease. I was pretty much raised between Liquid Gold and the mage school after that."

Toria and Kane exchanged a wordless glance. That fit the pattern they were seeing, in Limani and New Angouleme, of mages both not being born and dying before their time. "Mine died when I was young, too," Kane said. "Soon after I bonded with Toria. Her parents took me in."

Before the moment could turn awkward, Toria dragged them back to the subject at hand. "Think you can find Syri again, Kane?"

"I'll do my best," he said.

"Won't it need both of you?" Archer asked.

"The link we formed with Syri originated in my brain," Toria said. "I can't tell it apart from myself, but Kane has an outside perspective."

"Got it," Archer said. "I'll help where I can."

"You're probably going to have to be my power source, since you can draw from the ocean, and I don't have the earth to access," Kane said. "Toria, you focus on Syri again."

"I know, I know." Toria opened her mind to Kane's gentle touch. The power that flowed through her felt different, filtered through Archer's connection with water rather than Kane's with earth. The difference between dipping into a warm lagoon rather than tanning on the beach. She thought of Syri. Her snarky, impish almost-sister, who loved to dance and blossomed in the sunlight like a plant. Who crashed on their couch and in their beds instead of going home to her own empty apartment. Who dragged Toria to her workplace and let her play with kittens when she was stressed with schoolwork. Who painted Kane's scalp with makeup the first time he shaved off all his hair.

And she focused on what she had seen before: the inside of a metal shipping container. Syri's bright mind, dulled by magic or drugs. Toria reached, and Kane traced the path between them.

"Oh," Archer said, almost jolting Toria from her concentration. "I see her."

That was unexpected. Toria held steady whatever connection Kane had established. "Tell us," she said.

"She's in a forest, I think," Archer said. "It's dark, and there are branches and vines everywhere. She's trapped in them."

A jolt snapped through Toria's brain, and she jerked backward. When her hands left Kane's and Archer's, the connection between them failed. "Shit," she said, pressing the palms of her hands to her forehead. "That hurt." Bright flashes of light still echoed behind her eyelids. "What the hell was that?" When Toria managed to see again, she found that her companions had similar expressions of pain across their faces.

"She doesn't know me," Archer said. "I'd lash out, too, if I found a strange presence in my brain."

"Good girl," Kane said, managing a grin.

But something didn't add up. "You saw her in a forest?" Toria asked.

"Yep," Archer said. "But it was dark out. Middle of the night, dark."

As one, they all looked to the suite's windows. Evening was fast approaching, but they were less than a month past the summer solstice. There was still plenty of sunlight despite the late hour. "For it to be that dark where Syri is," Toria said, "she would already have to be somewhere in Europa. But Henry said he got word of her being put on a ship only a day before we left."

"She can't be more than two days ahead of us," Archer said. "There's absolutely no way she'd be across the ocean by now."

"Either what you saw is some sort of illusion," Kane said. "Or somehow she did make it across that fast. Either way, whoever has her has to be pretty damn powerful."

"I wish we knew what we were going up against," Toria said. If Syri was here, this would be where she cursed a blue streak. Instead, Toria could only sag back against one of the couches.

"Only thing we can do is wait until we make it to Calaitum," Archer said. "And hope that Hal's connections have some information for us when we get there."

#

This had turned into the longest week of Toria's life, and it was only halfway done.

She hid in her corner on the sky deck again. She came prepared this time, wearing the black bikini bought from one of the gift shops on the ship. Somehow, a bathing suit hadn't made the packing list when they left Limani.

After two days on the ship with no physical activity beyond a few miles around the running track, Toria's nerves jangled from that potent combination of stress and boredom. She'd used the handy Delacour all-access pass and gotten in contact with the troupe who performed every night in the ship's theatre. They had been more than happy to allow Toria access to their stage space in exchange for some help with their performance combat skills. That morning, with Kane's assistance since he was back to his regular self, she had done an assessment of which actors needed the most help with technique.

Archer had tagged along, and he and the troupe goaded the warrior-mage pair into accepting a pair of wooden practice blades to give a full-speed demonstration. After suitable warnings that what they were about to do was on the opposite end of the spectrum from flashy stage combat, Toria had tested the balance on her fake weapon and gone after Kane.

Twenty minutes of intense sparring, accompanied by nothing more than the strike of wood against wood or flesh and the impressed silence of their spectators, had left Toria exhausted and bruised. She felt amazing.

She had not missed the looks that passed between Archer and Kane as they rode the elevator back up to their deck. It appeared that watching Toria beat up her partner was a bit of a turn-on for a certain water mage.

When they'd gone back to their suite, she had declared her intention to change and hit the pool, then vacated the premises as soon as possible. She managed a short dip in the water to cool off before the phantom touches through the link became too much to ignore.

Thus, hiding in her corner again. This time with a cool drink and a comfortable chaise lounge chair and much better prepared for the heat. The "you can't see me" spell was active, saving Toria from any inappropriate glances based on the current state of her nipples.

A shadow fell across her, blocking her sun. "Why the hell do you have a hickey?"

Toria slapped a hand to the side of her neck, then looked up.

Archer grinned down at her, dressed in a set of swimming trunks with a towel tossed over his shoulder. "Other side," he said. He dragged a chair closer to her and dropped into it. "I guess I don't have to ask what you've been up to whenever Kane and I were otherwise occupied. Now you two are a matched set."

Toria prodded the side of her neck that Archer had indicated. The skin was a bit tender, but she hadn't been hit there during her sparring session with Kane. While pretending to have found a temporary companion on the *Lunar Queen* would save Archer and Kane from any awkwardness, that was not a charade she was willing to commit to for the three more days they were stuck on this ship. "You idiot," she said, fondness and amusement coloring her voice. "I guess the warrior-mage research you did never covered this sort of situation."

"Hmm?" When Toria didn't answer Archer's questioning noise, he looked over at her again. Toria saw the moment Archer put the pieces together when his olive skin flushed. "Oh. Oh!"

"Yep," she said. "Pretty much."

"I had no idea," Archer said. "Kane's passed out, by the way. I think he's still not back to one hundred percent. We'll get him up in time for dinner. But seriously. If I leave a mark on him, it'll show up on you?"

If only if were that simple. "Not quite," Toria said. "It's a bit more...in depth than that."

Archer coughed. "I find myself a bit embarrassed at this juncture."

It was adorable how Archer's speech became more formal whenever he became less than sure of himself. It made Toria want to do the complete opposite. "You two have kind of been fucking like bunnies."

Archer laughed at her bluntness. "That's one way of putting it. And you, wow. How do you put up with it?"

"Well, this is new," Toria said. "Usually we can get a lot farther apart, and everything gets duller with distance. No such option here. Don't tell Kane. He's happy. I like it when he's happy."

"I do, too," Archer said. "Need a refill?" He darted out of his chair without waiting for a response. The redness of his embarrassment had spread to the back of his neck.

He sat in silence for a few minutes after he returned with their drinks, and Toria didn't prod. Despite their conversation a few nights before, it seemed that Archer still had to wrap his brain around what being with half of a bonded pair would entail.

Finally, once most of his beer was gone, he said, "Talk about a mind-fuck."

Toria toasted him with her fresh cocktail. "That's putting it succinctly."

"I'll be more careful with him," Archer said. "No more hickeys."

"You do that," Toria said, taking a pull of her beer and sinking lower on her chaise.

She wouldn't mention that she'd noticed lovely set of scratch marks down Archer's back when he'd gotten their drinks. Her partner gave as good as he got.

\#

The forest had ensnared her. Vines wrapped around every limb, pinning Syri in a thicket. She'd never found a rock that could cut through them, even when she could still move her arms. Which frustrated her, because there were rocks everywhere she looked! And this thicket should be more uncomfortable, but behind her back she felt only smooth metal. And the lump digging into the small of her back. She'd rather have her knives, but she became trapped before she could go back for them.

The woman who felt like home never returned. Syri had planned to ask for help searching for her knives, but she never caught another hint of her presence.

Instead, there was someone else.

An unfamiliar man stood above her, tall and broad-shouldered. Thick ropes of black hair fell across his shoulders. She appreciated that some of them were dyed blue. She did not appreciate the fact that the man didn't speak, just stood over her and stared.

If he'd bothered to introduce himself, maybe she would have asked for help finding the woman. Or finding her knives.

But he was so impolite. She closed her eyes and screamed.

A blast echoed through the forest, shaking leaves down from the trees around her.

The man was gone when she opened her eyes. She was still no closer to finding her knives. Or getting out of this thicket.

\#

"That is the prettiest thing I've ever seen." Kane propped his elbows on the deck railing. The shoreline outside of Calaitum was lush with summer growth.

If they stood at the railing on the other side of the ship, they would be able to make out the white cliffs of Britannia herself on the other side of the channel. In fact, that's where most of the other passengers were gawking. But Kane had zeroed in on the greenery of the nearer shore and wouldn't look away.

"I won't take that as an insult," Toria said, hooking her arm around Kane's.

"I won't either," Archer said from Kane's other side.

They would arrive at port within the hour. According to the crew, the city would be in view soon, and they could depart soon after docking. Toria had expected to join the cattle line off the ship and through British customs, but the Delacour privilege came in handy once again. The same officer who had escorted them onto the ship in New Angouleme would meet them at this spot to whisk them through the special customs office that handled the Delacour family's private shipping business.

Toria needed to have to have a talk with Victory and Max about all their dramatic stories of camping in the mud. Except for that unfortunate stint at the New Angouleme mage school, her first two weeks of mercenary work had been first class all the way. And here in Calaitum, they'd be staying at the manor owned by Henry's parents rather than the local Mercenary Guildhall.

It turned out that Archer and Henry's mother regularly exchanged correspondence. Archer had laughed for a good five minutes at the expressions on Kane and Toria's faces when they learned that particular tidbit. Toria knew that Tristan, Limani's alpha werewolf, was as down to earth as a person could get, so not all werewolves were weird. Nope, turned out it was just the British nobility.

The *Lunar Queen* turned a bend in the shoreline, and the city of Calaitum spread before them. This was a true old city, different from Limani, New Angouleme, and the other cities Toria was familiar with in the Roman colonies. Buildings nestled together within a great wall, huddling along the coast. A watchtower at the center of the town towered above the other buildings. But the coast was far from defenseless, thanks to the great trebuchets Toria spotted amidst the docks.

A throat cleared behind them, and Toria pulled herself away from her first sight of civilization in the old world. Their escort had arrived. "If you'll follow me, sirs, madam," the *Lunar Queen* officer said, "we'll make sure you're first off the ship."

The officer helped carry Syri's packs, and as promised, it took less than ten minutes to disembark. He led them to a room within the office complex that serviced the *Lunar Queen* and her sister vessels. The private customs officer who awaited them was politely disinterested in giving more than a cursory glance at their passports, and he didn't question their weaponry. As if summoned by magic, a young man in a chauffeur's uniform appeared once the customs officer stamped their passports.

Toria and Kane exchanged glances. It was one thing to take advantage of the Delacour name while on the ship. It would be another to immerse themselves in the top end of British society. Coming from the bastion of equality and democracy that Limani tried to be, Toria wasn't even sure where they ranked in the grand scheme of things. Victory had once been Roman nobility, but she didn't think that extended to her, much less Kane. But while they might rank as journeymen mercenaries, they were still master mages in their own right, equal to Archer, and could follow his lead.

"Master Sophin, it's a pleasure to see you again," the man said, giving a short bow. He stepped forward to then exchange a less formal handshake with Archer. "Lady Delacour sent me with a town-car. She is pleased that you have arrived in time for supper."

"Thank you, Philippe," Archer said. "I'm looking forward to seeing her again. And it's a pleasure to see you as well." Archer made the introductions as they followed Philippe out of the shipping offices and to a small parking lot.

The *Lunar Queen* stretched above them, and Toria snuck one last look back at the ship. If they didn't screw things up with Henry's family here, perhaps that could be their ride back home once this was all over. Syri would get a kick out of it.

A sleek black town-car awaited them, much like the one that had driven them to the *Lunar Queen* back in New Angouleme. This one, however, came complete with a young man sitting cross-legged on the front hood, fiddling with something in his lap.

"Hey!" Philippe burst into a jog. "Get off there!"

The man slid down the hood of the town-car, and sunlight caught off his bright red hair. Familiar bright red hair. With a flash of magesight, Toria confirmed her suspicion. Elf, and possibly related to the woman who had approached them at the New Angouleme docks before cranky werewolves distracted them.

Philippe inspected the hood of the town-car as the rest of the group reached them. With a grave nod, the red-haired man handed a slip of paper out to Toria. She dropped one of her packs and accepted it. Not only was the red hair the same shade, but the delicate facial structure reminded her strongly of Brin, the elf in New Angouleme. Had to be a brother, if not some other blood relation.

When the man turned away, Kane dropped one of his packs and grabbed his arm. "Wait," he said. "Is Syri safe?"

"For now," the elven man said. "But she is still to be the sacrifice." He shrugged away Kane's arm and ran off, leaving the parking lot and ducking behind a building.

Toria flipped open the note as Kane and Archer peered over her shoulders. The elves had learned their lesson, and this time the writing was Loquella, the common language shared between the Roman and British Empires, in black ink. One word: *Parisii*.

British elves had kidnapped a Limani elf and hauled her halfway across the world to a Roman city. This got stranger and stranger.

#

An older couple greeted them warmly in the foyer of the grand Delacour estate, the man in an impeccable business suit and the woman in summer-weight linen slacks and a silk blouse. Their silver hair both matched the hue of Henry's fur in wolf form—these had to be his parents, confirmed by a quick glimpse through magesight that revealed shadowy lupine forms. Toria expected some sort of formal announcement from Philippe when he showed them in, and she was suddenly aware of the sword belted around her waist. Was that even allowed? Instead, Lady Delacour embraced Archer, and they exchanged kisses on both cheeks.

"Lovely to see you again, my dear," she said, as Archer bowed to Henry's father. "And this must be Limani's famous warrior-mage pair. Do introduce us."

Archer hadn't been kidding about his familiarity with Henry's mother. Toria had been braced for stiff awkwardness, not a family reunion. Archer tugged her and Kane forward. "It would be my pleasure. Earl Marcus Delacour and Lady Elspeth, may I present Toria Connor and Kane Nalamas, master mages and journeymen mercenaries of Limani.

It wasn't fair that she and Kane already had a reputation through nothing more than a quirk of fate. They hadn't done anything to become famous yet! Toria mimicked Archer's bow to Earl Delacour, Kane following less than a heartbeat later. "It is an honor to meet you, sir, madame," she said. "Unfortunately, we won't be able to join you for dinner as planned. We've received word that the friend we seek is in Parisii." Victory would smack her for her rudeness. But rudeness was preferable to losing Syri's trail. They needed to hit the road, now.

"Nonsense," Earl Delacour said. "The last train south left half an hour ago."

Crap.

"We would love to join you," Kane said.

After a few more pleasantries, in which Lady Elspeth exclaimed over Archer's hair and the earl complimented Kane's scimitar, a footman materialized in the foyer from a discreet servant's door.

"Please show our guests to the Cloud Suite," Lady Elspeth said, "so they may rest up after their journey. Philippe will have already sent their bags up. If they do not have appropriate clothing for dinner, please see to it that accommodations can be made."

"Don't worry," Archer said. "I wouldn't let us embarrass you."

"Good man, Sophin," Earl Delacour said.

The silent footman led them up the grand staircase, though it was clear that Archer already knew the way to their destination. "Appropriate clothing?" Toria hissed through her teeth, though that probably wouldn't stop the werewolves downstairs from hearing her clearly. "They barely let us in the dining room on the boat!"

"Don't worry," Archer said. He turned to the footman. "I'll show them the rest of the way. Master Nalamas should fit one of the earl's suits, if he doesn't mind, and Master Connor will be fine in one of last season's gowns if Lady Charlise has any here."

The footman nodded. "Lady Charlise is in Oxenafor for the summer semester, but I know she won't mind. I will check with one of the maids, and with the earl's valet for an old suit."

"Perfect, thanks," Archer said.

"What have you gotten us into?" Kane asked.

"Remember how good that dinner was at Liquid Gold, before all of this started?" Archer said. "This will be even better."

Well, this had all begun a bit before that. "We still don't have time for this," Toria said. "There's got to be another way to get to Parisii tonight."

Archer pushed open a door. "Sure, if you want to pay out the nose for a gas-powered vehicle. Sorry, but we're stuck for the night." He led them into an airy suite, decorated in light blues and silvers.

Toria and Kane gaped at the antique furniture and delicate décor. Light streamed through gauzy curtains, framing a view of expansive gardens behind the manor. "Wow," Kane said. He nudged Archer. "Sure you don't want to chase after Hal harder? This could all be yours."

Archer gave him a wry grin. "Not in the cards."

"Lucky me," Kane said.

After the past week, Toria knew what that delicate shiver down the link from Kane meant. "Don't even," Toria said. "I was promised rest before dinner."

#

Toria had gotten some of the promised rest, though it had been interrupted by sorting through laundry with a maid and seeing what could be cleaned before they left the next morning. By the last two days of the cruise, things had gotten a bit tight for weather-appropriate garb. That day, Kane had worn a band T-shirt borrowed from Archer, and Toria had nicked a pair of socks from Syri's gear.

The borrowed gown she wore now was a bit snug around the chest area, and Toria tried not to breath too deep. She and Henry's sister were of a similar height, but not the same dimensions in other areas. Kane, on the other hand, looked dashing in one of the earl's older suits, and it turned out that Archer already had a bespoke suit that he kept at the manor. Because of course he did.

As it turned out, the famous warrior-mages from Limani were a bit of a draw, and Lady Delacour had invited a host of local peerage to join them for supper. Toria would have kicked Archer, but he sat too far down the long table. She had the spot of honor on Earl Delacour's right, where she had the pleasure of listening to Lord Massey hold forth on the perils of visiting Parisii.

"It won't be safe," the elderly man said. "Not for a young lady such as yourself. Ever since it fell back in Roman hands at the end of the Last War, it's been a haven for vampires who want to distance themselves from the high families in Roma." He paused for a sip of wine. "Never trust a vampire, but especially never trust a vampire who's trying to stay far away from the Roman senate."

"I'm sure Masters Connor and Nalamas will be capable of taking care of themselves," Earl Delacour said. Toria saw him hide a smile behind his napkin. "Speaking of vampires, my dear," he said to Toria, "I did some checking this afternoon, and I discovered records that indicate your mother did pass through this estate during the Last War. I trust she's still doing well?"

"Yes, sir," Toria said, ignoring Lord Massey's sputter. "She's retired from mercenary work, and is the current Master of the City of Limani."

"I imagine she's pleased that you and Master Nalamas have followed in her footsteps," Lord Delacour said.

"She certainly liked to tell me stories designed to make me think twice about doing so," Toria said. "But yes, I think she is pleased."

"I'm sorry," Lord Massey said. "But am I to understand that your mother is a vampire?"

"Adopted mother, yes," Toria said. She braced for a negative reaction. Calaitum was constantly being traded back and forth between empires, and had in fact been Roman territory before the treaties that ended the Last War. While Lord Massey was old, he wouldn't have been alive then. But his parents certainly were. Who knew what stories of vampiric atrocities they had passed on to their son? Propaganda had been one of the war's most powerful weapons.

Lord Massey harrumphed into his wine. "Well, Master of the City is a respectable title," he said. "It's the wandering rogues you have to watch out for. And Parisii is full of them."

"We'll be sure to stay on our toes," Toria said.

That was another aspect of traveling to Parisii she and Kane would have to discuss tonight. While not vampires themselves, they were tied to Victory. Though they traveled as journeymen mercenaries, any vampires who identified them as Limani's warrior-mages might see them as representatives of her mother instead. Would they have to pay respects to the local Master of the City? How would they even find out who the local Master was?

Toria enjoyed another bite of her fish course as the conversation swirled around her. It was delicious, as promised, but sat heavy in her stomach.

For the first time since they left Limani, Toria wished she could talk to her mom.

#

Archer and Kane leaned against each other on the bench seat in the private train compartment. Toria had claimed the opposite bench, but she'd kicked off her boots and stretched her feet over to Kane's lap. If he was giving her a foot massage, he wasn't rubbing Archer's thigh. It seemed like a fair trade.

"I've never been farther south than Calaitum," Archer said, breaking the content silence. "I've never been in Roman territory at all. Are the vampires in Parisii as dangerous as Lord Massey said last night?"

Toria and Kane exchanged looks. Kane shrugged. This one must be on her. "I have the feeling that Lord Massey is a product of his upbringing," she said. "Are vampires dangerous? Hell, yes. Are they eating everyone in sight? That'd make a pretty terrible vampire, and the Master of the City would remove them as soon as possible."

"But I get the impression that your mother is a bit of an anomaly," Archer said. His fingers traced patterns on the seat's armrest.

He must be really nervous about this. "I promise we won't let any vampires eat you," Toria said. "It's only fair, since you didn't let the werewolves eat us."

Archer narrowed his eyes at her. "I can't tell whether you were legitimately concerned about that."

Toria shrugged. "I was almost killed by werepanthers in high school. That sort of thing sticks with you."

A look of morbid fascination crossed Archer's face. "Were they hunting you?"

"No," Kane said. "Civilized beings do not eat each other. No one is getting eaten in Parisii."

"Not unless we get our own hotel room," Archer said.

Toria chose to ignore that bit of innuendo. "Good luck with that," she said. "We can't afford a hotel in Parisii, at least not one we'd actually want to sleep in. We're staying at the local Guildhall. But Parisii is one of Europa's major cities, and I'll be surprised to manage a private room for the three of us."

Kane patted Archer's hand. "Welcome to the glamorous life of mercenary work."

Archer slouched lower in his seat. "And I'm not even getting paid."

#

The first thing Toria noticed about Parisii was that the skyline was much less impressive than in New Angouleme. The city was more spread out, with fewer modern buildings that scraped the sky and more historical structures that represented over two thousand years of culture. On the plus side, the urban miasma that had bothered Kane in New Angouleme was much less here, thanks to the copious amounts of green space within the city. More akin to a tickle at the back of the throat than a full wracking cough. Regular-strength shields would suffice rather than full combat levels.

They made their way through customs with no problems and entered the main room of the train station. Toria arrowed her way to a giant map of the city plastered on one wall. The selection in the train's dining carriage had been limited, and she wanted a direction as soon as possible so that food could be acquired along the way. She also wasn't looking forward to traipsing through the city burdened with four people's gear, and she hoped that taxis were as prevalent in this major city as in New Angouleme.

While she studied the map, trying to orient the train station with the memorized address of Parisii's Guildhall, Kane tugged on her belt loop.

"What?" She looked back at him, then followed the direction his finger pointed.

A group of hired drivers loitered around the station exit, holding signs indicating who they were there to pick up. An unassuming man in a black suit held a sign that simply listed *Connor-Nalamas-Sophin.*

Archer blew a dreadlock out of his face with a sigh. "I told Lady Elspeth not to worry about us, but she must have called ahead to arrange a town-car." He hoisted his packs higher and marched across the open space in the middle of the station, while Toria and Kane trailed behind him.

But when they approached, the man ignored Archer in favor of giving Toria a short bow. "Welcome to Parisii, Master Connor," he said through his bushy mustache. "The Lady Natalia Della Zanna sent me to escort you to her townhouse. She will meet you there after sunset tonight."

Toria glanced at the guys, but both of them had mystified expressions that must have mirrored her own. "I'm sorry," she said. "But I don't know of a Lady Della Zanna. There must be some mistake."

"She thought that might be the case, miss," the driver said. "She mentioned that you were probably more familiar with the name Serena."

Kane gasped, and Archer said, "What? Who?"

"Serena was one of the first vampires to make my father a daywalker," Toria said. "I guess that makes her my grandmother."

"Doesn't Mikelos think she's dead?" Kane asked.

"Yep," Toria said. "This better be good."

#

This was the second awkward dinner in as many days. At least Toria was much more comfortable in her own clothing this time. The three of them picked at their food in a large dining room. It wasn't huge, but the curtains drawn against the setting sun closed out all outside light, making the space dim. David, the driver who turned out to also be the butler for Serena's—Natalia's?—city residence, along with a silent maid served them dinner. David informed them that his mistress would arrive from her country chateau after sunset.

A clock ticked on the mantel, echoing in the silence. "We don't have to stay here, you know," Kane said. "We can still stay at the Guildhall."

"We're here," Toria said. "I have some things to say."

"And I am most interested in hearing them, my dear."

The three of them stood as a tall woman swept into the room. David shadowed her to pull out a chair at the other end of the long table. Sitting did nothing to diminish the woman's presence. "Welcome to my home," she said. "Please, sit, finish your meals."

Toria sank back into her chair and focused on the new arrival. She embodied every fictional cliché that authors loved to attribute to vampires. Alabaster skin.

130

Pale eyes. Expensive black clothing, cut in sharp lines that hugged an hourglass figure. The only unexpected feature was the vampire's pale, blond curls where Toria had expected more black. "You must be Serena," Toria said.

"I am indeed." A ghost of a smile crossed her face and that, more than anything else, convinced Toria that the vampire told the truth. Despite them not being biologically related, the expression was an exact match for the look Mikelos always got when he was being quietly amused by something. "But that is a name I haven't used in a long time. You may call me Natalia. Or Grandmere, I suppose." There was that smile again. Did Natalia know that Toria had grown up referring to Asaron as Grandpa? Or was it mere coincidence?

Kane and Archer nibbled at their dinners again. They seemed content to let Toria have the lead. Of course, Kane could feel her roiling, conflicting emotions bounding down their link. She hardly knew where to begin. "Seems like you already know us," Toria said. "Since David had that sign and all. How did you know we were coming?"

"I have resources in place to alert me if my dear Mikelos ever decided to return to this city," Natalia said. "Imagine my surprise when I receive word that his daughter has arrived in his stead. I couldn't pass up the opportunity to meet you. I know so little about you and your partner. You can imagine how difficult it must be, from such a distance."

It was a tad creepy how readily Natalia admitted to spying on her family from across an ocean. Victory wasn't exactly low-profile as the Master of the City, but Toria had never considered that her family would be of interest outside of Limani.

The maid entered the dining room and placed a delicate wine glass on the table beside her mistress. The liquid was too thick to be red wine. Toria and Kane didn't even blink, being used to Victory and Asaron's eating habits, but Toria could read the flash of discomfort that crossed Archer's face. Based on their conversation on the train earlier that day, being in the lair of a vampire was the last place he had expected to end up when he followed them out of New Angouleme.

Toria tried to remain polite, but never in a million years had she expected to sit across from this woman. Serena and Connor, the vampire whose name Mikelos had taken for his own after Connor's death, had featured in many of Toria's favorite childhood tales. Serena had been more of a shadowy background figure, despite the fact that Mikelos had been as much her daywalker as Connor's. Her father had never made a secret of the fact that he had been plucked off

Roma's streets by Serena to be a gift for her progeny. Mikelos was their most trusted companion for over two centuries, as he and Connor packed concert halls across the continent. But Serena had vanished when Connor died, and her father had always assumed that she perished as well. Did this woman even know that?

"You know Mikelos thinks you're dead, right?" Toria's fingers ached, and she became aware that her hands gripped the edge of the table. She placed them in her lap instead, willing herself to relax. "That's why he's never come back."

"And, we're not exactly here to see you, ma'am," Kane said. "We've come in search of a friend who was kidnapped in New Angouleme. We have reason to believe that she is here in Parisii."

"Oh?" Natalia licked her lips clean of red tinge after another sip from her glass. One delicate eyebrow arched, but otherwise that was the extent of her interest.

Perhaps a silver lining would come from this awkward encounter after all. If Natalia had the resources to spy on them from the other side of the world, she had to know even more about the city in which she lived. "Her name is Syrisinia," Toria said. "Syri. She's an elf, less than a century old. She was kidnapped by elves in New Angouleme. We've been contacted by another group, who seem to think she's been taken to be some sort of sacrifice."

Natalia set down her glass. "And you think she's been brought here." Her expression was shuttered and unreadable.

Toria dug the new note out of her jeans pocket and passed it to Kane to hand down the table. Archer was closer, but his back was still stiff, and he hadn't done more than shove the food around his plate since Natalia entered the room. She wouldn't push him.

Natalia accepted the note from Kane with one manicured hand and unfolded it. Considering it only read the one word, she took her time studying it. "This was given to you by an elf?"

"Yes," Kane said. "After we docked in Calaitum. He handed it to Toria and left before we could do more than verify that Syri was still alive."

"You believe that the elves have her?" Natalia asked. "What seems to be the problem? She is with her own kind."

"The whole 'sacrifice' thing is a bit worrying," Toria said. She failed to keep all trace of sarcasm from her voice. She appreciated that Kane was trying to turn this to their more immediate problem. Resentment on Mikelos' behalf had bubbled up within her, and it was hard to hold it all in. He had spent so long mourning the deaths of his family. To find out that one of them had abandoned him instead grated at Toria.

"The elves of the old world are different than what you are familiar with in Limani," Natalia said. "However close you might be with this Syri, I would advise against searching for her further. The elves here are not to be trifled with, and any actions against them would be taken amiss in the larger supernatural community of Parisii." She pushed her half-empty glass to the side and rose from the table. "I regret to leave you so soon, but unfortunately, I have a previous engagement scheduled for the evening. I will return later tonight. You are welcome to lodge here rather than going to the Mercenary Guildhall. I would be delighted to get to know the three of you better if you are still awake, or we make speak again tomorrow night." Without waiting for a response, she glided to the arched doorway, David on her heels.

Toria sprang to her feet. The legs of her chair scraped on the wooden floor. "Why did you abandon my father?" Her palms smacked the table, and the words surged out before she could stop herself.

Serena, or Natalia, or whoever she was, halted. She turned her face to the side, but did not look all the way back at them. "Because my son was dead. David will prepare rooms for you." Without another word, she swept from the room.

Silence reigned. "I'm going to admit to being really confused," Archer said. He grasped his water glass like a lifeline and drained half of it in one gulp. To Archer, it must be the most comforting and familiar thing in the room right now.

Kane placed a hand on one of Toria's where it was still braced on the table. "We don't have to stay here. We can go to the Guildhall and not have anything more to do with her."

"No, we're staying here," Toria said. "I mean, we're going after Syri now, but we won't go to the Guildhall. I'm not done with Serena yet."

#

Their packs were still piled in the entryway, and they geared up. Kane and Toria strapped on their swords and a few extra blades, while Archer leaned against the wall and shook his head in bemusement when Kane offered him a knife of his own.

"This is where I remind you that I'm a lowly mage," Archer said. "No fancy warrior training for me."

"You're a master mage in your own right, love," Kane said. "With more years of experience than we have. There's nothing lowly about that."

133

Toria suppressed a grin at the pet name that Kane had dropped, seemingly without thought. It seemed that Archer was moving up in the world. Instead, she busied herself settling the weight of her rapier around her hips.

David appeared in the foyer, and they accepted his offer to move their gear upstairs. He didn't blink at the weaponry they now bristled with, instead asking simply how many beds they would require. "If it pleases you to remain together, this house was built in the traditional style. The second owner's suite is vacant, and contains two beds," he said. "One larger, and a second in the dressing room."

"That would be perfect, thank you," Toria said. "I'm not sure what time we will back tonight."

"I am used to a nocturnal schedule, miss," David said. "Have no worries about disturbing me."

"Great. One more thing," Kane said. "Where's the nearest park or green space? Preferably some place with conifers."

David gave them directions to a large park a few blocks away, not blinking at the odd destination for an armed evening outing. He shut the townhouse door behind them, and the trio walked in the direction he had indicated. They found the public green space where expected, and Archer and Toria trailed behind Kane as he meandered through the dark. They were far from the lights lining the streets, so Toria dug a quartz crystal out of a small pouch she had attached to her belt. A trickle of magic activated the set enchantment, and the rock lit up, illuminating the area around them.

"Since Syri blasted you the last time we tried to contact her," Kane said, "we're going to try this the old-fashioned way tonight."

He found a clump of conifers, some variety of pine trees. Kane would know better than Toria. He pulled his belt knife and stripped a small branch of needles, dumping them in Archer's cupped hands. They followed him back to the gravel path.

"Do we need a circle for this?" Archer asked, eyeing the bits of plant life with trepidation.

"Nope," Kane said. "Welcome to the quick and dirty way to do magic that warrior-mages are known for." He pulled a piece of jewelry out of his jeans pocket. Toria recognized one of Syri's charm bracelets. Kane must have snagged it from one of Syri's packs while they geared up.

"Tracking spell?" Toria asked.

"If she's in the city," Kane said with a brisk nod, "we should be close enough."

"Let's do this." Toria reached out and melded her shields with Kane's, who meshed with her without a thought. Since they had left the ocean, her partner was back to being grounded the way he knew best, and didn't need to rely on filtering through Archer's power anymore. But magic remembered magic, and when they reached out, Archer's shields flowed into theirs without effort.

"On three, throw those up in the air," Kane said, pointing to the needles Archer still cupped in his hands.

"Seriously?" Archer asked. The dubious look on his face was almost comical.

This was so far out of his frame of reference. Toria would enjoy this. She activated her magesight and soaked in the magnificent triple structure of shielding that surrounded them. This would never get old. "Seriously," she said. "Trust the man."

"Don't worry, I do," Archer said. "Let me know when."

Kane dangled the bracelet in front of him with one outstretched hand. His other hand shimmered with an emerald glow, and tendrils of power stretched toward the silver jewelry. "One, two, three."

Archer tossed the needles up. Despite the gentle breeze, they all fell traight down. He froze, as if afraid that breathing would conflict with the spell Kane had cast.

"It's cool, it worked," Toria said.

Kane shoved the bracelet back into one of his pockets, and he and Toria leaned over where the dark green needles had fallen. Toria held the glowing quartz out, and the needles lay in stark contrast to the pale gravel. Every needle pointed in the same direction.

"Whoa," Archer said. "That was, indeed, quick and dirty."

"We have a direction," Kane said. He plucked a few of the needles from the ground and shoved them in the same pocket as the bracelet. "Let's get Syri."

#

Syri opened her eyes when she felt magic sniffing around her like a curious cat. Shimmery green tendrils wound their way into the tiny, dank cell through the viewing grate at the top of the metal door. They poked at the rough-cut stone walls and ceiling and investigated the cement floor that had cured with warped ridges and whorls that made sitting anywhere uncomfortable. But since the cell was otherwise empty but for her, Syri had no choice but to sit after she grew tired of pacing. The tendrils came to rest on her, now twisting down her arms like a cuddly garden snake.

It was the first thing to happen since she had awoken here an unknown number of hours before. She had no idea where "here" even was. She had dim memories of a dark forest, a dirty metal shipping container, and a world that would not stop shifting and rocking.

She also had no idea how much of what she remembered was truth or illusion, reality or drugs. Her last firm memory was of dancing in the club in New Angouleme. She didn't even remember leaving. She had no idea how much time had passed, or even whether she was still in the city. Or where the hell Toria and Kane were.

She curled in the corner of the stone cell, damp cold seeping through dirty jeans and a scuffed leather jacket that looked extra worse for the wear.

The palm pistol she clasped in her hands was real enough. When she woke, she discovered that it had still been tucked into the back of her jeans. The light-deflecting charm she set back in Calverton to shield it from sight should have worn off the first time she lost consciousness. While the fact that her mysterious captors hadn't searched her thoroughly should speak volumes about their intelligence, in reality, it scared Syri more that they probably had searched her but didn't view the gun as either a threat or a valuable to be taken from her. It was worrying that they would remove her knives but not that.

Despite the tendrils' reptilian appearances, they acted more cat-like, purring in the back of her mind when she traced a finger down one.

The purr sounded exactly like Kane did under the ministrations of one of her patented back rubs after a long evening of studying. Syri couldn't contain the relieved laughter that bubbled forth, but she shoved down the tears that threatened to follow.

She could be anywhere, held by anyone. But Kane was coming for her. Toria couldn't be far behind. Syri had witnessed first-hand Toria's dedication to rescuing her partner two years ago.

She had faith that her friends would fight just as hard for her.

#

The three of them wandered through the dark Parisii streets for over an hour. Every few blocks, Kane pulled one of the pine needles out of his pocket and studied it before marching in the correct direction. They kept up a steady stream of conversation through various neighborhoods and business districts, through classy shopping avenues and more decrepit-looking alleyways.

They passed more than one famous landmark, and Toria regretted not packing a camera. After they found Syri, she'd have to find a cheap one and play tourist for a few hours before they returned to Limani to report to Zerandan that mages weren't being born anymore. Then they would work out the next step in that particular quest.

She had no doubt in her mind that they would find Syri. The tracking spell wouldn't have worked if the bracelet's owner no longer lived. They were close.

"I think that's it," Kane said. He pointed across the street to a brightly lit café on the opposite side of the street. People spilled out the front doors and into the outdoor seating area in the warm summer evening, and they could hear the dance music from where they stood.

"Syri's in there?" Doubt colored Archer's face.

"The trail, well, focuses there," Kane said. "Either Syri is there, or something strongly tied to her is. And I don't know what else it could be, since I don't know that she's ever even been to this city before."

"Let's have a drink and see what we can find out," Toria said. She sauntered across the street and up to the café entrance.

Two men lounged against either side of the open doors, passing a cigarette back and forth. One had buzzed hair that did nothing to hide pointed elven ears, and the other flashed vampire fang when he took a drag on the cigarette. They made no secret of looking Toria up and down or of hiding the hunger of two different natures that seeped through their gazes. They must think the appraising expressions or the black leather they wore would intimidate her. They were mistaken.

"Good evening," Toria said. She was somehow unsurprised when an arm appeared across the doorway, blocking her path inside. She hadn't even seen the vampire move. But if he expected to startle her, he'd have to try that trick on someone who hadn't grown up practicing swordplay with two vampires who loved to trip her up by moving even faster.

"Can we help you?" asked the elven half of the pair. He flicked the cigarette butt to the sidewalk and ground it beneath the toe of his combat boot.

"My friends and I are in the mood for a drink, and this seems like the place to be," Toria said. She did her best to portray a party-girl persona, the type of woman who would wander into the seedy side of town in search of a good time. The vampire couldn't be that old, since she was able to meet his eyes for a full two seconds before she switched her flirty gaze to his friend.

"What's a pretty girl like you need the sword for to have a drink?" The vampire lowered his arm and stepped closer, looming over her.

Before she could respond, Toria felt Kane's fingertips brush her wrist. An image shoved down their link flashed in her mind—Kane had noticed that one of the elves leaning against the bar inside, past Toria's two new friends, had a long knife shoved through his belt, topped by a familiar silver hilt. Like called to like, and now that she knew it was there, Toria could feel the enchantment she had cast on the blade to prevent dulling sing through the café toward her. Kane's tracking spell had done at least part of its job.

She didn't let the smile plastered to her face waver. "Never can be too careful in a strange city," she said. "Buy me a drink and you can tell me all about what parts of Parisii I shouldn't miss while I'm here." Yes, tempt the strange vampire with the knowledge that she was a stranger in the city and might not be missed. Brilliant, Toria.

But the vampire laughed and waved her inside. "Can't leave my post, but I like your attitude. Welcome to Wyto's."

Kane and Archer stayed close on her heels as Toria entered the café. Loud music, loud conversation, flowing drinks, slightly seedy décor. It was a far cry from the class and elegance of The Red Eye in New Angouleme, and Archer probably felt a bit out of his element. Here, neon beer signs shone amidst posters of pinup girls and local bands. The dance floor, such as it was, consisted of a corner of the room near an electric music player. Overfilled tables crowded most of the space. Wyto's was a place for drinking and socializing. It could have been a bar back home, with one difference. While the majority of the patrons were human, a flash of magesight showed her that the two men at the door weren't a fluke. Vampires and elves were scattered everywhere.

Limani's few elves, with the possible exception of the always rebellious Syri, wouldn't have been caught dead in such a low-class establishment. Natalia was right. The elves of the old world, or at least of Parisii, were a breed of their own.

But they were here, and they had a job to do. Toria made her way to the bar, next to the elf wearing Syri's dagger. She ignored him, for now, and flagged down the bartender. They couldn't lose their edge, but they also couldn't stand out, so Toria ordered a round of beers for the three of them. "I need a distraction," Toria said, leaning against Kane to whisper in his ear.

"I don't like the sound of that," Kane said. "What sort of distraction? Bar fight?"

Bless him for not even batting an eye at what crazy thing she might have planned. "Not that extreme. Not yet. Make out with Archer."

"You have to ask?" Kane turned away from Toria, laughing. Without any warning, he wrapped his hands around the back of Archer's neck and pulled him closer, catching him in a lip-lock. Archer gave a surprised *oomph* sound before sinking into Kane's embrace and returning the kiss without protest.

Toria leaned against the bar with a dramatic sigh. When the bartender returned, wearing a bemused expression at the actions of her companions, she traded the three beers for cash. Kane and Archer were still making out, so she slid two drinks to the side and wrapped both hands around the third bottle. "Don't mind them," she said, twitching a finger in the boys' direction. "New couple. Can't get enough of each other. I'm a total third wheel, it's awful."

"My roommate's the same way with his girl," the bartender said. But he was called away to the other end of the bar before the conversation could continue.

Toria heaved another unnecessary sigh and sipped her drink. Was Kane nibbling on Archer's bottom lip? His dedication to this distraction now made even her uncomfortable. She spun on the bar stool and flashed a bright grin at the elf next to her. The one wearing Syri's knife. He stared at Kane and Archer as if watching a train wreck, but pulled his attention away to return Toria's smile.

"Can't take them anywhere," Toria said. "New couples are the worst."

"I think they've definitely abandoned you for the night," he said. He stuck a hand out. "Sten."

Sten wore black like most of the other elves, but the only leather was on his knee-high boots over black jeans. An unfamiliar logo, probably something Parisiian, decorated the black T-shirt. Nondescript blond hair was pulled back from his face in a short queue, but his lovely lavender eyes stood out from the rest of his face. Different, for an elf.

"Toria." She returned the introduction, refraining from offering her full elven name since he hadn't offered his, and accepted the handshake, dragging the pads of her fingertips down his palm as she released his hand. He already leaned into her space. She angled herself toward him as well, pitching her voice lower so that he had to lean in even more to hear her over the music. "Guess you'll have to keep me company instead."

"I'd offer to buy you a drink, but you already have one," Sten said. "Not sure how else I could show you a good time."

Toria took another sip of her beer, then pushed it away from her on the bar. With one fingertip, she traced a line down Sten's bare forearm. "Beer is certainly not necessary to have a good time."

Sten caught her hand in his and brought her knuckles to his lips, brushing a light kiss over them. Wow, this guy had moves. Toria almost felt guilty about taking advantage of him now. Almost. But if he thought this was all his idea, so much the better. "Does someplace quieter seem like a good time?"

Toria glanced back over her shoulder. Kane no longer held Archer's mouth captive with his own, but they were still draped in each other's personal space, trading whispers. Neither beer had been touched. She turned back to Sten. "I don't think they're going anywhere, and it's certainly not my job to babysit them. What did you have in mind?"

Since this wasn't the classiest joint in all of Parisii, Toria wasn't surprised at the response. "The bathrooms are in back," Sten said. Still gripping her hand, he hopped off his barstool and tugged her after him. Didn't seem like he expected her to turn down the romantic offer.

Never in a million years would Toria ever sink so low to having sex in a bar's bathroom. She repressed a shudder at the thought. But this wouldn't get that far. She kept her hand tucked in Sten's as they trailed their way through the loud crowd, ignoring the catcalls directed her way. Subtle, Sten was not. She directed reassurance at Kane when she sensed his mental query. At least her partner was no more than a thought away if this backfired.

Both of the restrooms off the back corridor were locked, so Toria let Sten push her against the wall and claim her mouth. On the plus side, he wasn't a bad kisser. To be fair, the fact that he appeared to be in his mid-twenties meant he was closer to two or three centuries old. A man better learn a thing or two in that time.

No one had ever complained about Toria's kissing abilities either, and Sten groaned into her mouth when she took his ass in her hands and pressed him closer to her. One hand brushed the hilt of Syri's dagger. He thrust one leg between hers, and she ground herself against his thigh.

One of those bathrooms better be free soon. She was not about to hump his leg in public.

As if answering her mental wish, one of the doors unlocked with a click and swung open, depositing a drunk woman who giggled at them as she brushed by in the narrow hall. Before she even disappeared from sight, Sten hauled Toria into the free bathroom. It...smelled like a bar bathroom. Old urine and stale beer, or was it the other way around? A definite mood killer no matter what the circumstances.

This time, it was Toria's turn to push Sten against the single wall that wasn't occupied by door, sink, or toilet. She resumed kissing him, because he really was a good kisser. His hands reached up to tangle in her hair. Perfect.

She grabbed his ass one more time with her left hand, shoving her leg between his and pinning him against the wall with her hip. With her right, she drew the dagger shoved through Sten's belt.

He stopped kissing her, finally, and jerked his body back when he felt the blade press to the side of this throat. But he was stuck between Toria and the wall. "What the fuck, lady?"

Toria felt his erection through his jeans, pressing against her. She tossed a prayer to any available deity that this didn't turn out to be some sort of crazy turn-on for him. But his hands left her hair, and the fear that bared his teeth was real. "Where did you get this knife?" She kept her voice pitched low.

"You want the knife? Take the knife," Sten said. "Let me go, bitch."

"I'm taking the knife," Toria said. "But I still want to know where you got it."

"My father found it," Sten said. "From the old mage school or something, I don't know. I just accepted the gift."

"When?"

"This morning! That's why I'm at Wyto's, I was showing it off to my crew."

This was turning out to be both more and less helpful than Toria had imagined. "Where's the other one?"

"The other what?" Now Sten had both hands pressed flat against the bathroom wall, and at least his penis was no longer an awkward distraction.

"The other knife," Toria said. "Like this one."

"I only have the one," Sten said. He tried to avoid her, but Toria kept the knife right where it was. "I had no idea it was a set."

"No siblings your dad might have given it to? Or other family?"

"If there's more than one knife," Sten said, babbling, "he either kept it or gave it to my uncle. I don't know, lady, I swear."

"Okay, okay, chill," Toria said. She withdrew the blade from Sten's neck, and he sagged against the wall, chest heaving. "I'm not going to hurt you. I wanted the knife and information." Adrenaline surged through her, and she wanted to gasp for breath as much as Sten was. She was not cut out to be a villain.

"You could have just asked, bitch," Sten said. "Get the fuck out of here. You and the exhibitionists you came in with."

"We're going," Toria said. She stepped back and slid the knife into her own belt. She'd find a more permanent home for it once she got out of this dump unscathed. "You and your crew going to come after us?"

"No," Sten said. "I don't need your crazy shit. I need a drink." He leaned against the grubby sink. "Just go."

Without removing her focus from him, Toria reached back for the bathroom doorknob. Neither of them had even locked it. She was lucky no one had burst in on that scene, which would have raised a hell of a lot more questions than the scenario Sten had been expecting to play out. In a matter of moments, Toria was down the hall and back through the crowd.

Kane and Archer still sat at the bar, now enjoying their drinks with much more decorum. The bartender leaned across from them, listening to Archer describe some drink or other.

"We have to go," Toria said. "Now." She dug some coins out of her pocket and slapped them at the bar.

"We're already paid up," Kane said.

"Not for us," Toria said. "The guy I was with? Get him a drink on me?" It was the least she could do after scaring him half to death. She was a terrible bad guy. At the bartender's confused nod, Toria grabbed Kane and Archer's hands and tugged them off their barstools. "Seriously, we've gotta go. Or did you want a bar fight tonight?"

Archer laughed, but he let her lead him through the crowd. "No, not tonight. Maybe another time."

"Did you get what we needed?" Kane asked, his tone more serious.

"The old mage school," Toria said, hoping that Parisii didn't have so many of them that Sten's information would be too difficult to decipher. "It's a start."

#

David opened the front door of Natalia's townhouse before Toria's hand even touched the bell. "Welcome back," he said, stepping away and gesturing them in. "Lady Della Zanna requests an audience in the parlor before you retire for the evening."

It had taken another hour to walk back from the bar, and they were exhausted. But despite the butler's wording, this rang more of an order than a request. Their packs no longer littered the foyer, so David must have moved them to the promised suite upstairs. "We would be delighted to," Toria said. She didn't have the energy for another strained conversation with her "Grandmere," but she followed David farther into the house, Kane and Archer close behind.

Natalia perched on the edge of a couch. The furniture was formal, and shelves filled more with decorative objects than books lined the room. Another delicate goblet, half-filled with blood, sat on the end table next to her. "Please, come in," she said. "Have a seat. May David fetch you any refreshments?"

There was nothing to do except as requested. Toria drew Syri's knife so that the naked blade wouldn't damage the upholstery and sat on the facing couch, the weapon balanced across her knees. Kane and Archer bracketed her, which was comforting. Her fingers sought Kane's, and reassurance flowed from him. "No, thank you," she said. "I think we'd rather go to bed soon."

A flash of unexpected humor crossed Natalia's face. "Yes, it is rather late," she said. "And you've had a long day of traveling. How was Wyto's?"

"The bar?" Kane asked. "Doesn't seem your sort of place."

"It's not," Natalia said. "But since it is a regular haunt of the younger vampires, I keep a weather eye on what happens there. Such as when elves get assaulted in bathrooms by guests to the city that I have personally vouched for."

Toria had filled Kane and Archer in on what happened during the stroll back, and neither of them blinked at the accusation. And she wouldn't quibble over the term assault, since she had threatened him, even if she did buy him a drink to try to make up for it. There was something else about what Natalia said that interested her much more. "I wasn't aware that our presence in Parisii needed vouching for," she said. "Our passports got us into Roman territory with no problems at either the train station in Calaitum or here. Was there some visa paperwork we missed?" Her sarcasm would be the death of her someday. The vampire sitting across from her was not the equally sarcastic vampire who had raised her.

"Three master mages, two of them warrior-mages, enter the city and expect to be nothing more than average tourists?" Natalia said. "Of course not. Do me, and yourselves, a favor. Stay out of trouble from now on. Don't antagonize the elves, or it will be me who must answer to the Master of the City for your actions."

"We can play tourist," Kane said. "In fact, we'd love to visit any local mage schools. Archer and I are interested in the libraries."

Natalia hid her silence behind a sip from her goblet. After setting it back down, she said, "I'd advise caution, but I cannot prevent you from visiting. Be aware that it will not be what you expect. The maid will have a breakfast laid out for whenever you rise in the morning, and David will summon a town-car for you whenever you're ready to leave. Good night."

She swept to her feet and had already left the room before Toria could do more than murmur "Good night," after her. They were left alone in the parlor.

"I'm pretty sure that she freaks me out more than Asaron," Kane said. "And that man terrified me for two years."

"I'm pretty sure all vampires still freak me out," Archer said. "And I'm exhausted. Let's go to bed."

When they left the parlor, David escorted them upstairs. There was no sign of where Natalia had gone, and Toria felt disinclined to ask. As promised, the suite contained both an enormous canopy bed and a second, cozier bed in the dressing room for a lady's maid. But rather than flop into the smaller bed after she'd had the last turn in the bathroom, Toria crawled in on the other side of Archer. There was more than enough room for all three of them.

"This okay?" she said, tucking her knees up and nestling her forehead against Archer's shoulder. Kane sprawled on Archer's other side, one foot sticking out from under the blankets as always.

"I find myself quite okay with being stuck between two warrior-mages while staying in a vampire's house," Archer said.

"Civilized vampires don't eat people," Toria said. Kane chorused the same phrase half a beat after her in a sleepy voice.

"Define civilized," Archer said.

Toria was tired, but her mind whirled. Natalia was the epitome of civilization, but where Victory embraced life in Limani, Natalia had more of a veneer hiding something deeper. But they were one step closer to finding Syri, and no threats would keep them from accomplishing that goal.

#

Their late breakfast the next morning consisted of fruit-filled crepes and coffee au lait. The maid they'd glimpsed at dinner the night before, a vivacioust young woman called Mellie, confessed that the crepes were from a café down the block. Lady Della Zanna did not often entertain guests in town who required the services of a full kitchen, but she provided an ample allowance that kept Mellie and David well fed.

True to her word, Natalia left the address of what appeared to be Parisii's only mage school, so at least there was no confusion regarding their next destination. Mellie also summoned a private town-car for them, indicating that the trip would go on the expense account Natalia kept with the service for times David was unavailable to drive her.

"We're getting spoiled," Kane said, muttering under his breath as they stepped into the luxurious vehicle.

Toria overheard him from her spot in the front seat. "Never turn down a rich patron," she said. "Max would be proud of us." She passed the driver the slip of paper with the address. The man pulled the town-car away from the curb.

"Max would be horrified to learn that we have yet to spend one night in a Guildhall," Kane said.

"You mean this is out of the ordinary for you?" Archer's voice contained genuine confusion.

Toria couldn't help but laugh. "Limani is mighty, but small. The Master of the City may have raised us in a house almost as big as the Delacours', but Kane and I aren't exactly nobility. Limani takes the whole equality gig seriously."

"Sorry," Kane said. "But if you stick with me, you'd be marrying down."

It took a mighty effort, but Toria did not turn around in her seat to gape at her partner. That had been unexpected. Before any awkwardness could ensue, she steered the conversation back to its original focus. "We still have a little over seventeen months to go," she said. "I'm sure we'll make up for all this luxury by sleeping in the dirt at least once by the time it's all over."

"Don't say things like that, you'll jinx us," Kane said.

The conversation tapered off as the sights outside the town-car's windows distracted them. Unlike New Angouleme, which had been a vertical city that brushed the sky, embracing modernity, Parisii blended old and new architecture. New Angouleme was a handful of centuries old, a baby compared with the millennia that Parisii had been continuously inhabited. Since the city had traded hands between the Roman and British empires many times over the past thousand years, it had echoes of both cultures everywhere Toria looked.

They soon entered one of the older districts. The broad avenue contained government buildings and houses of worship in between unmarked buildings that could have been anything from private homes to commercial offices. The mage school was a palatial estate set behind a groomed green space. In fact, the more Toria studied it as she stepped out of the town-car, the more it looked like it must have been a royal, or at least noble, residence at some point in the structure's history.

"Enjoy yourselves," the driver said through his open window after Kane thanked him for the ride. "I hear the tour isn't one to be missed."

He pulled away before Toria could ask what he meant. A mage school that catered to tourists? That was a new one. But as they traipsed up the gravel path that led to the entrance, a bronze plaque next to the door came into clearer view.

Parisiian Academy of Mages: Historical Site. A list of public hours, tour times, and prices for admission followed the name. Students and seniors saved some money.

They stood in front of the large wooden entrance, gaping at the sign. The doors and the sandstone façade were carved with fantastical depictions of the four elements. Storm was represented in the archway that framed the doors, with abstract electrical bolds highlighted with gold gilt. The door burst open as Kane reached for it, and a dozen children tumbled out followed by two harried adults.

The children streamed past them. Each of them wore a bright green sticker noting that they were Tour Group 2, and the babble of conversation included such gems as "I bet I would be a fire mage!" and more disturbing, "Don't be a dummy, Gerard, the elf lady said mages don't exist anymore!"

Kane caught the door before it could close, holding it open for the group's final adult chaperone who smiled in thanks. Toria's level of surrealism hit peak capacity, and while the snarky part of her brain wanted to spark some electricity to prove the kids wrong, the rest of her was too busy feeling bewildered.

"I am experiencing the strong temptation to make it rain," Archer said. "Not over the whole city, mind. Just right here. Over those kids."

"I refuse to accept responsibility for your mucking with the weather patterns," Toria said. "But I understand your impulse perfectly." She pulled some static electricity from the fabric of Archer's shirt and sparked him with a tiny shock. He jumped in surprise, then glared at her.

"Don't you two dare," Kane said. "Let's go find out what the hell is going on here." They followed him in, but ended up arrayed inside the door, once more taking in the unexpected.

Much like in New Angouleme, a desk dominated the large foyer. Rather than a simulacrum, however, two elves sat behind the desk. One typed at a computer, while the other accepted money from a human couple in exchange for a strip of green stickers. "The next tour is in about half an hour," she said with a bright grin. "It will be called here in the lobby."

On the other side of the grand foyer lay a gift shop.

The front display drew Toria, as if by a string. There was a T-shirt decorated with the same carved motifs as the front entrance. A historical treatise on the differences between the elemental magics. A set of magnets featuring a photo of the building. She picked up a coffee mug decorated with the official Parisii Academy of Mages Museum logo. She had been wrong. The surrealism could go further.

"Excuse me, miss. You'll want to make sure your admission is paid before you can join the next tour. It's best to visit the gift shop on the way out so you don't have to carry your purchases with you."

Toria returned the mug to the display table and looked up at the elven woman standing next to her. She wore a nametag that identified her as Giri, the gift shop manager.

"I'm confused," Toria said.

Giri's smile lost a bit of its enthusiasm but did not falter. "You'll need to purchase admission to view the museum with a tour," she said, as if explaining to a particularly dim person. "We only have open visiting hours on Saturdays and Wednesdays."

"No, no," Toria said. "That I get. But where's the school?" Kane and Archer had joined her. They also examined the items on display, but their focused body language said their attention was with Toria's.

"Why, this hasn't been a school for over a dozen years," Giri said.

"Where do Parisii's new mages go to train?" Kane asked.

"This hasn't been a school," Giri said, "because there are no new mages in Parisii." Her friendly persona was gone at this point. "I'm sorry," she said. "But what were you expecting?"

"I'll take it from here, Giri, thank you." Though elven faces did not show signs of age the way humans did, Toria sensed the aura of many years around the man that had approached them. Despite that, he stood ramrod straight in his impeccable grey suit. His hair was styled short, but his demeanor was nothing like Zerandan's back home. He smiled at Toria, but it never came close to reaching his eyes. Eyes a familiar shade of violet.

"Yes, sir," Giri said. She gave a demure bow before moving off to greet other gift shop patrons.

"If you'll follow me," he said, "I might be able to answer your questions more thoroughly in private. My office is this way." Without waiting for a response, he bustled through the foyer. The tip of his cane never touched the floor.

Toria sent a mental query down the link. Dare they follow? Kane shrugged, and Archer set the treatise back on the table. At a hurried pace, they accompanied the man through a door to the side marked "Private."

At the end of a short hallway, he gestured them into an office. Only two seats were available on the visitor's side of the desk, which Toria and Kane accepted while Archer leaned against the wall next to the door. Their host settled into a pretentious leather desk chair and rested his cane against the desk decorated with elaborate woodwork.

"My name is Rubinaril," he said. "You may call me Elder Rubin. May I please inquire what the three of you are doing in my museum?" His knuckles were white where he folded his hands on the desk.

Toria tried to be attentive, but something about the desk niggled at the back of her mind. "You know who we are?" Toria asked, hesitant. No, not the desk itself. Something inside the desk sparkled with magic and electricity. Something familiar.

"Of course I know who you are," Rubin said. "I'm not an idiot. You three are the first mages to step foot in Parisii in over a decade. Warrior-mages, no less. The Lady Della Zanna is hosting you. Word spread quickly when you arrived."

"Wait," Archer said, stepping forward. "There are *no mages* in Parisii? At all?"

"No," Rubin said. "They've either died of old age or moved on. The school was barely functioning as it was, when the last master died and the last student graduated. The elves of Parisii revamped it as a historical site before it could be turned into condos."

"What about the other cities?" Toria asked. "Roma? Londinium? Are the schools there still teaching?"

"I believe Roma still has a few masters, but I wouldn't know about student numbers," Rubin said. "And the school in Londinium merged with the one in Oxenafor a few years ago. Again, I haven't kept track of any numbers. I'm a museum curator, not a mage teacher. So I ask again, what are you doing here? Relic hunting? Searching for hidden power reserves? I assure you, there are none." He said that, yet Toria sensed the artifact hiding within his own desk.

"No, sir," Kane said. "We're searching for a friend of ours, and this was our most recent lead. It must have been a dead end."

"Quite," Rubin said. He stood up, the audience clearly over.

Kane and Toria followed suit. "Thank you for your time, sir," Toria said. "You'll understand if we don't stay for a tour."

"You missed it," Rubin said, without checking the clock on the wall. "You'd have to wait over an hour until the next one. Please see yourselves out. I have work to do."

They filed out of the office and Kane shut the door behind him. Toria cut him off with a slash of her hand before he could speak. "Not here," she said.

They exited the museum and ensconced themselves in another of Parisii's ubiquitous cafés across the street. Unlike Wyto's, this was more tea shop and less bar, with a family-oriented, upper-class atmosphere that matched the feel of the surrounding neighborhood. Their outdoor table gave them an unimpeded view of the museum entrance, and a bow-tied waiter brought the drinks and snacks they ordered without a blink at the blades they wore.

"Okay," Kane said after he savored a sip of café au lait. "Tell me you felt that."

Toria had the same beverage. She had a feeling this was going to be a new favorite. A perfect summer afternoon pick-me-up, despite the heat of the drink. It was all about the caffeine. "Kind of hard to miss."

"Felt what?" Archer had ordered a cool glass of water, requesting "no gas" at the waiter's query. However, when the waiter had brought the drink, he'd dipped a finger in the liquid and stirred three times. Now the water sparkled with carbonation, but Toria appreciated his conservation of their spending money. "I cast out when he said there were no enchanted objects in the museum, but I only sensed something in the room itself. I assumed it was his cane."

"Nope, that was a normal cane," Toria said. "The object was inside the desk. Syri's other knife, which also has my anti-tarnish charm."

"That was your friend from the bar's dad?" Kane asked. "Talk about falling far from the tree."

"Same eyes, though," Toria said.

"I guess you did get a good view," Archer said with a laugh.

"Don't remind me," she said. "We're lucky that Sten didn't tell his father what happened last night. Hell, I still want to know how Natalia knew." She pulled apart the fruit-filled pastry on the plate in front of her.

"I think there's a lot about that woman that's going to remain a mystery," Kane said. "What now?"

"Sten said his dad gave him Syri's knife. We've found the dad, and we've found the other knife," she said.

"Should we go after it?" Archer asked.

"Not worth it," Toria said. "When all is said and done, it's just a blade. I'd rather track the man than try to plan a crazy heist for something less valuable in the grand scheme of things."

"Well, it's a lovely afternoon," Kane said. "I don't mind waiting." He signaled the waiter and ordered another round of drinks.

It took a few hours, and more coffee than was healthy for any of them, but Elder Rubin finally left his museum as dusk fell over the city. They were in luck—he did not have a town-car, but instead set off down the avenue by foot. Toria and Archer abandoned the café to shadow him. Kane would catch up to them after he settled the bill. There was no danger of him losing them, thanks to his link with Toria. She hoped he left the waiter a decent tip since they'd monopolized his table all afternoon and never ordered anything more substantial than drinks and more of those amazing crescent-shaped pastries.

Trailing a body was not something Archer had ever been taught at the New Angouleme Center for Magical Education, and Toria worried that he would give them away. She relaxed after a few blocks. What Archer did excel at was following her lead. They'd make a decent mercenary out of him yet.

Kane reached them as they lurked in an alleyway. "What's going on?"

"Rubin's having dinner across the street," Toria said. "Looks like his private club. If he doesn't come out in a reasonable amount of time, we'll have to assume he keeps rooms there."

"We are not invading a club." Archer looked scandalized at the idea, and Toria remembered how attached he was to his own back in New Angouleme.

"We'll do whatever it takes to find Syri," she said, shrugging. "I'd be more worried, but it appears to cater more to local scholars than strictly elves. Those are wards I'd rather not tangle with, but this place has no magical protection." Though if there were no mages in Parisii, that didn't surprise her. Any magical warding would have to be elven by nature, unless a mage from outside of the city was contracted in.

The discussion became irrelevant less than an hour later when Rubin stepped out of the club. The attitude of full-stomached contentment that surrounded him was almost tangible. They ghosted down both sides of the avenue after him, which grew less challenging as the evening shadows deepened.

A few blocks away from his club, in a mostly residential area, Rubin turned into a courtyard and disappeared from view after nodding to the two men that bracketed the entrance. An elf and a vampire.

They kept moving. The elf might not notice them, but the vampire would note a trio of heartbeats lurking on the otherwise deserted street, even if they were out of immediate sight. Toria had assumed the situation at Wyto's had been a fluke, but here was the same combination once again guarding something. She looked with magesight as they passed, and had to blink away the dazzle of light that assaulted her magical senses.

She didn't have time to study them, but at first glance, they were the strongest elven wards she had ever encountered. They breathed with a life so strong that the building they guarded might as well have been a living object. Mixed within was another magic she couldn't immediately identify, something that tasted soapy and felt slick against her skin as they passed. Dark shadows she only caught out of the corner of her vision.

But they left the area before she could give more than a cursory glance. Kane had passed on the side of the street with the entrance, even going so far as giving a friendly nod to the men loitering outside. Perhaps he'd gotten a better idea of what they faced. Toria pulled Archer behind her at a faster clip. This would need some discussion.

#

Kane rendezvoused with them again as a waitress seated Toria and Archer in a cheery restaurant a few blocks away. "We're not going back to Natalia's to talk?" he asked, dropping into the empty seat beside Archer.

"We've had nothing but caffeine, sugar, and carbs to eat today," Toria said. "We need to get into that building, and I need a real meal before I even think about the defenses on that place. Something involving protein."

"I did get the impression this morning that Natalia's house was low on proper meals," Archer said. "And I may not have your fancy merc training, but even I know an assault on that place should probably wait until later at night."

"You're right," Kane said. "This isn't something that should be rushed. We'll have to go back to Natalia's to change and gear up anyway." But his fingers tapped a stacatto rhythm on the table, and Toria knew he was as anxious as she was.

Time to reel him in before he vibrated out of his seat. "I'm thinking the chicken parm," she said. "You?"

After they finished their meal, the waitress waved away their desire to call a taxi once she learned the address of their destination. Apparently they'd trailed Rubin most of the way back to Natalia's townhouse after he left the museum.

Full night had fallen, and Toria was unsurprised when Natalia herself opened the front door to the townhouse. She was, however, disconcerted by the sharp look that pinched the woman's face. "I would speak with you alone, Toria," she said. Without waiting for a response, Natalia stalked toward the parlor they'd met in late the night before.

"Upstairs," Toria said, when Kane and Archer made to follow her. "I'll be fine." She hoped her voice contained more bravado than she felt. Natalia's attitude was unexpected. What the hell had they done this time? Rubin had made no indication that he sensed or knew about followers that afternoon.

Natalia stood in the center of the parlor, arms crossed in front of her dress. Tonight, she was once again adorned in full black, but in a flowing gown that hugged every curve. Not willing to take a submissive position before the woman, Toria stood behind one of the couches, bracing her hands along the top. She knew better than to try to meet the gaze of a vampire possibly older than Asaron, so she fixed her eyes on a lighting fixture behind Natalia. "Good evening, Grandmere," she said. Perhaps the peace offering of that title would defer whatever distressed Natalia.

It didn't work. Natalia pursed her lips. "I trust your visit to the Academy of Mages was educational?"

"Not much of an academy anymore," Toria said. "We didn't stick around long."

"I wish that you had trusted my advice that the trip would be worthless," Natalia said. "Or are you still persisting in this fiction that your friend is in need of rescue?" She paced to the side of the room and poured herself a snifter of amber liquid from a glass decanter.

"We saw her get dragged off in New Angouleme," Toria said. Okay, they hadn't actually seen Syri leave the courtyard, but she had definitely been fighting with the elves they found there. "I'm pretty sure that even if Syri is with her own kind, she's not happy to be there."

"That is the problem," Natalia said, rotating the glass in her hands. "You don't understand the bonds of kindred. The closest you have to family are those two young men upstairs. "

"Of course I do," Toria said, bewildered by this sudden turn of focus. "My family isn't just Kane and Archer because they're mages. My mother is Victory, Master of the City of Limani, and my father is her daywalker Mikelos Connor."

Natalia snapped toward Toria. "Don't you dare say that name in this house. And despite the heights she has risen to, your mother has never been more than mercenary trash."

She ignored the dig at Victory, who would preen at the compliment if she was present. "It's my name, too," Toria said, focusing on Natalia's other comment. She crossed her arms over her chest, radiating defensiveness. "He lives on through Mikelos."

"That boy should have done his duty and taken his own life when he found his master dead," Natalia said.

"How can you say that?" Toria said. The stories she had grown up with whirled through her mind. "Dad loved Connor. He loved you. Why would you want him dead?" She laughed without humor. "At least he did you the favor of moving to Limani, even if it was because he thought you died with Connor."

"And now I have petulant little girls with my progeny's name showing up at my doorstep." Natalia drained the last of the liquid in her glass and slammed it down.

"What the hell is this about?" Toria said. "I'm sorry if you're still mourning Connor. I know Dad does, too. But you are making no sense right now."

"There is nothing for you to understand," Natalia said. "Mikelos did a poor job of raising you if you don't even know how to listen to your elders."

"I listen to my elders plenty," Toria said. "But they also taught me to think for myself and not blindly follow orders. I'm not inclined to follow what you say when I disagree with your assessment of the situation. Syri did not leave New Angouleme of her own free will. It's our responsibility as her friends to find her."

"And it is my responsibility to keep you from butting in where you do not belong," Natalia said.

"We appreciate the hospitality you have shown us since we arrived in Parisii," Toria said. "But if this is what it has come to, the three of us will leave. I'm sorry, Serena. Natalia." She corrected herself less than a heartbeat later, but the vampire's face darkened.

Natalia bared her fangs in a snarl. "If this is what it has come to, then despite your name, you are no child of mine."

By this point, Toria was already halfway to the doorway, but she paused to look over her shoulder. "You're right," she said. "I am my father's daughter. But if I have to claim a vampire line, I claim that of Asaron and Victory. I'm proud to be mercenary trash."

She escaped the room unscathed. Time to collect the boys. Their life of luxury for this trip was over.

#

"Pack up, we're leaving," Toria said as she entered the suite.

"One step ahead of you, hon," Kane said. He and Archer already had their bags on the bed, shoving gear into them. Syri's bags, having never been unpacked since their arrival in Parisii, already rested by the door. "We didn't think the conversation she wanted to have with you would be a good one. I figured packing was in order when I felt the ridiculous amount of stress pouring through the link."

"You guys are amazing." Toria shut the door behind her and stripped off her T-shirt. She caught the darker long-sleeved shirt that Kane tossed her and pulled it on. "How conspicuous do you think we'll be in our armor?"

"I don't care," Kane said. "We're wearing it. There was one vampire guarding that door, and I have the feeling that there will be more. We need every advantage possible." He already wore his reinforced leather pants, and Toria dug hers out of her pack.

"What happened downstairs?" Archer asked. He didn't have combat gear to change into, and his jeans and T-shirt would have to do. If he ended up in direct combat with someone, it would be because Toria and Kane weren't doing their jobs.

"The highlights of the conversation were when she insulted my mother and wished my father had committed suicide," Toria said. "Fun times."

Years of "surprise attacks" by Asaron had trained them to be in their gear and ready to go in less time than Toria needed to brush her teeth on most mornings. As Toria buckled her sword belt back in place, Archer loaded himself up with both his and Syri's bags and reached for the doorknob. Toria felt a bit guilty for leaving a mess for David and Mellie. They had been nice.

"Oh, hell," Archer said.

Toria's head snapped up, as did Kane's from inspecting the backup knife strapped to his ankle. "What?" she asked.

"Door's locked," Archer said. "From the outside."

"You have got to be kidding me." Toria settled the weight around her waist with a final shimmy of her hips, then joined Archer. She believed him, but tried the door anyway. Yep. Locked from the outside.

"Why would she do this?" Kane's forehead wrinkled in a confused glare.

"I'm betting it has something to do with how badly she wanted us to *not* go after Syri," Toria said. "She harped on that again tonight."

"There's got to be something bigger going on," Archer said. He dropped his gear to the ground. "We're not letting a door stop us, are we?"

Kane laughed. "No, it will take more than a door." He worked the tip of his belt knife between the door and the frame. Toria held her breath, but let it out in a rush when Kane sank back on his heels. "Nope," he said. "This should work, but something feels…soapy."

Toria snapped her fingers. "There was elven magic warding the building Rubin entered, but something else, something I'd never seen before. That felt soapy, too." That was the problem with describing the indescribable. The wording often got wonky.

Kane rested his hands on either side of the doorknob. The door was wood, so he would have best chance of teasing out whatever enchantments had been laid on it. But soon he looked up at them, defeat crossing his features. "That is nothing I have ever felt before. It's not elemental magic, or storm. It's not elven magic, or whatever the hell it is that Syri does. This feels dark. Damaged somehow."

"Let me try." Archer dropped to the floor next to Kane, tailor-style, and also pressed both hands to the door.

They didn't have time for this. Kane and Archer had fallen into the typical mage's trap, something that Natalia had probably counted on. Toria saw the broader picture. The large window on the other side of the room that looked over the townhouse's tiny garden was double-paned for insulation, but when she laid her fingers on it, she felt nothing out of the ordinary, magically speaking.

Kane and Archer still murmured at the door behind her, but she didn't need them for this. She picked up the seat that paired with the graceful writing desk in the far corner of the room. Yep, this would do. She hoisted the chair by its backrest and swung it toward the window.

With a satisfying shatter, glass sprayed over the back garden. Momentum carried the chair after it, and it crashed onto the archway that covered the patio, probably to disintegrate into kindling by the time it reached the paving stones below that. Toria laughed at the beauty of the destruction and clapped her hands together. That had been *awesome*.

"You are a freak," Kane said, coming to stand next to her. "But a freak who gets things done."

"That's what I'm here for." Toria matched his wide grin.

Archer emerged from the bathroom, wrapping a towel around his arm. "Let me clear some of this away," he said. Using his protected fist, he punched out the remaining shards, removing most of the rest of the glass from the window. He peered out below. "We're lucky we're not in the next room, which is a two-story drop onto rose bushes. From here, we can climb down to the patio and it's an easy drop into the garden. You are, indeed, a maniac," Archer said. He unwound the towel from his arm and dropped it on the floor to the side of the window. He pressed a kiss to Toria's hair. "But we're lucky you're our maniac."

"Let's get out of here," Toria said, tying a purple bandana over her hair to keep it out of her face. "Grandmere can go suck a lemon."

#

The logical place for them to go next was Parisii's Mercenary Guildhall, which eliminated that as an option. Unfortunately, Natalia's neighborhood was a bit too swanky for any of the youth hostels that were supposed to be prevalent in the old world, so they made their way back to the park they had visited the night before.

"This seems like a terrible idea," Archer said, eyeing the darkest copse of trees Kane could find with skepticism.

"Well, it's what we've got," Kane said. He dropped his packs in the divot between some roots, and Toria and Archer followed suit.

"Is this going to be too much of a drain on you?" Toria asked. "We still have no idea what we're facing tonight."

Kane pressed both palms against the tree. Toria tried to toss some energy his way, but she felt it turned back on her. Oh, she understood now. Kane's hands glowed for the briefest of seconds, and then—their gear was gone. He'd used Syri's ever-so-handy "don't look at me" charm, but tied it into the tree itself. Its life force would power the spell, and their gear should remain undetected through the night.

If this final push to find Syri took longer than one night, they'd have to reassess the situation anyway.

"There, that should do it," Kane said. "Good to go."

"You have got to teach me that," Archer said, peering at where their packs should be from one angle and another. "It's elven magic."

"Syri doesn't do elven magic," Toria and Kane said, in chorus, chanting her oft-repeated refrain.

"But...she's an elf?" Archer didn't look like he bought it.

"Yep," Toria said. "We don't ask too many questions. You guys ready?"

She felt Kane pulse one more bit of power into the tree before he stepped away and nodded at his work. "Good to go."

They left the park and returned the way they came earlier in the evening. Toria's fears that they would stand out in their combat gear went unrealized. Unlike the night before, when they'd been wandering through less elite districts of the city, plenty of those out for a night on the town around here had their own armed escorts. Seeing this, Kane and Toria positioned themselves behind Archer, bracing him as proper bodyguards. The ruse would work better had Archer been in clothing fancier than jeans, but it played well enough. No one blinked at them twice.

"What's the plan if the vampire is still at the door?" Kane asked, pitching his voice to carry forward to Archer as well.

"We have to assume that he will be," Toria said. Tension radiated from Archer's stiff walk. Poor guy. This was nothing he had ever trained for. "We've sparred with Grandpa and Mama at full speed before. We know we can handle one vampire together. Archer, can you at least keep the elf distracted until we can get to him?"

"I'll see what I can do," he said. Now the set of his shoulders was more determined, echoing the firmness in his voice. "Do we have to kill them? We don't even know if Syri is down there."

They closed in on the block in question. The fact that it was all residential was on their side. If they contained the combat within the courtyard the duo guarded, and kept the fight quick and dirty, the risk of witnesses to sound the alarm diminished drastically. Of course, no plan survived engagement with the enemy. All Toria could do was cross mental fingers and pray to all the gods of which she knew about that the three of them could pull this off.

"We have no way to restrain them, and there's no way the three of us can keep control of both an elf and a vampire for long," Kane said.

The fight back in New Angouleme had been so unexpected that there had been no nerves to contend with, just action and reaction. Toria had seen Syri under attack, and she had engaged. This felt much more like waiting to confront the Roman forces two years ago. That time, it had been Syri and Toria on their way to rescue Kane. If the two of them could manage after less than forty-eight hours of friendship, Toria and Kane's decade-long bond could handle this without a problem.

She hoped.

Did Toria like the fact that they planned to kill two men in a strange city in cold blood? Of course not. But this was where all clues led, and the fact that Natalia wanted them to do anything other than investigate told them loud and clear that this was where they needed to be. They marched toward the mysteriously warded building, keeping up their patron and bodyguards pretense. The same two guards still lounged against the wall to either side of the courtyard entrance. The vampire ignored them as they approached, but the elf exchanged a cordial nod with Archer.

As if taking that as a cue, Archer paused on the sidewalk. "Pardon me, sir," he said. "But are you familiar with this neighborhood? My fiancée is in love with the buildings on this block, and keeps hassling me to find out whether there are any vacancies or owners interested in selling."

Before the elf could respond, the vampire said, "Nothing for sale," with a grunt.

"Oh, but someone is always interested for the right price," Archer said. "What a sweet courtyard! Hallie will love that." He crowded the two men, peering over their shoulders into the area beyond.

The vampire bared fangs and lunged at Archer, placing his back to Kane and Toria. That was his fatal mistake. Moving as one, Toria and Kane drew knives from their belts and darted forward. They each snagged one of his arms, pulling him away from Archer. The vampire's linen shirt afforded no protection against the blades that pierced both kidneys.

The elven guard turned in surprise at the vampire's snarl, but Archer impeded his attempts to help his companion by kicking a leg in his path. When he pitched forward, Archer directed his fall into the courtyard entrance, following him to the ground and pinning him beneath his own bodyweight. With one problem out of the way, Toria directed her attention back to the man struggling in her grasp. Even if they had been silver, the double knives to the kidneys wouldn't disable a vampire, though it did slow him down. They needed to get him out of sight, fast.

Still in sync, Toria and Kane shoved him forward, following Archer into the more shielded alcove. Once inside, they forced him to his knees. With his larger bulk, Kane hung on, keeping the vampire low. Toria released him, leaving her dagger where it was. "Are you going to chill the fuck out?" she said.

He hissed low in his throat. "Under orders to keep the two of you out of the Catacombs at all costs." He struggled in Kane's grasp, but Kane used his own larger mass to keep the vampire down.

This wasn't sustainable. "Kane?" Toria asked. This had escalated too fast, but they didn't have any other choice.

"Do it."

She reached over the vampire to draw Kane's scimitar, ignoring the fangs that snapped at her. With one motion, putting the force of both arms into the blow, she decapitated the vampire. Blood sprayed Kane as the head fell to the paved ground with a thunk, and her partner dropped the body after it. If the body made any noise as it fell, she couldn't hear it over the sound of Archer vomiting.

Archer had seen Wick's body back in New Angouleme, so this certainly wasn't the first corpse he'd ever seen. But he had not seen Toria make the tackle that smashed the back of the woman's, and they'd been too busy making their way out of the mage school afterward for what he'd seen to sink in. This was up close and personal. Toria had puked the first time she'd seen someone get killed, too. She'd made her own first kill soon thereafter. If they were lucky, Archer wouldn't be in the same situation.

Despite his distress, Archer maintained his focus enough to keep the elven man pinned to the ground. He also had his forearm jammed over the man's mouth, transforming his shouts into muffled grunts.

Kane yanked his knife out of the vampire's torso and approached them, side-stepping the pool of vomit. Reversing the blade, he slammed the pommel into the elf's temple. He slumped under Archer, now silent. The blow was a recipe for a traumatic brain injury with long-lasting health effects in a human. With luck, the elven man would shake off a headache in a few hours.

Archer accepted Kane's hand, using the leverage to pull himself to his feet. Without a word, Kane wrapped his empty hand behind Archer's neck and embraced him. The two men stood still for a moment.

Toria busied herself wiping the blade of Kane's scimitar down with her spare bandana. Eyeing it with disgust, she dropped the cloth next to the vampire's body.

The men drew apart, and Archer made a face as he examined his shirt. "I think you've gotten blood on me."

"Sorry," Kane said. "Occupational hazard." He accepted his sword from Toria and slid it back in its sheath.

They had succeeded in one goal—the entire incident had occured inside the entrance, and there was nothing to backlight the scene for any random passersby. Toria dug her handy quartz out of its belt pouch and activated the light cantrip with a mental touch. The three of them peered into the darkness.

What they had assumed to be an entrance to a courtyard within the building revealed itself to be a tunnel that burrowed into the depths instead, twisting into a spiral staircase. However, there was an entrance into the building to their right. Down or in? Toria really hoped it was in.

Kane pulled one more pine needle out of his pocket and tossed it in the air. Rather than falling straight to the ground, it arced through the air and landed on the top step of the stairs.

"Oh, hell," Toria said.

"Claustrophobic?" Archer asked.

"You have no idea."

#

This being held captive thing was boring as fuck.

Syri sat on the ground as far from the cell's door as she could get. Kane's magic had been gone for hours, but knowing that her friends were closing in calmed her.

Holding the pistol was pretty damn calming, too.

Elves could survive much longer than humans or werecreatures with little food or water, and even exist without both provided they had a reasonable magical source to sustain them in its stead. She had no idea how long she had been captive, but based on the state of her hair, it had to be much longer than the amount of time she'd remained in this underground cell. Despite the way it made something itch in the back of her brain, she'd been turning over the memories of the forest illusion, trying to gain some clue as to where she was. The rocking motion was the only thing that stood out. Had she been on a ship? For how long? Someone must have fed her magical energy while she was drugged or delusional.

Syri twirled the gun on her finger like the star of one of those ridiculous action vids Toria liked to watch. Keep her in this cell long enough, and she might get good at that.

So say she had been provided with magical energy. The churning in her gut told her that it hadn't been the right sort. Like the small number of other elves Syri knew within a few decades of her own age, she needed a certain amount of time in the sun to be happy and healthy. It's why she had seasonal affective disorder in the winter and wore as little clothing as possible in the summer. She was a delicate fucking flower.

Zerandan had always hinted that she would grow out of it. But despite how he must have gone through the same phase at her age, he was never able to answer all of her questions about how it worked. Seriously, she knew he was old, but his memory wasn't that poor.

With a metallic click, the cell door unlocked. Syri shot to her feet and aimed the palm pistol at the door. She braced herself against the wall when the world spun around her, leaving her unbalanced and dizzy.

The door swung open, revealing an unfamiliar woman who entered the cell. She glanced down at the gun, but dismissed it to focus on Syri's face. "Put that toy away, little girl," she said. "We don't have time for this."

"Who the fuck are you?" Syri did not, of course, lower the gun.

The woman *tsked*. She was dressed casually, in jeans and a loose cotton blouse. Her blond hair, close in shade to Syri's own, was pulled back in a tail at the nape of her neck. Despite her informality, her attitude did little to put Syri at ease. "Such language, Syri. I see Zerandan has failed in your upbringing in more ways than one. I am your cousin, Ayannastia, Ayanna."

"Never heard of you."

Ayanna scratched her nose. "That does not surprise me. Our sides of the family are not exactly on speaking terms."

"That why you kidnapped me?" Syri asked. "To make me play peacemaker? I hate to say, but you haven't made the best impression so far."

"No, not at all," Ayanna said. "We have been forced to search farther afield for this cycle's sacrifice. We were lucky to stumble across you in New Angouleme, away from the protection of your uncle."

"Excuse me?" That sounded ominous. "Sacrifice?" Damn, the pistol wobbled in her hand, which didn't add to her show of rebellion. It wasn't heavy, but her body had been strained to its limits.

"I see," Ayanna said. "There appear to be more holes in your education than we anticipated. You have been taught about the world spell, yes?"

"Every elf knows about that. I'm not an idiot." The spell the elves cast that prevented new technology from advancing beyond a certain limit. Why guns still existed, but not the tanks or rockets that had dominated the Last War, which she only learned about in history books. Why Syri had never seen an airplane except in old films. "It's our responsibility to prevent another world war. The planet can't handle the destruction that created the Wasteland. I've seen the Wasteland, lady. Have you?"

"I have not had the privilege," Ayanna said. "But you don't think a force like that exists in a vacuum, right? It must be maintained. Power is expensive."

"Why do I get the honor of being sacrificed?" Syri asked. She had the feeling she wouldn't like answer.

"Because you are one of the Broken," Ayanna said. "Your magic differs from that of most elves. You will never be able to take your place maintaining the world spell, but you can serve your people by feeding it instead. You have a responsibility to your people and this planet." She checked her wristwatch. "I can't believe I have to explain this to you now. This was Zerandan's duty."

"No, I have a responsibility to myself," Syri said. "You really think Zerandan was grooming me to die?"

"Honey, you were supposed to be the sacrifice three cycles ago." Pity shone on Ayanna's face. "But Zerandan kept claiming that you weren't ready. We were able to switch in substitutes, but eventually it had to be your turn. Removing you from Limani would have been difficult, which brings us back to how lucky we were that you were spotted in New Angouleme in time. But enough talk." Ayanna lifted her right hand, and light glowed at the tips of her fingers.

Syri pulled the trigger.

The shot echoed in the enclosed space, but the ringing in Syri's ears didn't impede her view of what followed. Blood blossomed from Ayanna's torso. The light from her hands blinked out when she pulled them to her chest. Ayanna fell to her knees, then to the floor. She didn't scream, but a whimper escaped her lips.

Someone had to have heard the gunshot. Someone would come running to Ayanna's aid any moment now. Syri didn't move from her position in the back of the cell. She would be ready to defend herself if anyone else came. Ayanna had been right—Zerandan had left key information out of her history lessons. Such as the fact that elven lives fed the world spell every three years.

"Help me. Please." Even with her exceptional hearing, Syri barely caught the rasp from Ayanna's lips.

How long had this been going on? Despite their long lives, the elven population could barely support itself as it was. If this cost in lives kept going, they would soon reach extinction levels.

No one came to investigate. Ayanna died in silence, blood pooling around her on the rough stone floor. One hand reached for Syri.

She stepped away from the wall and transferred the gun to her other hand. As she shook out cramped fingers, Syri stepped around the body on the floor of the cell and neared the door with caution. She didn't have any firearm training beyond point and shoot, so it was time to mimic more of Toria's vids. As she peeked out of the tiny room, she held the gun up by her face, pointed at the ceiling.

The hallway beyond was clear in both directions. Electric bulbs hung from the ceiling at intervals, casting islands of light in the darkness. The floor and ceiling were more of the same rough-cut stone as the cell at her back, but deep alcoves featuring intricate carvings lined the walls.

Syri stepped out of the cell and focused on the carved stone in the dim light.

Not carvings. It was all bones. Bones stacked from floor to ceiling, so that the joints faced outward, creating a delicate pattern. The pile reached six or more inches above her head, and the skulls lined at the top peered back down at her with vacant eye sockets. Syri read a lot of horror novels, but this was like nothing she had ever imagined. This wasn't the dumping ground from some massacre. These bones were organized with skill and intent. Thousands and thousands of bones. Hundreds of skulls within view of this hallway alone. Humanoid skulls, not animal.

Where the fuck had she ended up?

#

Toria descended into the darkness, step by step. The quartz she held in front of her washed the stone walls in pastel purple light. It was the curve of the spiral staircase that blocked her view beyond the next few steps. Archer followed close on her heels, and Kane guarded their rear. Only the fact that they were at her back kept her moving. One step at a time. The stone beneath her feet was worn by years, perhaps centuries, of passing feet and slick beneath her boot treads.

Were the walls closing in? She took another cautious step down. Another.

She shook herself all over, fighting back the anxiety that preyed at her brain.

"You okay?" Archer whispered in the darkness.

"This really, really sucks," Toria said, also keeping her voice low. Though anyone below them would see the light before hearing their voices. "Kane, I take back every uncharitable thought I had about you back on that boat."

"About time." Kane's voice drifted down to her from the shadows.

"Wait, are you having the same problems?" Archer asked.

"Being underground is the equivalent for a storm mage," Kane said. "We can link shields, and we can try to ground you into the earth, like Archer did for me with the water."

Salt stung her eyes, and Toria wiped her forehead with the back of her hand. She didn't realize she'd been sweating. The air itself felt cool and dry. "I'm not sure we have time for that. I'll let you know if it gets worse. Right now I'm just uncomfortable."

They rounded one last curve, and finally, the walls stopped pressing in. Toria halted at the foot of the stairwell, holding the quartz high to illuminate the space. The light didn't penetrate the entire cavern, but she saw all she needed to.

Artfully displayed bones lined the walls that spread out on either side of the staircase. Not individual skeletons, but hundreds of bodies' worth. Skulls, possibly human, possibly elven, lined the tops of the rows. In some cases, the tops had fallen back, leaving the jaws gape-mouthed.

There was no immediate threat, but Toria drew her rapier anyway. Because this was nothing she had ever dreamed in her worst nightmares. She heard the reassuring sound of Kane drawing his scimitar behind her.

"Oh my gods," Archer said, hardly breathing. "The Catacombs. I thought this was a legend."

A female voice answered from the depths. "Not a legend, water mage. Very real indeed."

Natalia emerged from the darkness, anger etched in the planes of her face. She continued, "And I am disappointed to see the three of you here."

Light followed Natalia out of the expanse, as electric bulbs hanging from the ceiling clicked on one by one. They seemed out of place in a macabre cavern that should have been lit by torches or grand mage lights. But torches would require ventilation, and if there were truly no more mages left in Parisii, no one was around to maintain magical lighting. Toria cut off the trickle of power flowing in the quartz and shoved the crystal back into its belt pouch, leaving her off-hand free. Archer paced forward, craning his neck to see every nook and cranny of the room. Kane stood on his other side, but directed his gaze at Natalia.

"What the hell is this place?" Toria asked.

"It's a—" Archer cut himself off with a look to Natalia. When the vampire gestured for him to continue, he said, "It's a burial ground. For the centuries that Parisii was an independent human city, the rulers would not allow any supernaturals to be buried in the graveyards in the city. The communities placed their dead in this system of old quarries instead."

"He is correct," Natalia said. "This stopped being necessary when the city passed into Roman hands three centuries ago, but the tradition continues."

A trio of elves poured out of a tunnel to the side of the cavern, led by Elder Rubin. While he wore another stylish business suit similar to the one they saw him in yesterday, the man and woman who followed him wore robes of long, flowing silk in jewel tones. Rubin took up the thread of the conversation without missing a beat. "The elven community maintains the Catacombs and uses it as one of our primary ritual spaces. Lady Natalia, the sacrifice area has been prepared and awaits your arrival." He aimed a disdainful look toward Toria and the others. "After you determine what should be done about these intruders."

"They appear to have bypassed your guards, Rubin," Natalia said. "Do they still live?" She arched a manicured eyebrow in their direction.

Toria and Kane traded short glances. "Yes and no," Toria said.

A stricken look crossed the face of the elven woman behind Rubin. "Harn?"

Elven name. "Alive," Toria said. No reason to panic the woman without cause. "Bit of a headache soon, though."

Natalia flicked the fingers of her right hand in the air. "If Jean-Pierre could not do his duty, he deserves his final death."

The chill in Natalia's voice struck Toria to the core. The illusions were gone, and her grandmere showed her true colors. This was the woman who had abandoned Mikelos. She could believe that now.

"They shall accompany us to the sacrifice," Natalia continued. "They've come this far. They deserve to see out the futility of their quest. Come, children." She turned on her heel and stalked to the back of the cavern, to the third and final exit from the bone-lined room.

Deeper underground. Toria drew a shuddering breath as the walls inched in at the edge of her vision. Archer grasped her empty hand with a reassuring squeeze as they followed Natalia. Elder Rubin and his two companions fell in behind them. They trooped past the empty gaze of dozens of skulls, darkened by age. The hallway that stretched before them was shorter than the cavern ceiling, lined on both sides by more bones, more skulls. Toria could have brushed the ceiling with her hand without stretching to her tiptoes.

Everything pressed in, and she suppressed a gag in the back of her throat. But she kept moving forward.

#

Despite the fact that they retained their weapons, Toria knew they were prisoners in this underground warren. Natalia led the group, certain in her path despite the halls that branched in every direction. Toria did note elven runes burned into the wall at each interchange that appeared to be directional notations, but until they found Syri, the signs were useless to them. The fact that Natalia could read them did not surprise Toria, who revised the vampire's age upward once again. Mikelos had never had an exact age for her, instead estimating that she was at least as old as Asaron. Now, even if she had Asaron at her back, she wouldn't lay all her odds on her grandfather against the woman.

As long as they kept moving, the walls stayed put. That didn't prevent the oppressive feeling of the air itself from pressing down on her, but for now, she could still breathe. And if she could breathe, she could talk. They still needed more information about what was going on down here.

Pitching her voice to be as submissive as possible, Toria said, "Can you please tell us more about this ritual, Grandmere?"

"That's your department, Rubin," Natalia said, calling over her shoulder. "Enlighten the girl."

Rubin sniffed, and Toria heard his cane tap the ground once. "What purpose would that serve?"

"You have in front of you three of the last remaining mages in the world, Elder," Natalia said. "And possibly the last warrior-mage pair, unless there are some in the Qin lands that we don't know about. I would hate for them to miss this opportunity to learn what all of our peoples have sacrificed. We're here."

Finally, the group emerged from the cramped tunnels. Though this room still contained plenty of remains, it showed more of the cave system's origins as a quarry. The ceiling soared above them, atop natural pillars of stone. Scattered about the cavern were delicate structures consisting of balanced bones, hundreds of bodies made into works of art that cast intricate shadows in the light of more bare electric bulbs. About half a dozen adult elves, equally split between male and female, moved about the room, inspecting both statuary and the walls and floor. They also wore flowing robes.

Toria dragged her attention away from the dead and examined the floor more carefully. Those displays were not scattered about the room without purpose. Carved into the floor was the largest ritual circle she had ever seen. However, this was an entirely unfamiliar school of magic, and was a many-pointed star rather than a simple circle. The bodies aligned with the points and intersections important to whatever magical system worked best here. Judging from the many runes also etched into the floor and on the walls above the piled bones, this was a nexus of elven magic.

The stone altar in the center of the ritual area was the right size for a body. Toria had a good idea of where the sacrifice was supposed to occur now.

"I can see from the expressions on your faces that the pieces are falling in place," Rubin said. He wandered farther into the room, coming to a stop between two of the sculptures. His escort joined the other elves in inspecting and cleaning. Rubin placed his cane between his feet and rested both hands atop it. "But do you truly wish to learn the real story about the way this planet functions?"

"I think we're a captive audience," Archer said. "Please go on."

"You are aware of the world spell, yes?" Rubin asked. "That limits the expansion of technology?"

"The elves created it after the Last War," Kane said. "And considering Toria and I came across one of the remnants that you folks missed, which would have wiped out an entire city, even I can appreciate your motives."

"The three of you are relatively accomplished mages for your ages," Rubin said. "Having each attained the rank of master. You must know that all magic comes at a price."

"Of course we know," Archer said. "Were you going to give us a lesson in magical theory, or would you prefer to get to the point, sir?" Toria touched his arm, hoping the gesture would reel in his attitude. He glanced at her and nodded, some of the irritation draining from his shoulders. But the thumb on his left hand tapped each of the fingers on his hand in turn, back and forth down the line. Magic stirred against Toria's skin, where her body intersected the area contained within Archer's shields.

"To put it simply," Rubin said. "The cost of the world spell was magic itself. There is less magic in the world, and fewer mages are born every year. Europa has been the epicenter, but I'm sure you are even beginning to see the effects on the New Continent. Magic itself has been warped, and all elven children born since the world spell was cast have been cut off from their innate abilities. Instead, they have access to a lesser power."

The pieces fell together. It was like one of those abstract pictures with hidden objects. Once seen, they could not be unseen. The threads were pulling in, and now Toria could never go back to being an innocent bystander. "That elf back in New Angouleme called Syri 'broken,'" she said. "And the whole reason we were in New Angouleme is because Syri's uncle sent us there to find out why there were so few mages these days."

"He knew." Kane's face was ashen, and his shock and betrayal slammed through the link to Toria, reverberating agains her own. "Zerandan knew what was going on the whole time. We thought he did something, and that he was pointing us in the right direction. But he knew about the problem with magic itself."

"Correct," Rubin said. "And he was hiding that girl of his the whole time. We don't know what possessed him to send her out of the safety of Limani, but her time to be the sacrifice was years ago."

Zerandan had sent Syri out of Limani because he had trusted Toria and Kane to protect her. Toria's stomach clenched, and this time it wasn't because of the stone and earth squeezing her from every side. They had failed Zerandan. They had failed their friend. "That's why Syri was taken?" Toria asked. "You were planning to murder one of your own kind?"

"The broken barely deserve to be called one of our people." The corner of Rubin's lip lifted in a sneer. "But they will serve their purpose for the greater good."

"You think you're saving the world, but what if you're the ones killing it?" Kane asked. "Is the loss of all magic a fair price?"

Natalia had stood apart from them, watching the other elves move about the room, but at that she whirled on the group. "What would you rather instead?

Another nuclear war? One not limited to the center of a sparsely inhabited continent? You would prefer the loss of millions of lives instead of a few tens of thousands?"

"You do not have the luxury of the long view that the elves and vampires have," Rubin said with a firm nod. "Despite your greater power, you are still human. And humans must be protected from themselves."

"Then why are you even here?" Toria asked. Vampires and elves were never a combination people expected, and whatever was going on here didn't bode well. "What do the vampires have to do with this? Or do you just deliver the killing blow?"

"You think mages and elves are the only ones with magical power in the world?" Natalia lifted her hands, and dark clouds slid out of the shadows created by the bone sculptures.

Toria's stomach clenched again, this time with a sharp inhalation of breath. The moving shadows gave off the same soapy taste in the back of her brain that she had sensed in the wards protecting the entrance to the Catacombs and in the locked door in Natalia's townhouse. It wasn't some form of obscure elemental magic after all. "You were a mage? I thought that was impossible." Years ago, Toria had asked Victory whether her mother would change her once Toria became an adult. Pain had shown from her mother's eyes as she explained that it was impossible to turn a mage into a vampire. Victory would watch her daughter grow old and die.

"No, child," Natalia said. At her gesture, the shadows whirled around her once before dissipating into nothingness. "Just very, very old."

"Lady Della Zanna's abilities allow us to transmute the death of the sacrifice into the power that maintains the world spell," Rubin said. "None of this would be possible without her. But I assure you, where it comes to young Syrisinia, I will be the one to make the final strike. That is not a responsibility I would pass off—"

Rubin's face exploded in a mass of blood and tissue, spraying Toria and Archer. He pitched forward, falling to the stone floor in a tangle of limbs and cane. A female elf screamed.

Toria and Kane closed ranks on Archer, scanning the perimeter of the room. They wouldn't let another person under their protection fall to these insane elves.

#

Syri drifted through endless dim passages, one hand clutching the palm pistol and the other brushing the bones that lined the walls. So many bones. Something about the place, some description, tickled the back of her brain, but she couldn't place it. These tunnels could be some historical landmark she'd never bothered to remember, or it could be the stuff of which nightmares were made.

One thing was for sure: that one skull, tipped back with the jaw open wide, would haunt her dreams for years to come. It was either screaming or laughing. Syri couldn't decide which was worse. She hurried past. She didn't touch that one.

She could wander these tunnels for days and never find the surface. Never see a living being. She could die under here, without ever being this so-called sacrifice she was destined to be, never seeing Toria or Kane again, never feeling sunlight touch her skin.

Pausing at another intersection, she inspected the runes that marked the walls. Street names, mostly, with a few addresses. They probably corresponded with landmarks on the surface, none of which were familiar. And without even knowing what city she was in, the runes were useless as a map out of here.

She picked another tunnel at random. Perhaps that lightbulb was a bit brighter than the ones in tunnels to either side? As good a reason as any to go that direction.

Two more twists to the left deposited Syri in a room that, for once, was not lined with remains. Instead of bare bulbs from the ceiling, two spotlights were bolted to the wall. Both aimed at the opposite side of the room, highlighting the epic carving that spanned the length of the wall. She leaned against the wall between the spotlights. If she was going to have a two-minute breather, she might as well do it in a room that creeped her out slightly less than the rest of this bizarre warren.

The relief showed a stately manor, at the top of a switchback road. Or was the road an aqueduct? Syri didn't know anything about architecture, she was a vet tech. But the colonnaded palace was reminiscent of pictures she had seen of the royal estates to the south. This might narrow down her location—perhaps she had found herself in Roman territory? The Roman colonies to the south of Limani, or even in the Empire itself? Either would explain the possible boat ride.

Regardless, the carving was intricate and amazing and completely out of place in this underground maze of death. Three other passages emanated from this room, which appeared to be a major intersection. Rouch stone stacked floor to ceiling sealed one of them. Bones lined the way she had come and the third hall. But the fourth was a much larger hallway, nary a rib in sight. She looked up a narrow ramp to the other end of the hall. While she could have brushed the ceiling in the tunnels she had traversed so far, this hall was spaced with archways that soared twenty or more feet above her.

Gripping the handy rail, Syri climbed the ramp. It wasn't a long hall, but it would make a nice break from the bones.

At the top, of course, were more bones.

But was it her imagination, or were these bones more deliberate? Where before the piles had been more arbitrary, with skulls perching along the top, here were organized stacks of femurs and tibias, with narrower fibulas filling in the cracks. Pelvic bones lined the ground like eerie floor molding, and the skulls were patterned into the walls in elegant rises and falls. Ribs curled in starbursts in random spots, and she saw no sign of the random smaller bones that Syri had accidentally trod upon in this clean-swept hallway. Perhaps she was reaching civilization?

For whatever measure of civilization maintained such a bizarre fucking place.

But no! Were those voices?

Syri crept forward, keeping the pistol at the ready. If it was more of Ayanna's ilk, she wouldn't be overpowered easily. Sacrifice was not on the day's menu.

One last curve, and the hall opened to a larger space. There were still plenty of bones, this time in delicate artistic piles. But there were also people. The man she heard speaking stood between two of the piles, which obscured her view of his immediate companions. However, she saw others scattered about the room, doing arcane and unknowable things to the remains in the room and—was that a ritual star on the floor? If so, it was the most intricate she'd ever seen.

She refocused on the man speaking when her name reached her ears. "—young Syrisinia, I will be the one to make the final strike—"

Oh, hell no.

Syri raised the pistol and took her shot.

The speaker's head exploded, and only then did she realize how much her hand shook. She had aimed for his chest.

#

More shadows came to life around the room. Some converged on Natalia, but the rest swooped toward Rubin's body. His form blurred, obscured by the twisting darkness. The soapy taste was back, stronger than ever, but a sudden rush of more familiar magic at her back made Toria relax. She could tell from experience that Archer had pulled up physical shields around the three of them. If any more bullets came out of the darkness, none of them would be hit. Shimmering blue edged her vision even without magesight, representing the strength of the physical shields.

The elves in the room scattered, hiding behind bone statuary. Kane herded the three of them for one of the larger pieces in a corner of the cavern. It wouldn't provide much cover, but it was better than nothing.

Natalia darted past them and fell to her knees next to Rubin's body, heedless of her expensive clothing on the blood-spattered ground. She held both hands above the corpse, but they disappeared into the shadows. Since Kane and Archer focused on defense, Toria kept an eye on whatever mischief Natalia was cooking up. But seeing the shadows was difficult, and her sight kept sliding to the side. This magic was so foreign that she had no idea what the vampire was attempting, good or bad.

At her side, Kane gasped. He straightened from his crouch and left the limited safety of their defensive position. Toria made a futile grab for the back of his shirt, but he slipped away too soon.

Even worse, Kane lowered his scimitar. But then he called, "Syri!"

What? Toria turned from whatever Natalia was doing in time to see Syri break into a run across the cavern. Kane had a heartbeat to move his blade to the side before Syri crashed into him. He wrapped his free arm around her in a tight hug and buried his face in her hair.

Syri pulled away and stretched a hand to Toria. But before she could step toward her, another elf screamed. This time it was a male voice, filled with rage instead of fear. Syri fell back a few paces to keep out of range of the dagger the robed figure slashed at her. The other elves had rallied as well, and more long knives appeared from within the depths of their silk robes.

Toria's first instinct was to run to Syri's side, to defend her friend, but Kane was closer. Archer remained at her back, doing something magical based on the swirls of power she could feel on all sides. She held her ground to protect the mage.

The attacking elf lunged again, and Syri bought up the pistol still clutched in her hand. She fired three times in quick succession. Two bullets missed, but the third hit, and a bloom of red stained the emerald of his robes at the shoulder. She pulled the trigger a fourth time, but the chamber clicked empty.

He howled in pain and dropped the knife. Kane slipped between him and Syri to engage with his longer blade, but a second male elf hurled toward him. This one still wielded a long knife, and the injured man kept attacking, heedless of his injury or disarmed state.

Syri swooped to pick up the discarded knife. No sooner had her fingers closed around the hilt than she yelped in pain and dropped the weapon again. "Fuck!"

Instead, she kicked the knife out of range so that it wouldn't tangle Kane's feet. Toria noted a flash of red skin. Somehow the weapon had burned Syri's flesh on contact. The elves didn't wear gloves, which meant it couldn't be steel. Some sort of set spell, then.

This gave an opening for two more elves to make their assault. They came from Toria's left, and she placed herself between them and Archer.

Syri ducked to Archer's side. "The elves have fucked shit up, Tor," she said.

Before the elves could enter physical range, Toria drew Syri's own knife from where it was still tucked into her belt. "Yeah, we know. Catch!"

Syri plucked her knife out of the air with grace and dropped to a defensive crouch in front of Archer. The water mage's eyes were closed, and flickers of blue continued to appear in the corners of Toria's vision. More interestingly, her hair frizzed where it escaped its bandana, evidence that the humidity level in the underground cavern had skyrocketed.

Syri would protect Archer. Toria's focus narrowed to the two elves advancing on her.

Red Robe ducked with supernatural grace under the reach of her longer blade. But years of practice with vampires had honed Toria's reflexes. She was also not a traditionally trained rapier dueler. Though Red Robe was close enough to swipe at her chest with his knife, he was also close enough for Toria to slam the hilt of her sword into his arm, deflecting the blade away from her

But an elf in green was also at her side, and she was an inch too late in dancing away from his slashing knife. It caught her off shoulder, gouging her protective leather armor.

Green Robe pressed his attack, forcing Toria back another step. The wall of the cavern was too near. She couldn't allow herself to be cornered away from Archer and Syri. Red Robe followed a step behind, ready to take advantage of any opening his friend gave him.

When he lunged again, Toria parried with her longer sword. But before he could press forward, his entire body stiffened in shock. The tip of a sword erupted from his stomach, run through by Kane's scimitar.

In the space between one breath and the next, Toria met her partner's eyes over the impaled elf's shoulder. A mental touch: okay? Okay. A quick scan beyond Kane showed his own two attackers already on the stone floor of the cavern, dead or dying.

When Green Robe's knife fell from a useless hand, Toria met the final attack the elf in red threw at her. His knife slid down the edge of her sword's blade, bringing Toria in close. She caught his wrist with her empty hand and used her forward momentum to swing them toward the wall. Now she cornered him, and Toria slashed at his chest before he could wrest his knife free. The silk parted like cobweb, and the skin beneath offered no real resistance either. Blood poured down his chest, and the elf sagged against the cavern wall. Another knife dropped as his hand spasmed in pain.

Toria left him sagging against the wall, hugging his arms to his chest. She kicked his knife away and turned to Kane. Giving him a once-over, she noted a slash in his jeans, but no blood. And though the bicep of his sword arm was bloody, the grip on his scimitar was still strong.

She caught a whiff of evergreen as his magic coursed down her body in his more arcane method of a health check. But he had no immediate cause for concern. They had one moment to catch their breath. Then they turned to face the cavern. Four elves had fallen, but there were more.

But the three remaining elves, all female, clustered around Natalia and ignored the bloodshed. The vampire still knelt next to Rubin's body.

At least Toria was pretty sure Rubin's body was in there somewhere. Shadows swirled in a thick pea-soup fog that enveloped Natalia's knees. Natalia's hands and arms gestured above the darkness, and her lips moved. But whatever she chanted was so low that the words did not reach Toria's ears.

The soapy feeling that tickled her brain grew stronger and coated the back of her throat. This did not bode well.

"Natalia!" Archer's voice rang out across the cavern. "Whatever it is you're doing, I recommend stopping."

The stone beneath Toria's feet shuddered, and small cracks arced through the walls. One of the nearby sculptures collapsed in a rattle of bones. A lone femur rolled toward Kane, who stopped it with the toe of his boot.

Natalia's soundless chanting did not cease. Her left hand continued its dancing pattern, but the right gestured toward Archer. As one, the three female elves turned to the water mage.

He was on the opposite side of the cavern, with only Syri's knife to protect him. Kane kicked the femur out the way and broke into a run, Toria fast on his heels.

Archer didn't need Syri to protect him. Stone crackled again, and he lifted his hands from his sides. A torrent of water erupted from the stone at his feet. Instead of shooting straight up, the wave curved toward the approaching elves. The weight of the water slammed them to the ground.

The water spread with the movement of Archer's hands. But when it reached Natalia, it crashed against an invisible dome of energy. The water steamed and crackled where it beat at her, filling the cavern with fog. The bone sculptures around the cavern collapsed one by one as the steam enveloped them. Considering the source, it had to be more than just super-heated water.

The lead elf was still down, having taken the brunt of the initial burst of water. Hundreds of pounds of force, if not more. But now that it had spread, Toria and Kane waded into the spray and engaged the other two who rose before they could continue their way to Archer.

But the water meant that Toria could no longer see the stone floor. Her boot slid, possibly on one of the tiles that made up the ritual star. She fell to one knee and lost her grip on her sword as she splashed into the current. The elf she had aimed for saw her chance and tackled Toria. She caught a shoulder in the sternum, which forced her back into the water. Toria coughed and inhaled liquid, which tightened her chest more. She tried to push herself up, but hands closed around her throat, forcing her back below the surface.

Panic and lack of oxygen spurred drastic measures, and she activated one of the fail-safes worked into her shields. Pure energy flared from her skin, arcing electricity through the water and up into the body above her. Sparks lit her vision, and the hands loosened. She surged up and out of the water, gasping air and hacking up rackish liquid. The elven woman lay in the water next to her, eyes open and unseeing, where Toria had pushed her away. Hundreds of watts must have coursed through her body, killing her instantly.

That last ditch measure had exhausted Toria, but she was alive. She rubbed water out of her face and looked for the others.

Her partner faced her from where he stood over the body of the remaining female elf, his chest heaving and his sword held loose at his side. The swirling mass of shadows had grown again, rising almost to the cavern's ceiling. Natalia stalked out of the darkness. In one swift movement, she gripped Kane by the shoulder and pushed his head to the side. Her fangs closed over his throat.

Toria screamed. Sharp pain sliced through her neck, cutting off the scream as her vocal cords stopped working. A different sort of darkness engulfed her.

#

The city of Limani spread out before Toria from the top of city hall. Fireworks exploded in the sky. The air bit her skin with autumn's sharpness.

Toria stood at the edge of the roof, once more in the body of a young girl. She looked up at the warm presence at her side. An adult Kane smiled at her, his teeth white in the darkness. His eyes sparkled with the rainbow bursts over them. He twined his fingers in hers and squeezed her hand.

"Don't go," she said.

"Never," Kane said.

He released her hand and stepped forward.

He fell.

\#

Someone was screaming.

Oh.

That someone was her.

Someone shouted her name.

Toria opened her eyes.

She sat up, still soaked from head to toe. The water had receded, leaving large puddles across the cavern. Archer stood before her, holding a familiar scimitar to Natalia's neck.

Natalia sat cross-legged, demurely, cradling Kane's limp body in her arms and unconcerned by either her damp clothing or the blade at her throat.

Toria opened her mouth again, but no sound came out. She coughed, then tried again. "Where's Syri?"

Archer jerked his shoulder in one direction. "One of the bastards was still alive. Came up behind us and slit her throat. Kane's dead." Toria followed the line and saw a crumpled body that wore a familiar black leather jacket. She touched a hand to her neck, and her fingers came away tinged with blood. The sympathetic injury she had felt before passing out.

Of course Kane was dead. That went unsaid. There was a giant gaping hole where Toria's heart belonged. Her power, her soul, kept reaching for him and finding nothing. Her power would keep reaching for him, until it drained her dry.

Warrior-mages always came in pairs. Toria would follow her partner shortly. She was surprisingly okay with this. But she would do one thing first.

Despite the gnawing numbness that spread through her body, Toria pushed herself to her feet. Her rapier lay abandoned in the water. She staggered over to it and scooped it up before turning on Natalia.

But as Toria stepped forward, Natalia raised one hand. An invisible wall repelled Toria. She pounded against it with the hilt of her sword, to no avail.

"Calm yourself, granddaughter," Natalia said.

"I thought you said I was no child of yours," Toria said.

Natalia started to nod, but caught the motion before her chin touched the sword still held at her throat. "You are not," she said. "But your passion inspires me."

"You killed Kane," Toria said. "Your fucking minions killed Syri. I mean to do a lot more than inspire you." She placed a palm on the invisible shield and pushed power at it, brute-strength. She had nothing left to lose, no power to hold back in reserve. Sparks erupted from her fingertips but died against Natalia's shield.

"Syri's death was unfortunate," Natalia said. "Kane's death, however, was necessary. The shadows had gone too long without their tribute."

Toria scanned the cavern. Most of the bone sculptures had collapsed, and loose bones scattered the floor around elven bodies. But the swirling mass of shadows was indeed gone.

"What was that?" Toria asked. "Was that the world spell?"

"It is a great many things," Natalia said. "But I fear that was the last time the world spell will be activated. Perhaps Zerandan did know what he was doing when he dangled Syri in front of Rubin, knowing the two of you would be close behind."

"But you fed it Kane, instead," Archer said.

"Before it took us all," Natalia said. "But all is not lost. I can return one of your friends to you."

Blackness licked at the edges of Toria's vision, and someone screamed again. Oh.

It was her.

She slumped against the invisible shield, losing steam all at once. Archer had jumped away from Natalia during her short blackout. He shook the scimitar at her, also yelling, demanding to know what the vampire meant.

Natalia waited until Archer fell silent. She cradled Kane, brushing his smooth scalp with one hand. If not for the awkward angle, he could almost be sleeping.

The sucking emptiness inside Toria belied that pleasant wishful thinking.

"What the fuck do you mean, Grandmere?" Toria spit the last word.

"I have no idea what damage has been done to the world spell," Natalia said, "by feeding it a warrior-mage rather than one of the broken. But I can feel it inside me. It's feeding back on me, and I signed my own fate when I killed your partner. But I can bring one of them back before I go." She smiled, close-lipped, and shook her head. "What magic would a vampire have, other than to bring life back where there was none?"

"But you can't turn a mage or an elf into a vampire," Toria said. "It's impossible."

"*Life*, child," Natalia said. "Not death. You have only to choose."

Syri. Her best friend, her partner-in-crime, her sister.

Kane. Her partner, her brother, her soulmate.

It was an impossible choice.

Except her life was on the line. There was no choice.

Archer's eyes were shuttered as he looked at her, but he nodded once.

"Kane," she said, forcing the name out through sobs. "Please bring him back."

After all that, it was quick. Natalia touched Kane's chest. Magic pulsed through the cavern, echoing in the empty space of Toria's heart. The vampire's body faded into nothing, and her clothing drifted to the damp stone.

Toria fell forward as the shield shattered.

Kane surged up, gasping for breath. Panic and pain and confusion swept through their link. "Toria? What happened?"

But what mattered was that the emptiness inside her vanished. She shoved away his pain and replaced it a sense of love and peace that filled them to the brim. Kane's magic melded with hers, back where it should be. Together, as one, the energies of storm and earth dancing together in two bodies. All of the power she'd expended in the battle was back, fivefold, tenfold.

She stepped on feet no longer numb and dropped to her knees next to Kane, collapsing into his arms. A third arm crossed her back as Archer held them both.

Her soul felt full again, but now she noticed a vacant spot in the back of her brain. Syri's loss would not go unfelt.

Toria looked over Kane's shoulder. The elven bodies remained scattered, except for one.

A sodden leather jacket lay next to a lone silver knife.

\#

The gardens wilted in the late afternoon sunshine. While power still shimmered in the air, the plants themselves emanated an aura of benign neglect. The grass a little less green, the flowers a little less fresh. But otherwise, the New Angouleme Center for Magical Education was as impressive as the first time Toria entered the grounds.

After the events in the Catacombs, the three emerged from underground to find dawn. With Syri and Natalia's bodies gone, nothing showed what had happened except a bunch of damp elven bodies, destroyed ancient remains, and the scorched ruins of the ritual circle. Toria had burned a lot of power setting her lightning to it before they left. She didn't view it as a waste.

They collected their packs from the park, finding them undisturbed. Toria shed more tears as she slung one of Syri's bags over her shoulder. They wouldn't be the last tears for a long time to come. They debated whether to return to Natalia's house and let her staff know not to expect her return. But that path invited too many questions. Instead, they hustled for the station and and purchased tickets for the first available train back to Calaitum.

That's when they learned about the first of the effects of the shattering of the world spell. Long-distance communications fueled by elven magic had cut out all over the city, and when they reached Calaitum, they learned that the issue was not limited to Parisii alone.

They had no idea what other effects the world spell's collapse had on the planet, but they figured that would come in time. For now, Toria, Kane, and Archer resolved to watch and wait.

Henry's parents were glad to see them again. They didn't ask any questions. Though Lady Delacour begged Archer to stay for the rest of the summer, he was adept at making excuses requiring his presence back in New Angouleme. They were stuck in limbo for three days until the next ship departed for the New Continent, but the ride home on the *Lycan Queen*, the *Lunar Queen's* sister ship, was filled with the same luxury they'd experienced on the way out.

They didn't enjoy it much. After bolstering Kane's shields before they left the dock, the three of them mostly spent time on deck, staring out across the waves. And if Toria got drunk and danced the night away while Kane holed up with Archer in their suite, well, neither partner called the other on it.

Alexei, the headman of Liquid Gold, met them at the docks in New Angouleme. Archer requested that they be driven straight to the mage school. He didn't comment when Toria and Kane strapped on their swords in the back of the town-car. When last she had been in the mage school, Toria had left the dead and broken body of the woman who had mind-raped her and tried to steal her power. They had no idea what they'd find when they got there today.

But they passed through the gardens without incident. Archer jumped the front steps two at a time and pushed open the main doors. They followed him into the front lobby, blinking in the darkness after the late summer light.

"Greetings, Master Sophin. Welcome home." An uninflected voice reached them out of the dim room.

Archer tried the switches next to the door, but no lights flicked on. Toria dug out her trusty quartz and powered it up. Pastel light shimmered into the corners of the dusty room. Even the enchanted fireplace lay dark. But a familiar figure stood behind the reception desk.

"Greetings, Fee," Archer said, approaching the simulacrum with caution. "Are you okay?"

"I am functioning adequately, Master Sophin," Fee said. "Thank you." Her neutral business suit hid any dust, but specks of dirt in her eyebrows caught in Toria's magical light.

"Where is everybody?" Toria moved in a slow circle, holding the quartz at eye level. Nothing jumped out of the shadows at them, and she felt some of the tension leave her spine. Kane rested a hand on her back, and she leaned into his comforting presence.

"Fee?" Archer said. "Where are the students and staff?"

"Master Sherman Burrows has left the premises," Fee said. "Master Lana Wick is deceased. Staff member Heather Murphy has left the premises. Staff member Kriscinda Sundberg has left the premises. Staff member Blake—"

"Yes, thank you, Fee," Archer said, cutting her off. "What about the students?"

"Senior student Laurel O'Dwyer has left the premises. Senior student Kathleen Betts has left the premises. Apprentice Thomas Daniels has left the—"

"Thanks, Fee," Kane said. "Is anyone still on the premises?"

"No."

"When was the last time anyone was here?" Archer asked.

"Staff member Heather Murphy left two weeks, three days, and four hours ago," Fee said.

Archer leaned against the desk, considering. "Fee, did Master Burrows leave with any of the students?"

"Master Burrows left three days before any registered students."

"Huh, he didn't bring along his portable batteries," Toria said. "That's good news, at least."

"What are you going to do now?" Kane said, leaning next to Archer.

"I didn't set out to be a teacher, and I may have been training them partly under duress," Archer said, "but I've got a responsibility to those kids. I need to track them down and make sure their education gets finished before they burn themselves out. I also need to find Burrows and make sure he doesn't set up shop somewhere and take advantage of anyone else."

Toria finished her circuit of the room and joined them on Archer's other side. Except that put Fee at her back, and the simulacrum's blank gaze made the back of her neck itch. She stepped away to face the men. "We should probably also make sure this place is fully shut down and cleared out."

"Yes," Archer said, nodding.

"Need help?" Kane asked.

"Probably," Archer said. "But you two need to get back to Limani and talk to Syri's family. Besides, you're still on journeyman status. Until I get access to the school's funds, if Burrows left any, I have no way to pay you."

Kane bumped Archer's shoulder with his own. "I am happy to accept payment in the form of sexual favors."

"I'm not!" Toria raised her hand. "But I do accept chocolate."

"Deal," Archer said. "I'll get in contact if I need you."

"What about after?" Toria asked. "You'd shut this place down only to reopen once you've taken care of Burrows and rounded up all the students?"

"No, I'm done with this place," Archer said. "I love the city, but I have no more family here, and these grounds will carry too many bad memories. But I hear Limani has a mage school and students looking for a master. Since its two most famous students won't step up to the job, the prodigal son will have to return and do it for them."

Kane captured Archer and Toria's hands in his own. "That sounds perfect."

EPILOGUE

Toria launched herself off the ferry, landing on the wooden dock with a heavy thud, before the crewmembers could lower the exit ramp. She ignored Kane's shout behind her.

"I'll get our gear then?"

She waved at him, but kept running.

Max waited next to the Limani customs house, basking against the wall in the warmth of the setting sun. Toria slid to halt in front of him. He opened one eye, and said, "You two are back early. I distinctly remember saying eighteen months."

"And yet you still came to meet us," Toria said. "Do I get a hug or not?"

"You get a hug," Max said, opening his arms wide.

Toria melted into his strong embrace. She'd feel even better when she got a hug from her father, but Max was enough to tide her over. "Thanks." He squeezed her tight, but released her at the sound of packs hitting the ground behind her.

"Welcome home," Max said, gripping Kane's hand.

"Thanks," Kane said. "It's good to be back. Feels a lot longer than a month."

"Your message from New Angouleme wasn't that detailed," Max said. "What have you guys been doing up there all this time?" When neither of them responded, he continued, "Oh, I have the feeling this is gonna be good. Where's your partner-in-crime? Leave her up north?"

Toria choked back the tightness in her chest. She wasn't going to cry again. "That's part of why we're back. We need to see Zerandan first thing."

"That's a bit of a problem," Max said. "He took off, oh, about two weeks ago. Left me with the balance payment on your contract and said to hand it all over whenever you guys got back, no questions asked. Wouldn't tell me what that was all about." He ducked to look more closely at Toria. "What's going on, kid?"

"Syri's dead," Kane said. "She died about the same time you say Zerandan left. He must have been able to tell somehow."

"Shit," Max said. "I'm sorry to hear that."

"Thanks," Toria said. She chased away the threatening bout of sadness with a clap of her hands. "Mind giving us a ride back to the manor? And how come Dad

181

isn't here?" She hoisted her packs, and they approached Max's truck. The bags had held up well for a month. They would see how they handled for another seventeen.

"Well, Asaron's home waiting for you," Max said, as they tossed all the bags into the back pallet of the truck. "Victory and Mikelos are not."

Toria hopped into the back seat, allowing Kane the privilege of shotgun for his longer legs. She leaned between the two front seats. "Where'd they go?"

"Asaron's got a better handle on that one," Max said. He pulled out of the parking lot, puffing diesel exhaust in his wake.

After so much time in the luxurious town-cars in New Angouleme, Calaitum, and Parisii, the truck's nonelectric engine was loud to Toria's ears. "Gotcha," she said.

"But before I leave you in your grandfather's clutches," Max said, "I've gotta ask. Seems like it's been a rough month on you two. You've still got seventeen more to go. You going to keep on this path?"

A shimmer of excitement rushed through Toria, magnified by what she felt through her link with Kane. "Absolutely."

"Good," Max said. "Because the second you checked into the Guildhall in New Angouleme, word got out that two warrior-mages were looking for work. I've got three contracts waiting for you to look at back in my office."

#

"Grandpa! We're home!"

No one responded to Toria's shout from the manor foyer. She dropped her packs to the floor, and this time, they would stay there until she was good and ready to tackle the laundry. It would be nice not to lug her life around with her for at least a day or two, until she and Kane could look at the contracts on offer.

Max pulled the front door shut behind him and Kane. "He's probably in that creepy basement lair of his."

"It's not creepy, it's cozy," Toria said. She also unbelted her sword and dropped it, scabbard and all, in the umbrella stand next to the front door. Kane's weapon followed shortly after. They didn't look out of place next to the spare cutlass Victory kept there in case of unexpected visitors.

"No, it can be pretty creepy," Kane said. "I'm surprised Asaron's still home. He doesn't usually stick around Limani more than a week or two at a time."

Kane's voice faded behind her as Toria sprinted through the house to the stairs at the back of the kitchen. She bounded into Asaron's basement apartment in time for him to catch her in his arms, swinging her around. "We're home," she said again, burying her face in his shoulder.

182

"I heard," Asaron said. He dropped her back onto the carpet to catch Kane in his arms for another tight hung, minus the swinging.

While a handshake might have been more appropriate for Max, their mentor in all things mercenary, even Kane could unwind enough for a hug from his foster grandfather.

"Where're Mama and Dad?" Toria asked as the men broke apart.

Asaron glanced at Max, who had followed them down at a more sedate pace and now held up the wall at the bottom of the stairs. "You didn't tell them?"

"Nope," Max said. "You're the big boss now. Figured it was your call?"

"Big boss?" Kane asked.

"You're looking at Limani's Master of the City, Kane," Max said. "Best be respectful."

Kane laughed, but Toria's mind churned. She might not have known all the crazy things the elves on this world were up to, but one thing she knew was vampire lore and traditional vampire politics. "But that usually only happens if—"

Asaron interrupted her. "Your mother is fine," he said. "But it took her less than a week to go stir-crazy once the two of you set forth. I figured that might happen, so Max and I had a contingency plan."

"Yeah, you think you two are a hot commodity in the mercenary business right now?" Max said. "Try putting the infamous Victory back on the market."

"No way," Kane said. "She always says she's retired."

"Indeed," Asaron said. "But we needed something to keep her occupied while her babies were out in the big bad world. I found her a job and promised to keep the city safe while she was gone. Now I know why she's always complaining about those damn council meetings."

"You knew what you were getting into," Max said.

"And Dad went with her?" Toria asked.

"Of course," Asaron said. "Daywalker's got a job to do, and it's to be by her side. And he brought that violin of his. With his music, he'll probably be more of draw where they're going."

"Which is where?" Kane asked.

"South," Max said. "Asaron's got more connections that even I do."

"Your mother was hired to bodyguard the princess of Jiang Yi Yue," Asaron said.

"But that's a Qin territory!" Toria said. "The whole southern continent was closed off after the Last War."

"Not to everyone," Asaron said. "Not to me. And this job was a personal favor from Victory to the former governor. The princess is one of his granddaughters. He preferred for a woman to be her protector. Mikelos got himself an invitation to be a visiting bard to the court."

"They left less than a week after the three of you left for Calverton," Max said. "Have you gotten any word since—?"

"I would let you know if I had," Asaron said.

"Why?" Toria said. "What's going on?"

"They were three days out of Fort Caroline when all the communications spells crashed," Asaron said. "And there's been no contact from them since."

ACKNOWLEDGMENTS

Publishing a book is a long shot. Publishing a second book is winning the lottery.

Many thanks go out to those who helped me beat the odds:

My amazing beta readers and critique partners—Chris Stout, K. W. Taylor, Breeanna Pierce, and Chelsea Stickle—who read all or parts of this novel. Your invaluable comments and support only improved my work.

Everyone who cheered me on during National Novel Writing Month 2014, especially the local chapter for Columbia, Maryland.

My mother-in-law, Iolany Gonçalves, for letting me share in so many of her travel adventures and introducing me to the city of Paris.

My wonderful editors, Jennifer and John, for encouraging me to explore the world outside of Limani.

And finally, my husband Erik. You didn't know exactly what you were getting when you married a novelist, but your love and support have been invaluable.

ABOUT THE AUTHOR

By day, J. L. Gribble is a professional medical editor. By night, she does freelance fiction editing in all genres, along with reading, playing video games, and occasionally even writing.

Previously, Gribble studied English at St. Mary's College of Maryland. She received her Master's degree in Writing Popular Fiction from Seton Hill University in Greensburg, Pennsylvania, where her debut novel *Steel Victory* was her thesis for the program.

She lives in Ellicott City, Maryland, with her husband and three vocal Siamese cats. Find her online (www.jlgribble.com), on Facebook (www.facebook.com/ jlgribblewriter), and on Twitter and Instagram (@hannaedits). She is currently working on more tales set in the world of Limani.

CPSIA information can be obtained
at www.ICGtesting.com
Printed in the USA
LVOW12s1928140716

496335LV00008B/912/P